Between the Lines of Shadows

STACY SAFIRT MCGINNIS

Disclaimer

This book is a work of fiction. Names, characters, organizations, places, events, and incidents are either the product of the author's imagination or are used in a fictitious manner. Any resemblance to actual persons, living or dead, or to actual events, locales, or organizations is purely coincidental. The author makes no representations or warranties with respect to the accuracy or completeness of the content, and shall not be held liable for any loss, damage, or disruption caused by reliance on any material contained herein.

www.dawnspirepublishing.com

LIBRARY OF CONGRESS CATALOGING-IN-PUBLICATION DATA
MCGINNIS, STACY SAFIRT
Between The Lines Of Shadows / BY Stacy Safirt McGinnis
FIRST EDITION
p. cm.
ISBN 979-8-9930372-0-2
1. Romance 2. Mystery 3. Fiction.
I.   Between The Lines Of Shadows
Library of Congress Control Number: 2025919580

Forward

Life, in all its unpredictable turns, often presents us with challenges that test our very core. Yet, within these trials lies an incredible wellspring of hope and courage. In navigating the darkness that this world brings, we truly discover the resilience of the human spirit, learning that even after the most profound storms, the sun will rise, illuminating a path forward. These experiences, no matter how daunting, are not meant to break us, but to sculpt us, refining our character and revealing the immense strength we possess.

This journey is an invitation to embrace your own narrative, not as a series of unfortunate events, but as a rich tapestry of learning and growth. Each chapter, each setback, each moment of triumph, contributes to the unique story that only you can tell. By understanding and accepting your experiences, you unlock the potential to transform them into powerful lessons, launching you into the greatest, most fulfilling chapter of your life yet. The courage to face your past, to learn from your present, and to bravely step into your future is within you.

This book aims to be a beacon, inspiring you to see your life as an unfolding epic, where every experience is a stepping stone, and every challenge is an opportunity to write a more courageous, hopeful, and magnificent story for yourself. Embrace your narrative, and let it propel you toward the extraordinary life you were always meant to live.

Contents

Chapter 1

The Unraveling Thread

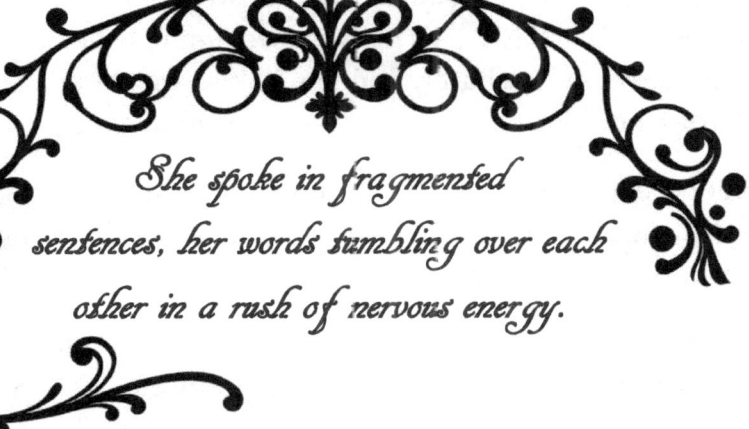

She spoke in fragmented sentences, her words tumbling over each other in a rush of nervous energy.

First Session with Emily

The scent of old books and faint dust motes danced in the single shaft of afternoon sunlight slicing through the blinds of my office. Emily sat opposite me; a delicate porcelain doll perched on the edge of the plush armchair. Her hands, clasped tightly in her lap, trembled almost imperceptibly. At twenty-three, she possessed a fragility that belied a strength I sensed simmering just beneath the surface, a strength she was desperately trying to conceal. She was here for anxiety, she'd said on the phone, crippling anxiety that left her breathless and unable to function. But something in her voice, a subtle tremor of fear masked by forced composure, had alerted me to a deeper, more unsettling current.

"So, tell me about your anxiety, Emily," I began, my voice soft, encouraging. I leaned forward, my posture open and inviting, mirroring her fragility while maintaining a professional distance. The years spent honing my skills in counseling had taught me the delicate balance required; empathy without intrusion, guidance without imposition.

Emily hesitated, her gaze flitting nervously around the room, avoiding my eyes. "It's… it's just overwhelming," she finally whispered, her voice barely audible. "Like a weight on my chest, suffocating me. I can't… I can't breathe sometimes."

I nodded, encouraging her to continue. "And when does this feeling usually come on, Emily? Is there a trigger, a specific situation or thought that seems to bring it about?"

She spoke in fragmented sentences, her words tumbling over each other in a rush of nervous energy. "It's… unpredictable. Sometimes it's nothing, just… being here. Other times, it's… it's like something's watching me. Following me." She paused, her eyes widening slightly. "It's irrational, I know. But it feels so real."

The feeling of being watched, that primal fear of unseen eyes, was a common thread in anxiety, but the way Emily described it – the chilling certainty, the lack of a specific trigger – raised a flag in my mind. Her descriptions lacked the usual accompanying symptoms – the rapid heartbeat, sweating, panic attacks – which made the case more perplexing. It felt... calculated. Controlled.

"Tell me more about this feeling of being watched," I prompted gently, my intuition telling me this was the key.

She shifted uncomfortably in her seat, her fingers tracing nervous patterns on the worn fabric of her skirt. "It's not a person, not exactly," she explained, her voice laced with a disquieting mixture of fear and uncertainty. "It's... a presence. Like someone is close by, even when I know I'm alone." She paused, then added in a low voice, "It started... about a month ago."

The timeline was significant. A sudden onset of this intensity warranted further investigation. I steered the conversation toward her daily routine, her relationships, any recent stressors, but her answers remained vague, inconsistent. She would offer details, then contradict herself moments later, leaving gaps in her narrative that felt deliberate, not accidental. One moment she described spending her evenings alone, reading; the next, she claimed she was always out with friends.

Her fidgeting intensified as the session progressed. She constantly adjusted her jewelry, twisting her wedding ring – a simple gold band – around her finger. The ring itself seemed unremarkable, but the way she manipulated it – a subconscious gesture, perhaps – hinted at underlying anxieties. She was clutching at something, trying to hold onto a sense of control in a world that felt increasingly unpredictable.

As the hour drew to a close, I felt a growing unease. This wasn't the presentation of a typical anxiety case. Emily's evasiveness, the inconsistencies in her story, the chilling undercurrent of fear – it all pointed to something far more complex, something that lay beyond the realm of clinical diagnoses.

"Emily," I said, my voice quiet but firm, "I have a feeling that what you're experiencing is more than just anxiety. There's something else going on, something you may not even be fully aware of." I paused, allowing my words to sink in. "I want you to trust me. We need to explore this further."

She looked at me, her eyes wide and filled with a mixture of fear and desperation. "I... I don't know," she stammered. "I don't want to tell you what's really going on."

I waited patiently, understanding the reluctance, the deep-seated fear that often accompanies the unveiling of painful truths. "It's okay, Emily," I reassured her gently. "There's no rush. But know this: I'm here to help you, whatever it is."

As she left, her shoulders slumped, the feeling of something unresolved hung heavy in the air. I sat for a long time after she was gone, reviewing her file, her nervous gestures, the inconsistencies in her story. Something was deeply wrong, and my gut told me that my work was no longer confined to the boundaries of my office.

That night, an anonymous letter arrived. It was slipped under my door, a thin, cream-colored envelope bearing no return address. The paper felt unusually thick, almost cardstock in its texture, the handwriting elegant but anonymous – looping script that seemed both familiar and unnervingly strange. The contents were even more unsettling, a cryptic message hinting at a connection between Emily and a former client, a case that had haunted me long after its conclusion – a case involving a similar pattern of anxiety, a similar feeling of being watched, and a recurring symbol, a specific type of flower – a rare, almost extinct white moonflower. The letter ended with a single, chilling sentence: "Some things are better left buried." A shiver ran down my spine as I realized that whatever Emily was hiding, it was far more dangerous than I had initially imagined. The unraveling thread had begun to pull me into a web far deeper and more complex than anything I had ever encountered. The quiet solitude of my office, once a sanctuary, now felt like a precarious perch on the edge of a dark, unknown abyss. My therapeutic instincts were battling with a growing sense of dread, and the lines between professional curiosity and personal danger were blurring fast.

The Anonymous Letter

The crisp autumn air, carrying the scent of decaying leaves and damp earth, seeped under the door, a stark contrast to the warmth of my apartment. The silence of the night was broken only by the rhythmic ticking of the grandfather clock in the hall, each tick a tiny hammer blow against the stillness. I sat at my kitchen table, the anonymous letter spread before me, its cream-colored surface illuminated by the soft glow of a desk lamp. The paper itself was intriguing – thicker than standard stationery, almost cardstock, with a slightly textured finish. I ran my fingertip across its surface, feeling the subtle grain, the slight unevenness. It felt deliberately chosen, almost as if the sender wanted the physicality of the letter to be part of the message.

The handwriting was elegant, a looping script that possessed a peculiar familiarity, a ghost of recognition that eluded my grasp. The individual letters were carefully formed, each stroke deliberate, yet there was a fluidity to the writing, a graceful arc that suggested a practiced hand. I'd seen similar handwriting before, but where? My mind raced, searching through a sea of faces, a kaleidoscope of past clients, each one a unique puzzle piece in the complex mosaic of my professional life. I examined the script under a magnifying glass, scrutinizing the subtle variations in stroke width and pressure, looking for any microscopic clue that might betray the writer's identity. There was nothing out of the ordinary, no trembling strokes, no wavering lines that might indicate nervousness or haste. The letter was the work of someone calm, deliberate, someone who knew exactly what they were doing.

The message itself was a series of carefully chosen words, a cryptic puzzle designed to unsettle and intrigue. It spoke of Emily, referencing her recent anxieties in vague, almost poetic terms, hinting at a connection to a past case, a case I'd tried to bury deep within the archives of my memory. The case of Sarah Jenkins. Sarah, with her haunting eyes and whispered secrets, had been a source of considerable professional and emotional turmoil. Her case involved a pattern of anxiety, a similar feeling of being watched, and the recurring symbol that now gnawed at my subconscious: a white moonflower, a rare nocturnal bloom, almost extinct in this part of the country.

The letter mentioned Sarah's anxieties, her recurring nightmares filled with the image of the moonflower, its luminous petals glowing in the darkness, a symbol of both beauty and dread. Sarah's descriptions, much like Emily's, had been fragmented, unreliable, shrouded in a veil of fear and obfuscation. There had been a tangible sense of unease in Sarah's therapy sessions, a chilling current of dread that had permeated our interactions. She would often speak of a "presence," a feeling of being watched, a sensation of being followed even in the most public of spaces. She never explicitly mentioned a perpetrator, never provided any concrete details that could lead to a tangible identification of a stalker or threat. Her fear was far more insidious than that, woven into the very fabric of her anxieties, a deeply rooted, almost existential dread.

The anonymous letter's veiled references to Sarah's case sent a chill down my spine. It was more than a simple coincidence; it was a deliberate attempt to draw a connection, to weave a sinister thread between two seemingly disparate lives. The writer was playing a game, testing my knowledge, gauging my response. The closing sentence – "Some things are better left buried" – echoed Sarah's own haunting words, a chilling reminder of the secrets she had taken to her grave.

The implication was clear: there was more to Emily's anxiety, more to Sarah's death than met the eye. The letter wasn't just a threat; it was a carefully crafted provocation, designed to draw me into a dangerous game, to force me to confront a truth that had been carefully concealed for years. A truth that seemed inextricably linked to both Emily and Sarah. The letter left me with a profound sense of unease, a feeling that went beyond professional curiosity. The lines between counselor and investigator were becoming increasingly blurred. The rational part of my mind, the one trained in years of psychological assessment and therapeutic practice, told me to remain calm, to proceed cautiously, to collect evidence before jumping to conclusions. Yet, a deeper, more primal instinct – a gut feeling fueled by a sudden, sharp increase in adrenaline – urged me to act.

I spent the rest of the night poring over Sarah's files, rereading her transcripts, searching for any overlooked clues, any hint of a connection between her case and Emily's present situation. I reviewed Sarah's medical history, searching for any possible underlying conditions that might have contributed to her anxieties, any physiological or psychological factors that could explain her vivid nightmares and persistent feeling of being watched. I found nothing definitive, nothing that could definitively link the two cases. However, certain similarities remained – the recurring presence, the unsettling nightmares, and the elusive moonflower that continued to appear as a disturbing motif in both narratives.

As I lay in bed, the soft glow of my bedside lamp illuminated my long, brown, wavy hair as it cascaded around my shoulders. My gentle, inquisitive nature was evident in the way my soft green eyes scanned the ceiling, lost in deep contemplation of Emily's recent session. The recent discoveries about Emily's case being so intricately tied to the Sarah Jenkins investigation had clearly weighed on me. Even in repose, the professional me was present; the faint silhouette of a trench coat and knee-high boots, visible in the periphery of my eyes, draped over a nearby chair, testament to the dedication and adventurous spirit that pushed me to seek answers beyond the usual boundaries of therapy. As a hard-working therapist, driven by a desire to understand and heal, the complex web I'm unraveling with Emily is a challenge I embrace with both my mind and my adventurous heart.

The next morning, I arrived at my office earlier than usual, the weight of the anonymous letter heavy on my mind. I needed to see Emily again, to explore her story further, to uncover the truth that the letter had so subtly suggested. I felt the growing apprehension that gnawed at the edges of my professional curiosity. Was this just another case of severe anxiety, or was something far more sinister at play? The unknown that loomed over my investigation threatened to engulf me. This was no longer just a matter of unraveling psychological threads; it was a confrontation with the unseen, the potential presence of danger in the quiet, almost predictable rhythm of my professional life.

Emily's appointment was scheduled for noon, yet I found myself restless, pacing my office, unable to settle. I reviewed the letter again, studying the handwriting, the paper, the cryptic message, looking for some hidden meaning, some clue that could illuminate the shadows surrounding Emily's case. I even checked my own handwriting, comparing it to the elegantly looping script of the anonymous letter. Nothing matched. The sender was clearly someone skilled at masking their identity, someone who understood the art of deception.

The thought of the white moonflower kept returning to me, a recurring motif in Sarah's nightmares. It was more than just a symbol; it felt like a key, a piece of the puzzle that refused to fit. I recalled a botanical journal article I'd read about the near-extinction of the white moonflower in our region, mentioning isolated pockets in remote areas of the nearby forest, a detail I had never considered before.

As the clock ticked towards noon, my anxiety mirrored Emily's, the lines between therapist and patient becoming blurred. The anonymous letter had achieved its purpose: it had stirred the waters, creating ripples of unease that spread through my professional life and threatened to consume me entirely. My office, once a sanctuary of calm and understanding, now felt like a stage set for a drama whose plot line remained stubbornly shrouded in darkness. The waiting room felt unusually cold; the usual comforting familiarity of the space replaced by a growing sense of apprehension. The familiar scent of old books seemed suffocating, the quiet tick of the office clock suddenly echoing with an ominous resonance. I waited, bracing myself for the arrival of Emily, a woman whose story was slowly revealing a potential danger that extended far beyond the confines of her own anxieties. The anonymous letter was not just a warning; it was a call to action, a summons to a game of shadows where I was forced to question my own intuition, the boundaries of my profession, and the safety of my own life. I waited, and the weight of the unknown pressed down on me, a tangible force that seemed to suffocate the air in the room.

Building Rapport with Emily

The door opened, and Emily entered, her shoulders slumped, her gaze fixed on the floor. Upon our first meeting, I thought she was younger than I'd initially imagined, barely out of her twenties, with large, expressive eyes that held a weariness far beyond her years. Her clothes were simple, almost drab, a muted reflection of the subdued emotions she carried. She sat down on the plush couch, her hands clasped tightly in her lap, her knuckles white. The scent of vanilla and something else, something faintly floral and unsettling, hung in the air around her. It was a perfume I couldn't quite place, adding to the enigma that shrouded her.

My initial approach was one of calm reassurance. I began with gentle, open-ended questions, allowing her to guide the conversation, to set the pace. "Emily, thank you for coming in today. I understand from our previous conversation that you've been experiencing some... anxiety?" I said, my voice soft, measured, my tone deliberately non-judgmental. I avoided the word "fear," opting instead for a softer, less intimidating term.

She nodded slowly; her gaze still fixed on the floor. "Yes," she whispered, her voice barely audible. "It's... it's like I'm being watched. Like someone is always there, just... watching."

I leaned forward, maintaining eye contact, but not in a way that felt intrusive or overwhelming. "Can you tell me more about that feeling? What does it feel like to be watched?" I asked, my voice a gentle counterpoint to the palpable tension in the room.

She hesitated, then began to describe the feeling, her words halting at first, then gaining momentum as she spoke. She described a pervasive sense of unease, a feeling of being observed, scrutinized, even judged, in every aspect of her life. It wasn't a specific person, she stressed, but rather an omnipresent sensation, a vague feeling of being under constant surveillance.

I listened intently, employing active listening techniques, mirroring her body language subtly to convey empathy and understanding. I nodded, offered encouraging murmurs, and used reflective statements to demonstrate that I was fully engaged with her experience. "So, it's not a specific person you're afraid of, but rather a feeling of being observed, a constant sense of being watched?" I confirmed, summarizing her feelings to ensure accuracy and understanding.

She nodded again, a tremor running through her shoulders. "Yes," she repeated, her voice trembling slightly. "It's...exhausting. I can't relax. I can't sleep. Everywhere I go, I feel like they're there."

I introduced the concept of generalized anxiety disorder, explaining its symptoms in simple terms, avoiding technical jargon that might overwhelm her. I gently pointed out the similarities between her symptoms and those commonly associated with the condition. I made a point of acknowledging that her feelings were real and valid, and that experiencing them didn't make her weak or flawed. Building rapport was paramount, ensuring she felt safe enough to share more deeply.

Our conversation continued for a considerable time, delving deeper into the nuances of her anxiety. I steered the conversation towards specific details, but always gently, carefully probing without pushing too hard. I asked about her daily routine, her relationships, and her environment, looking for any potential triggers or stressors that might be contributing to her anxiety. I paid close attention to her body language, her vocal tone, and her choice of words, searching for clues beyond the surface level of her narrative.

As the session progressed, Emily began to reveal more, her reticence slowly giving way to a hesitant trust. She spoke of recurring dreams, vivid and unsettling, filled with images of shadows and fleeting glimpses of a figure she couldn't quite make out. She described a recurring symbol that haunted her subconscious: a white moonflower, its petals luminous in the darkness. The same moonflower mentioned in the anonymous letter.

The mention of the moonflower sent a jolt through me. It was a deliberate choice of words, an unexpected confirmation of my suspicions. My role shifted subtly, the lines between therapist and investigator blurring further. I had to tread carefully, balancing the need to gather information with the ethical obligations of confidentiality and client well-being.

I responded with carefully chosen words, maintaining my professional demeanor while subtly guiding the conversation. "Emily, that's a very powerful image. Can you describe it in more detail? What does the moonflower represent to you? What feelings does it evoke?" My questions were designed to tap into the emotional significance of the symbol, to uncover any latent meanings or connections that might provide clues to the source of her anxiety.

She struggled to articulate her feelings, her words laced with confusion and apprehension. The moonflower, she explained, represented both beauty and dread, a sense of otherworldly enchantment tinged with an underlying fear. It was a symbol of mystery and unease, a persistent presence in her subconscious, a reminder of something she couldn't quite grasp.

I acknowledged her difficulty articulating her emotions, validating her feelings without dismissing the significance of the symbol. I suggested we explore this further using techniques like free association, allowing her subconscious to guide our conversation.

The next hour became a carefully orchestrated dance between therapeutic techniques and investigative inquiry. I utilized different therapeutic approaches, seamlessly weaving them into our conversation. I asked her to describe the moonflower in detail, focusing on the sensory aspects—the texture of the petals, the scent, the luminescence in the darkness. Through this, she inadvertently revealed more, sharing snippets of fragmented memories and sensations—the chill of the night air, the rustling of leaves, the unsettling sound of footsteps in the distance. These seemingly insignificant details were in fact crucial puzzle pieces.

By subtly shifting the focus, I encouraged her to recall memories associated with the symbol. I used techniques like guided imagery, helping her visualize the moonflower in vivid detail, encouraging her to explore any related emotions or sensations. I asked about places she might have seen a similar flower, or any places that evoked a similar feeling of unease.

Gradually, as trust between us deepened, Emily began to connect her feelings of being watched with certain locations and memories, although they remained fragmented and imprecise. She mentioned a specific park, a place where she often went for walks, but only at night. The park was near the location of Sarah Jenkins' house, a house she had never explicitly known, or thought she'd known, though the symbol, the very existence of the moonflower, tied them in a way she had yet to understand.

As the session concluded, Emily seemed calmer, more at ease. She had disclosed significantly more than she had intended, and there was a discernible shift in her emotional state. The heavy weight of her anxiety seemed marginally lighter. But I knew that our work was far from over. The anonymous letter, the moonflower motif, Sarah Jenkins' case—all the pieces were beginning to coalesce, forming a chilling pattern that extended far beyond Emily's individual anxieties. The investigation was now far beyond the confines of the consulting room; it was becoming increasingly personal, potentially dangerous, and more entwined with my own life than I had ever anticipated. The unraveling thread had become a tangled web, and I was firmly caught within it.

A Recurring Symbol

The session ended, but the image of the white moonflower remained imprinted on my mind. It wasn't just a symbol in Emily's subconscious; it was a recurring motif, a thread weaving its way through the fabric of her anxiety, and now, strangely, into my own investigation. Its presence in the anonymous letter, its emergence in

Emily's dreams, and the stark realization that I'd actually seen a similar flower pressed delicately between the pages of Sarah Jenkins's case file – it was all too much of a coincidence to ignore.

The next few days were a blur of research and reflection. I revisited Sarah Jenkins's file, poring over every detail, searching for any mention of moonflowers, any connection, however tenuous, to Emily's case. There was nothing explicit, no mention of the flower in her personal belongings, or in the accounts of her friends and family. But the absence of direct evidence didn't diminish the unsettling feeling that the symbol held a key. The way Sarah's murder had been meticulously staged, the almost theatrical precision of the crime scene—it suggested a level of planning and obsession that resonated with the intensity of Emily's anxiety and the obsessive repetition of the moonflower.

I found myself gravitating towards botanical websites, searching for varieties of white moonflowers, studying their morphology, their flowering periods, and their geographical distribution. I even consulted a local botanist, a charming but eccentric woman named Dr. Michelle Braden, whose expertise in rare and unusual flora was legendary. She confirmed that the type of moonflower I described— a large, pure white bloom with a subtly intoxicating fragrance—was relatively uncommon in our region, blooming primarily during late summer and autumn. This temporal detail, although seemingly insignificant, added another layer to the mystery. The letter had arrived in the spring, and Emily's anxiety had begun around the same time, months before the typical moonflower's blooming season.

Intrigued, I revisited Emily's notes, meticulously examining them under a bright lamp. I had initially dismissed them as nothing more than scribbled thoughts and anxieties, but my perspective had shifted. I scrutinized every word, every drawing, searching for any hidden clues, any recurring themes. And there it was, etched subtly in the corner of a page—a tiny sketch of a moonflower, barely visible, yet undeniably present. It was a smaller, less detailed version of the one described in her dreams, but the essence was the same: the ethereal beauty juxtaposed with an underlying sense of unease.

The following session with Emily was pivotal. I decided to directly address the recurring moonflower symbol, gently confronting her with the evidence I'd uncovered. The sight of the tiny sketch in her notebook brought a wave of shock and apprehension across her face. She visibly recoiled, her hands trembling as she stared at the drawing. The silence hung heavy in the air, thick with unspoken fears and half-remembered memories.

"Emily," I began softly, "I've been doing some research. I've found some interesting things related to the moonflower." I showed her the picture I'd taken of the pressed flower from Sarah Jenkins's file, the delicate petals seemingly whispering secrets. I cautiously showed her Dr. Braden's notes on the flower's uncommonness and blooming season, emphasizing the seeming discrepancy between its seasonal presence and when her anxieties began.

Her reaction confirmed my suspicions. The symbol was more than just a random image in her subconscious; it was a deeply ingrained trigger, a link to a traumatic event, a memory she couldn't fully access, or perhaps, a memory she desperately wanted to suppress. She confessed that the sight of the moonflower, in any form, sent a chill down her spine, a wave of fear that paralyzed her.

Through carefully guided imagery and free association, we slowly began to peel back the layers of her repression. She started talking about a childhood memory, vague and fragmented at first, filled with shadows and half-remembered sounds. She spoke of a night walk in a park, a place that resembled the park near Sarah Jenkins's house—the same park I'd found mentioned in her session notes. She recalled the scent of moonflowers, a cloying sweetness mingled with something sharp and unsettling, the rustling of leaves in the night, a fleeting glimpse of a dark figure in the periphery. The details were hazy, blurry, like a half-forgotten dream.

I used therapeutic techniques to guide her towards clarifying these memories, helping her to unpack the emotional weight associated with the symbol. I used metaphors, art therapy, even guided meditation to access her subconscious. We explored different interpretations of the moonflower—its beauty, its mystery, its association with both life and death, its nighttime blossoming. I validated her feelings, reminding her that her memories, however fragmented, were real and valid, and that it was okay to face her past, even if it was painful.

The image of the moonflower became a focal point of our therapeutic process. It was a shared symbol, a conduit to her unconscious, and a powerful tool in unpacking her trauma. Her feelings of being watched, her anxiety, her nightmares—they were all inexplicably linked to this symbol, to the place where she'd experienced something traumatic, something she couldn't fully recall, but that haunted her nonetheless.

As the sessions continued, Emily revealed more details, slowly connecting her fragmented memories to the unsettling reality of what had happened in the park that night. It was slowly emerging that the feeling of being watched wasn't just anxiety; it was a lingering presence, a constant reminder of a threat that never truly left. The moonflower, in its ethereal beauty, had become a morbid reminder of that threat, its haunting presence a constant echo of a past trauma. Its recurring appearances in the letter, her dreams, and her own subconscious became less of a puzzle and more of a roadmap, guiding us toward a truth far more sinister than we could have imagined. The moonflower, a symbol of beauty and dread, was leading us down a dark path, one that connected Emily's anxieties to the enigmatic case of Sarah Jenkins, a path I was becoming increasingly determined to follow. The unraveling thread was becoming a terrifying tapestry.

Initial Investigation Begins

The weight of Emily's case pressed down on me, a palpable sense of urgency replacing the initial cautious curiosity. My role had shifted, subtly but significantly. I was no longer just her therapist; I was, in a sense, her investigator. The ethical considerations were a constant companion, a silent voice whispering warnings in the back of my mind. Yet, ignoring the chilling connection between Emily's trauma and Sarah Jenkins's murder felt impossible. The anonymous letter, the recurring moonflower, the uncanny similarities – these were not mere coincidences; they were clues.

My first step was discreet. I started with Emily's background information. Her file, meticulously kept, revealed a relatively stable childhood, a loving family, and a consistent academic record. There were no glaring red flags, no hints of past trauma that would explain the intensity of her current anxiety. This lack of overt indicators fueled my determination. The deeper the mystery, the more compelling the pursuit.

I then turned my attention to the anonymous letter. The handwriting analysis I commissioned yielded little beyond confirming the author was female and likely right-handed. The paper type was common, the ink unremarkable, all of which pointed towards an attempt at anonymity, which was hardly surprising. However, the forensic examination of the letter revealed a faint trace of pollen adhering to the paper's fibers. It was sent in the spring, a time when most moonflowers, according to Dr. Braden, were not in bloom, further deepening the mystery. I sent the pollen sample to a specialist for analysis.

My investigation branched out from the confines of my office. I spent hours at the city library, poring over old newspaper archives, searching for any unsolved cases involving missing persons or unexplained deaths in the vicinity of the park Emily described. I checked police records, focusing on incidents that involved moonflowers—a long shot, I knew, but the symbol's persistent presence made it a worthwhile pursuit.

Days turned into weeks; each one filled with a meticulous piecing together of fragments. I learned that Sarah Jenkins, besides being a talented artist, had also been involved in a local environmental group focused on preserving the natural areas surrounding the city, specifically the park where Emily's fragmented memories were centered. This connection, albeit indirect, was another piece of the puzzle, further linking the two women's lives.

I revisited the park myself, walking the paths Emily had described, attempting to visualize the scene she had recounted. The place was serene by day, but I could imagine its eerie beauty under the cloak of night. The air, even in the daylight, had an almost tangible stillness, a hush that seemed to echo with unspoken secrets. I meticulously examined the area, searching for anything out of place, any sign of disturbance, anything that would unlock the mystery shrouding Emily's memory.

I spent a day with Dr. Michelle Braden, engaging her not just about the moonflower itself, but about the park's ecosystem. She revealed a keen awareness of the park's delicate balance, particularly its diverse nocturnal wildlife and the prevalence of certain insects and arachnids. While initially seeming unrelated, this information provided a new perspective. Could Emily's fragmented memory involve a nocturnal creature, a sound, a detail that held the key to understanding the threat she had experienced?

The pollen analysis results arrived. The pollen was indeed from a moonflower, a rare variety whose specific location was limited to a small area in a remote part of the park, an area infrequently visited. This wasn't a common moonflower; it was an uncommon, almost isolated variety. The fact that the pollen was found on the anonymous letter hinted at a deliberate connection, a subtle message deliberately woven into the fabric of the letter itself. The location of this rare moonflower was not something that the average person would know.

I continued to visit with Emily, our therapeutic sessions interwoven with my discreet investigation. She was slowly but surely recovering, finding solace in the process of piecing together her memories. The moonflower, though still triggering fear, had also become a pathway to healing, a symbol of her past trauma, and yet a symbol that was leading her towards a sense of resolution. My role was to guide her and protect her, but also to understand the connection to Sarah Jenkins's case, a case that was more than likely intrinsically linked to her own fragmented memories.

While I maintained the strictest professional boundaries, the line between therapist and investigator became increasingly blurred. I justified my actions by reminding myself that I was acting not only in Emily's best interest, but to prevent further harm. The very real possibility of another victim loomed, a dark shadow that underscored the urgency of my actions. It was a delicate dance between ethical considerations and the relentless pursuit of truth, a pursuit that pushed me to the edge of my professional comfort zone.

The next session with Emily was remarkable. The fragmented memories were coalescing. She spoke, hesitantly at first, about a figure who had been watching her, a figure that had appeared on several occasions, lurking in the shadows, near the location of the rare moonflowers. She described a distinct feeling of being followed, of being stalked. The feeling of dread and paralysis that had characterized her anxiety was not simply a manifestation of her inner turmoil; it was a genuine feeling of imminent threat.

Emily's fragmented memories started revealing details – a glint of metal, the sound of snapping twigs, a lingering scent of tobacco. This information was not only emotionally difficult for Emily but was offering me more clues. I started to wonder if there was a pattern to these incidents. Was this a stalker? A predator? Someone who was deliberately using the moonflower as a sinister symbol? The answers were still buried, hidden beneath layers of trauma and repression. But the unraveling thread was bringing me closer to the truth, a truth that was far more sinister than I had initially imagined.

The moonflower, in its fragile beauty, was no longer just a symbol of anxiety and repressed memory. It was now a trail, leading me down a dangerous path, a path that entangled Emily's life with Sarah Jenkins's murder, and that demanded resolution. The pieces of the puzzle were falling into place, but the full picture remained elusive, a terrifying, yet compelling enigma. The night was still young, and the unraveling of this terrifying tapestry had just begun.

Chapter 2

Shadows of the Past

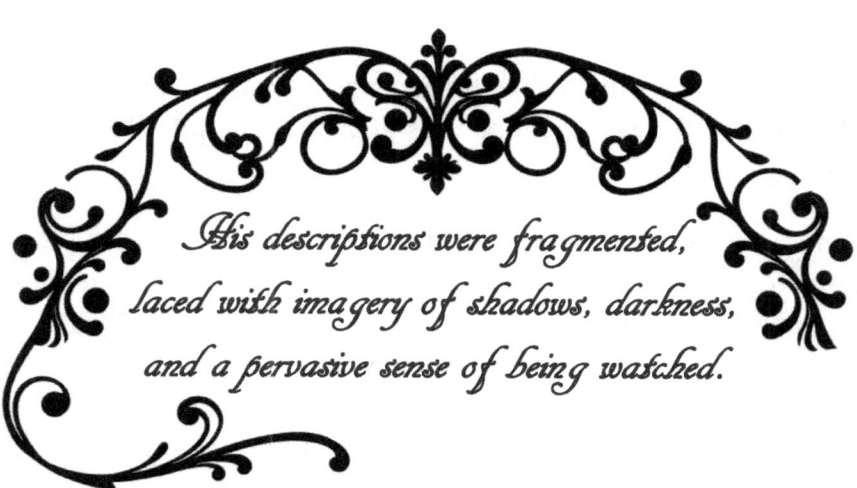

His descriptions were fragmented, laced with imagery of shadows, darkness, and a pervasive sense of being watched.

Exploring Emily's Childhood

Our next session began with a gentle exercise in guided imagery. I asked Emily to close her eyes and take slow, deep breaths, focusing on the sensations in her body. I guided her to a safe place, a memory of a time when she felt peaceful and secure. This was crucial; I needed to build a foundation of trust and safety before delving into the potentially traumatic memories. We spent several sessions establishing this baseline, gently chipping away at the layers of anxiety that shrouded her past.

Once a sense of calm had been established, we cautiously began to explore her childhood. Her initial descriptions were vague, fragmented images flitting across the canvas of her mind – sunlit rooms, the scent of baking bread, the sound of laughter. These were pleasant memories, seemingly innocuous, but they were a vital starting point, a way to help her navigate the path to more difficult recollections.

I used a technique called "timeline therapy," mapping out significant events of her life on a visual timeline. This helped to organize her memories chronologically and to identify potential periods of stress or disruption. Emily's early years were marked by stability, as her file had suggested. She described a loving family, a comfortable home, and a supportive community. There were no major upheavals, no traumatic events that readily presented themselves as possible root causes of her current distress. This only served to deepen the mystery.

As we progressed, however, the idyllic picture began to crack. Emily started mentioning fleeting feelings of unease, sensations of being watched, a recurring sense of being followed. These were initially dismissed as childish fantasies, but as we explored them further, a pattern began to emerge. The feeling of being watched intensified around the time of her seventh birthday. Around this period, her descriptions became less vivid, her memories more fragmented, punctuated by moments of intense anxiety.

Using narrative therapy, I encouraged Emily to tell her story in her own words, without interruption or judgment. This approach allows the individual to become the active agent in their narrative, and in Emily's case, was particularly beneficial in reducing her sense of helplessness and vulnerability. We began to notice a recurring theme: the presence of a shadow, a vague and ill-defined figure lurking at the edge of her awareness. She described seeing it flitting between trees, appearing in dimly lit corners of her house. She was uncertain of its form but vividly remembered the disconcerting feeling of being observed.

"It was like… a presence," she explained, her voice trembling slightly. "Not a person, exactly. More like… a feeling, a shadow. It never got close, but it was always there, watching."

These shadows were not only visual; they manifested as sounds and smells as well. She described the sound of rustling leaves, even in the absence of wind; a peculiar scent akin to old wood and damp earth; and an almost imperceptible chill in the air whenever the shadow was near. I made note of these sensory details, recognizing that they could be critical in reconstructing the events. The recurring sensation of a chilling presence, however, was more than just a fear response; it hinted at a potential traumatic encounter.

Through careful prompting and the use of relaxation techniques, I helped Emily delve deeper into these sensory memories. We revisited her seventh birthday party in detail, analyzing the events, people present, and the overall atmosphere. The party itself seemed unremarkable—a standard celebration with friends and family. However, during a period of playful hide-and-seek, Emily recalled a distinct sensation of being watched from a distance, a feeling that transcended simple observation and instilled a primal fear. She remembered hiding in a darkened shed located near a moonflower bush, the aroma of the flower, cloying and sweet, lingering in her memory.

The memory of the shed remained fragmented, yet the underlying fear was palpable. The details were blurred, yet the feelings—fear, vulnerability, and a deep sense of violation—remained profoundly potent. Her initial discomfort in the shed became more distinct. It was more than just a case of hiding; there was a feeling of being trapped, of being observed, of something dangerous, although unseen.

The moonflower, which had initially surfaced in her adult anxieties, found its roots here, in the obscured memory of her childhood. The connection was striking, and unsettling. The same flower she had seen in her adult night terrors, the same flower found at the scene of Sarah Jenkins's murder, and the same flower mentioned in the anonymous letter—it was all converging, hinting at a possible link between Emily's past and the present-day mystery.

Emily remembered a specific detail about the shed: an old rusty tool lying on the ground; it was vaguely familiar to her. It wasn't until a few sessions later that this detail became meaningful. She described the tool as resembling a shovel. This seemingly trivial detail suddenly took on a sinister significance. A shovel, an instrument used for burying things.

I encouraged her to explore the emotions associated with this detail, which triggered a wave of fragmented memories. She described feeling cold, alone, and deeply afraid in the shed. She recalled seeing a shadowy figure at the edge of her awareness, a figure that didn't seem fully formed, as if made of smoke and mist. The feeling of paralysis returned. She felt utterly helpless.

We then explored the period immediately following her seventh birthday. Her demeanor shifted subtly. She spoke of increased anxiety, nightmares, and a general feeling of unease. Her previously exuberant personality became withdrawn and subdued. This marked a notable shift in her development. She withdrew from social interactions, becoming more isolated and introspective. Her academic performance, which had been consistently excellent, began to decline.

The symptoms were consistent with the effects of trauma. I suspected that whatever occurred in the shed on her seventh birthday had a profound and lasting impact on her psyche. The fragmented memories, the recurring shadows, the persistent anxiety – it all pointed towards a concealed traumatic event.

Our sessions continued, each one a carefully orchestrated step towards uncovering the truth. I used a range of therapeutic techniques – EMDR, cognitive behavioral therapy, and narrative therapy – to help Emily process her memories and work through the associated trauma. The therapeutic process was slow and meticulous, requiring patience, empathy, and a careful balancing of pushing her to confront her fears while ensuring her safety and well-being.

Gradually, the details started to coalesce. While the complete picture remained elusive, the fragments were forming a clearer narrative. The shadowy figure, initially seen only in her fragmented memories, became slightly more defined. She began to remember glimpses of clothing—dark, nondescript clothes—and a sense of the figure's size and build. It was still hazy, but the image was becoming less amorphous, less akin to a nightmarish figment of her imagination and more like a recollection of a real presence.

The details of the shed also became slightly more vivid. She recalled the texture of the old wooden floor, the damp smell of soil, and the feeling of cold, hard earth beneath her fingers. She also remembered the taste of the moonflower as she hid, a cloying sweetness mixed with a metallic aftertaste that remained disturbing. The metallic aftertaste added another layer of complexity to the unfolding mystery, and I noted it down meticulously.

Through this painstaking process of memory retrieval and therapeutic intervention, Emily's childhood began to reveal its secrets. The stability she had initially described masked a concealed trauma, a lurking darkness that had shaped her life in ways she had yet to fully comprehend. The path to uncovering the truth was challenging, but every session, every shared memory, brought us closer to understanding the profound connection between her past and the present, a connection that remained as chilling as it was compelling. The next steps involved further investigation into her family history and revisiting the park, an endeavor that promised both healing and potential danger. The moonflower, once a symbol of her fear, had become a pathway to the truth, a potentially dangerous yet undeniably vital path toward healing and justice.

The Second Client Daniel

My next client, Daniel, was a stark contrast to Emily. Where Emily presented a fragile exterior masking a deep well of suppressed trauma, Daniel projected an almost aggressive defensiveness, a carefully constructed wall designed to keep the world – and me – at bay. He was a tall, wiry man in his late twenties, with eyes that darted nervously and hands that fidgeted constantly. His initial intake form revealed a history of anxiety and paranoia, but it lacked the depth of detail Emily's had provided. He'd presented himself with a curt, almost hostile brevity, which initially made me question his commitment to therapy. His reluctance to disclose details hinted at something deeper, something he was desperately trying to conceal.

Our first session was a tense affair. Daniel sat rigidly on the edge of the couch, his gaze fixed on a point somewhere beyond my shoulder. He spoke in clipped sentences, offering minimal information about his background or the nature of his distress. I began with open-ended questions, attempting to create a safe space for him to express himself without feeling pressured. However, each carefully crafted question met with a guarded response, a wall of resistance subtly reinforced with every terse answer.

"I have nightmares," he finally admitted, his voice a low growl. "They're... vivid. Too vivid." He paused, his gaze flickering towards the window as if expecting to see something lurking outside.

I probed further, inquiring about the content of his nightmares. His descriptions were fragmented, laced with imagery of shadows, darkness, and a pervasive sense of being watched. He mentioned recurring symbols – a moonflower, surprisingly – and the unsettling sound of rustling leaves in the absence of wind. This detail sent a shiver down my spine. The moonflower motif, so deeply embedded in Emily's subconscious, now surfaced in Daniel's night terrors. The eerie coincidence was striking, almost too coincidental to ignore. It deepened the already unsettling mystery connecting Emily's trauma to a larger, as-yet-undefined pattern.

"It's always the same," he continued, his voice barely above a whisper. "The shadows, the leaves... and the smell. It's like...damp earth and old wood." This mirrored Emily's descriptions with chilling precision. The sensory details were nearly identical, despite the two individuals having no apparent connection.

His paranoia extended beyond his nightmares. He spoke of feeling constantly watched, of sensing a presence in his apartment, even when he knew he was alone. He checked locks repeatedly, slept with a knife under his pillow, and avoided walking alone at night. His anxiety levels were significantly heightened, bordering on debilitating. His heart raced even when engaging in simple daily activities, indicating a heightened state of physiological arousal. His responses suggested a chronic hypervigilance; a condition often associated with severe trauma or prolonged exposure to dangerous situations.

Unlike Emily, who had gradually opened up during our sessions, Daniel remained guarded and resistant. His defensive mechanisms were entrenched, and I realized that a direct approach would be counterproductive. I shifted my therapeutic approach from the narrative and timeline therapies used with Emily, towards a more gentle and exploratory strategy designed to build trust and to create a safe therapeutic relationship. I opted for techniques that emphasized self-soothing and mindfulness, focusing on helping him manage his immediate anxiety and panic.

Bottom-up processing proved to be an effective strategy that allowed him to understand his immediate surroundings as safe space.

We spent several sessions focusing on breathing exercises and grounding techniques, gradually working towards a point where he could talk about his feelings without feeling overwhelmed. I used somatic experiencing, focusing on helping him connect with his bodily sensations, and then learning to manage the associated emotions. This approach avoided forcing him to confront his traumatic memories directly and allowed him to process his anxieties at his own pace.

Gradually, through consistent engagement with these calming techniques, Daniel started to relax somewhat. His posture eased, his fidgeting decreased, and his eyes held mine for longer periods. This shift, though subtle, was significant, providing a vital foundation of trust upon which we could build our therapeutic relationship. He admitted feeling safe and assured that there was no pressure to disclose information that he was not yet comfortable sharing. His hesitations did not mean a failure of the therapeutic relationship; they underscored his trauma-related reluctance to trust others.

As the sessions progressed, Daniel's stories, although still fragmented, provided glimpses into the possible source of his distress. He mentioned a childhood spent mostly alone, a solitary existence characterized by frequent moves and a lack of consistent social connections. He recounted moments of intense isolation, feelings of vulnerability, and a deep-seated fear of abandonment. He described the feeling of being watched throughout his childhood, an omnipresent dread that had intensified with time, particularly during specific periods. This chronic anxiety, coupled with the night terrors and sensory hallucinations, suggested a significant traumatic event in his past, one that remained shrouded in ambiguity and concealed by his defensive responses.

He described vague memories of his early childhood, memories that were both fragmented and emotionally charged. He spoke of a shadowy figure, very similar to Emily's descriptions, only occasionally recalling aspects of the figure's appearance, always in short fragmented images. He remembered shadowy figures lingering in the periphery of his vision, fleeting glimpses of dark clothing, the feeling of being observed from a distance, and a peculiar smell. The scent was remarkably familiar – again, damp earth and old wood.

One particular memory, while still hazy, stood out. He recalled a scene involving a shed, very much like Emily's description, a place of hiding, a place of terror. It seemed as if the memories were triggering both a sense of terror and a feeling of paralysis; he couldn't fully recall the events that occurred, however, his emotional reaction revealed the trauma he had endured. He described the same cloying sweetness of moonflowers and the metallic aftertaste that Emily had described. He, too, vaguely recalled the presence of a rusty tool, possibly a shovel, lying on the ground. The consistency in sensory details across both clients was uncanny. It suggested a common experience, a shared traumatic event, but the question was, how? And what was the commonality linking them both?

Daniel's sessions weren't as easy to navigate as Emily's had been. His guarded nature and intense anxiety required a delicate approach. I needed to carefully balance the need to explore his past trauma with the vital requirement of maintaining his sense of safety and security. The use of somatic experiencing and mindfulness strategies allowed for slow but steady progress. Through guided imagery, mindfulness, and self-regulation techniques, I hoped to help him build a foundation of safety before we attempted to directly confront his traumatic memories.

His therapy was a slower and more complex process than Emily's. He presented with a greater depth of defensive barriers and a more pronounced distrust of others. The similarities, however, between his symptoms and Emily's continued to nag at my mind. The shared imagery, the consistent sensory details, and the underlying themes of shadows, isolation, and a profound sense of violation strongly suggested a potential link between their cases. This shared narrative, although fragmented, was too compelling to ignore. The possibility that they shared a common traumatic experience or perhaps even shared a common perpetrator was becoming more and more plausible. The investigation, I felt, was rapidly shifting from a question of individual trauma to a broader search for a pattern that transcended the individual and suggested a wider issue at play. The implications were far-reaching and profoundly unsettling. The moonflower continued to act as a chilling link, connecting their trauma to the Sarah Jenkins case and the anonymous letter, all converging into a terrifying pattern of events.

Connecting the Dots

The recurring motif of the moonflower, initially a striking coincidence, now felt like a crucial piece of a larger puzzle. Its presence in both Emily and Daniel's narratives, interwoven with the descriptions of shadows, damp earth, old wood, and the unsettling rustling of leaves, painted a disturbingly consistent picture. The sensory details were too specific, too similar to be mere coincidence. This wasn't just about individual trauma; it was about something far more sinister, something that linked their experiences, their nightmares, and their anxieties in a way that I couldn't yet comprehend.

My mind raced, attempting to connect the dots. I reviewed Emily's detailed sessions, searching for any overlooked detail, any nuance that might illuminate the connection. Her descriptions of the shed, the metallic taste, the overwhelming sense of violation—all mirrored in Daniel's fragmented memories. The shared sensory experience, the recurring imagery, and the consistent emotional responses were simply too compelling to ignore. This wasn't a coincidence; it was a pattern, a terrifyingly consistent pattern that hinted at a shared traumatic event. But what was it? And who, or what, was responsible?

The anonymous letter, with its cryptic reference to the Sarah Jenkins case, resurfaced in my mind. The moonflower mentioned in the letter—was this a deliberate clue, a breadcrumb leading me toward a larger, more sinister truth? The Sarah Jenkins case, unsolved for years, seemed to cast a long shadow over these seemingly unrelated cases. Could there be a connection? Was there a common thread binding them together, a common perpetrator operating under the cloak of secrecy?

I spent hours poring over police reports from the Sarah Jenkins case, comparing details to the narratives provided by Emily and Daniel. The reports were sparse, the investigation seemingly incomplete. However, several details resonated with the stories of my clients: the secluded location of the crime scene, the prevalence of moonflowers in the vicinity, the mention of a disturbed area of earth near the discovery of Sarah's body. The details, while seemingly disparate, coalesced into a disturbingly cohesive pattern when viewed through the lens of Emily and Daniel's shared experiences.

The shared imagery of shadows also struck me. Both Emily and Daniel described shadowy figures lurking in the periphery of their vision, figures they couldn't quite make out, figures that seemed to embody their fear and anxiety. These shadows weren't just metaphorical; they were real, present in their memories, in their nightmares, in their waking moments. They were a constant, pervasive reminder of the trauma they had endured. The pervasive feeling of being watched also echoed through both their narratives—a constant sense of surveillance, a feeling of being preyed upon, an almost tangible sense of dread. This element of fear and vulnerability, consistently present in both their experiences, added a further layer of complexity to the mystery.

The differences between Emily and Daniel's personalities and their approaches to therapy were also revealing. Emily, initially fragile and withdrawn, had gradually opened up, trusting me with intimate details of her past. Daniel, on the other hand, remained guarded, his defensive mechanisms firmly in place. This contrast highlighted the complexity of trauma responses, the diverse ways in which individuals cope with overwhelming experiences. Emily's trauma had manifested in a sense of paralysis and a deep-seated emotional vulnerability, while Daniel's had led to heightened anxiety, paranoia, and a deep-seated distrust of others. Both responses, however, pointed to a history of profound violation and a deep-seated need for safety and security.

The sheer consistency of the sensory details—the smell of damp earth and old wood, the cloying sweetness of moonflowers, the metallic taste—was particularly striking. These details were not simply elements of their individual narratives; they were common threads weaving their experiences together, creating a shared tapestry of trauma that transcended individual differences. This shared sensory experience suggested a shared location, a shared perpetrator, or perhaps a shared traumatic event that had imprinted itself deeply into their subconscious.

My own background in psychology and counseling informed my approach to this unfolding mystery. I understood the complexities of trauma, the ways in which memories are fragmented, distorted, and suppressed. I recognized the power of shared sensory experiences in creating strong, lasting emotional connections. The convergence of these details was not simply a matter of chance; it suggested a shared experience, a connection that was far too intricate and specific to ignore.

The fact that both Emily and Daniel had experienced periods of isolation and vulnerability further reinforced my suspicions. Their solitary childhoods, the frequent moves, the lack of consistent social connections—these elements created a fertile ground for exploitation and trauma. It suggested a vulnerability that might have been exploited by a predatory individual, someone who preyed on isolated children, someone who used their vulnerabilities to inflict unimaginable harm. The sheer consistency of the sensory details between the two patients was beginning to point towards a singular traumatic experience or a singular perpetrator. The question of how they were connected remained a chilling mystery.

I began to sketch a tentative timeline, cross-referencing details from both clients' accounts with information from the Sarah Jenkins case. The potential connections were unsettling. The timeframes, while not precisely aligned, overlapped in certain key aspects. The locations, though geographically separated, had some commonality - both clients' memories indicated rural settings. The timing of the experiences, based on their memories, suggested a potential pattern of behavior, a methodical approach to targeting and victimizing isolated individuals.

The more I delved into the mystery, the more I realized that I was not simply dealing with individual cases of trauma. I was grappling with something far larger, something that extended beyond the confines of my therapy practice and spilled over into the realm of criminal investigation. The moonflower, once a simple, striking coincidence, had become a macabre symbol, a terrifying link in a chain of events that suggested a broader pattern of abuse and violence. The pattern, the consistent sensory details and the shared emotional responses were all undeniable, suggesting that these seemingly disparate cases were linked in a way I could not have imagined. The implications were profound, far-reaching, and deeply unsettling. My role as a counselor was now inextricably intertwined with the need to uncover a larger truth, a truth that could potentially lead to justice for multiple victims, including those yet to come forward. The search for the truth had begun.

Threatening Encounters

The unsettling feeling of being watched intensified. It wasn't the imagined paranoia of a stressed therapist; this felt different, more tangible, more menacing. It started with small things—a car slowing down as it passed my house, its occupants staring intently; a shadow flitting across the periphery of my vision while I walked home from work, a fleeting glimpse of movement that was gone before I could focus on it. Then came the phone calls. No message, just the sound of heavy, ragged breathing, punctuated by the click of the phone disconnecting. These weren't the accidental misdials or wrong numbers that occasionally plagued my landline; these were deliberate, chilling intrusions.

My initial reaction was to dismiss them as the product of a frayed mind, a byproduct of my deep dive into Emily and Daniel's cases. The intensity of their trauma, their shared nightmares, the unsettling parallels between their experiences—it was all taking its toll. But even as I reasoned with myself, a cold dread settled in my stomach. The calls were too consistent, too precisely timed to be merely coincidental. They felt like warnings, escalating reminders that my investigation was attracting attention, attention of a kind that made my blood run cold.

One evening, as I watered the plants on my porch, a small, crumpled piece of paper caught my eye. It lay nestled amongst the flowerpots, almost camouflaged amongst the terracotta and the green foliage. I picked it up, my heart pounding a nervous rhythm against my ribs. It was a single, dried moonflower, its delicate petals brittle and brown, a stark contrast to the vibrant blooms I'd seen in park's garden and in the old photographs from the Sarah Jenkins case. The difference in their color was unsettling. This one wasn't vibrant; it was dead, desiccated, a stark symbol of decay.

There was nothing else on the paper; just the single moonflower. But the implication was clear. Someone was watching me, someone who knew about my investigation, someone who was sending a message, a chilling, silent threat. The moonflower, once a curious detail, had now become a symbol of terror, a macabre calling card.

The next incident felt more blatant. I was walking home from a late night at the library, engrossed in a particularly dense article on dissociative disorders, when I heard footsteps behind me. I quickened my pace, the sound of my own heartbeat echoing in my ears. The footsteps matched my pace, neither slowing nor quickening. I glanced over my shoulder; there was no one there. But the feeling persisted, that unnerving sense of being watched, of being followed, of being stalked.

I broke into a run, my breath catching in my throat, the fear clawing its way up my throat. I didn't stop until I reached my apartment building, my hands trembling as I fumbled with my keys. Once inside, I bolted the door, the familiar click of the lock a small but significant victory against the encroaching darkness. The adrenaline coursed through my veins, leaving me shaken and breathless.

That night, sleep evaded me. The images of the moonflower, the anonymous calls, the relentless footsteps haunted my dreams, twisting into nightmarish scenarios where shadows danced and figures lurked in the periphery of my vision. The line between my waking hours and my dreams blurred, the fear seeping into every facet of my being.

The following day, I contacted Detective Miller, the lead investigator on the Sarah Jenkins case. He seemed surprisingly receptive, his initial skepticism tempered by the sheer coincidence—or perhaps not coincidence—of the threatening encounters. He agreed to meet me, his eyes narrowed with a hint of concern as he listened to my account of the escalating threats.

"It's not just you, Dr. Adams," he said, his voice low and gravelly. "We've had reports of similar incidents in the area, seemingly random acts of intimidation. A series of strange occurrences, mostly late at night. Nothing concrete, nothing we can pin down, but enough to raise eyebrows."

He listened intently as I detailed my findings, the connections between Emily and Daniel's cases, the shared symbolism of the moonflower, the disturbing parallels between their narratives and the details from the Sarah Jenkins case. He leaned back in his chair, considering my words.

"It's starting to sound like we're dealing with something more than just coincidence, Dr. Adams," he admitted. "A pattern, maybe. And it seems like this pattern is now targeting you."

The weight of his words settled on me, confirming my deepest fears. I was no longer simply a counselor untangling the threads of her patients' pasts; I was a target, a pawn in a game I didn't understand, a game with stakes far higher than I had ever imagined. My investigation had somehow escalated beyond the realm of therapy, pushing me into the chilling territory of a criminal investigation. My professional life and personal safety were now inextricably linked.

We decided to increase security around my apartment. Detective Miller assigned a patrol officer to keep a close eye on my building. This small measure of comfort did little to alleviate the underlying anxiety. The pervasive feeling of being watched intensified. The knowledge that I was being targeted, that someone was systematically escalating their threats, filled me with a sense of foreboding that defied logic.

Days turned into nights, each moment filled with a growing sense of unease. The anonymous calls continued, the breathing growing more ragged, more menacing, each call closer to my home. I found myself constantly checking my surroundings, my senses heightened, my vigilance unwavering. The simple act of leaving my apartment became a fraught exercise, each step outside a potential confrontation.

One afternoon, while driving home, I noticed a car following me. A beat-up sedan, nondescript, blending in with the other vehicles on the road. I tried to shake it, changing lanes, accelerating, even pulling into a side street. But it stayed with me, persistent, unwavering, a constant shadow clinging to my rear bumper.

My heart pounded in my chest. This was no longer a subtle threat; this was open intimidation, a blatant display of power and control. I drove directly to the police station, the sedan following close behind. As I pulled into the parking lot, a uniformed officer immediately approached my car, his expression serious.

The car behind me stopped abruptly, and a figure emerged. He was tall, his features obscured by shadow, but something about his gait, his posture, his deliberate movements filled me with icy dread. He didn't try to run, or to hide. He stood there, watching me, a silent, menacing presence, a figure straight out of a nightmare. He looked at me, and a chilling smile spread across his face. It was brief, almost imperceptible, but it was enough. I recognized the malevolence in his eyes.

The officer apprehended the man, who refused to give his name. This encounter, far from reassuring, only increased my sense of danger. This wasn't some random act of intimidation; it was planned, orchestrated, and clearly aimed at silencing me. The game had shifted to a far more dangerous level.

The investigation into Emily and Daniel's cases had become far more than a therapeutic pursuit; it had become a fight for my own survival. The shadows of the past were not only haunting my clients; they were closing in on me, threatening to engulf me in their darkness. The moonflower, once a symbol of eerie coincidence, had blossomed into a sinister emblem of fear, a chilling reminder that I was playing a game with stakes far higher than I could have ever anticipated. The weight of the case pressed down on me; heavier than any other case I've ever handled.

The Romantic Entanglement

The persistent dread clung to me like a second skin, seeping into every aspect of my life, even bleeding into my relationship with Liam. He'd noticed the change, the subtle shift in my demeanor— the way my eyes darted nervously, the way I flinched at sudden noises, the almost imperceptible tremor in my hands. Liam, a history professor with a gentle nature and a calming presence, had always been my anchor, my safe harbor in the storms of life. But lately, even his comforting presence couldn't fully dispel the shadow of fear that had settled over me.

"You're not yourself, Elara," he'd said one evening, his voice laced with concern as he watched me meticulously check the locks on my apartment door for the tenth time. The usual ease in our evenings had been replaced with a tense silence, broken only by the rhythmic click of the locks and the sound of my own racing heart.

Liam pulled me gently to a seat, kissed my forehead and sat across from me, his dark, wavy hair falling around his forehead, framing his earnest hazel eyes. His short, well-kept beard gave him a distinguished yet approachable look. I could see his tall, toned body even as he leaned forward, his voice a low rumble as he shared his concerns. My heart swelled with affection as I watched him. I love his loving and playful nature, the way he surprises me with little treats or tries to make me jump with his little tricks. Even in this serious conversation, a small smile played on my lips, touched by the familiar warmth of his presence and the gentle love that always seems to radiate from him.

I tried to reassure him, to brush off his concerns as the result of stress, the inevitable consequence of dealing with particularly difficult cases. "It's just work, Liam. A few unsettling incidents, nothing more." But even as I spoke the words, I knew they were a lie. The weight of the investigation, the relentless threats, the constant feeling of being watched – it was all consuming, slowly eroding the foundations of my sanity.

He didn't believe me. He heard me speak of the way my sleep was plagued by nightmares, the way I'd wake up screaming in the dead of night, the dark circles under my eyes that spoke volumes of sleepless nights spent staring at the ceiling, haunted by visions of moonflowers and shadowy figures. He saw the way I'd jump at the slightest sound, my senses perpetually on high alert, my body taut with anticipation.

"Elara, you need to take a break," he insisted, his voice firm but gentle. "This case... it's taking over your life. You're neglecting yourself, neglecting us. This isn't healthy."

His words were a mirror reflecting the truth I desperately tried to ignore. My obsession with Emily and Daniel's cases, the relentless pursuit of answers, had become all-consuming. My work had bled into my personal life, pushing Liam to the periphery of my existence. The lines between my professional and personal worlds had blurred, the boundaries dissolving under the relentless pressure of the investigation. I spent hours poring over case files, analyzing photographs, searching for connections and patterns long after he had gone, the glow of the laptop screen illuminating my face in the darkness. Even during the day, my thoughts were constantly preoccupied with the cases, leaving little room for anything else, least of all Liam.

Our conversations, once vibrant and filled with laughter, had become stilted and strained, laced with unspoken anxieties and simmering resentment. My focus on work was not just consuming my time and energy, but it was affecting my ability to be emotionally present with him. Our intimate moments, once filled with passion and tenderness, had become infrequent, overshadowed by the chilling fear that had taken root within me.

The distance between us widened with each passing day, a chasm that deepened with every cryptic phone call and every unsettling encounter. His worry was palpable, his concern a tangible weight in the air between us. He'd try to engage me in conversations, to break through the wall of anxiety I'd inadvertently built around myself, but my responses were often short, distracted, my mind far away, racing through the details of the case. He didn't deserve this, this neglected shadow of a woman he once knew and loved.

One night, after another sleepless night haunted by the chilling image of the man who had followed me to the police station, I found Liam sitting on the front porch, his eyes filled with a mixture of concern and sadness.

"Elara," he began, his voice soft, "I'm worried about you. This isn't just a case anymore. It's… it's consuming you. You're losing yourself."

His words cut deeper than any threat I'd received. The truth of his statement struck me with the force of a physical blow. He was right. I was losing myself, losing the woman I was before this investigation had consumed me, before the shadows of the past began to encroach on my life. I was becoming a shadow of my former self, haunted by the moonflowers, the phone calls, and the ever-present feeling of being watched.

The weight of his words, coupled with the relentless pressure of the case, brought tears to my eyes. I didn't want to lose him. He was everything to me, my rock, my safe haven, and I was pushing him away.

"I know," I whispered, my voice choked with emotion. "I'm scared, Liam. I'm scared for myself, and I'm scared for... everything."

He reached out, his hand gently cupping my face. His touch, usually a source of comfort, now felt foreign, distant, as if I had become a stranger even to myself. The chasm between us felt wide and unyielding.

"We'll face this together," he said, his voice filled with unwavering support. "But you need to let me help you. You need to trust me."

His words offered a glimmer of hope, a tiny spark in the suffocating darkness that had enveloped me. His love, his unwavering support, offered a lifeline, a beacon in the storm. But even as I clung to that lifeline, I knew that the storm was far from over. The shadows of the past were still closing in, and the fight for my own survival, and for the preservation of my relationship, had only just begun. The weight of the case, both professionally and personally, felt insurmountable. The threats continued, and the strain on our relationship was evident, and yet, the strength of his love and his commitment to help was palpable.

The next few days were a blur of therapy sessions, police interviews, and sleepless nights. Detective Miller continued to investigate, offering what little comfort he could. He understood the increasing danger, the systematic escalation of the threats, and the toll it was taking on me, both professionally and personally. He acknowledged the strain it was putting on my relationship with Liam. He even suggested I take a leave of absence, a suggestion I initially resisted, clinging to the case like a life raft in a raging sea.

But Liam's unwavering support, his constant reassurance, eventually chipped away at my resistance. I finally agreed to take a temporary leave, to step away from the relentless pursuit of answers, to focus on myself and on rebuilding the connection with Liam that was slowly unraveling before my eyes.

Leaving the case behind was agonizing, a wrenching act of self-preservation. But even as I stepped away, the feeling of being watched remained. The unsettling quiet and lack of action on the case was, at first, incredibly stressful. The silence only accentuated the ever-present feeling that the unseen predator was still lurking just out of sight, its intentions as menacing as ever. The relief was temporary, and the fear still lingered. It had permeated every aspect of my life, leaving a residue of terror that refused to dissipate.

Despite the temporary reprieve from work, the emotional toll was immense. The nights were still filled with anxiety, the days punctuated by moments of intense fear. But Liam was there, patiently guiding me through the darkness, providing the emotional support I desperately needed to heal and recover.

Slowly, tentatively, we began to rebuild what had been broken. We talked, sharing our fears and anxieties, opening ourselves up to one another with a vulnerability that had been absent during the height of the investigation. His love and support was a beacon of hope, guiding me through the darkest moments.

The path to recovery would be long and arduous, but with Liam by my side, I knew I wasn't alone. The shadows of the past still lingered, but I was determined to face them, together, not letting them consume me. The road to healing would be a long and difficult journey, and the threats might return, but with Liam's love and support, I finally felt I had a chance to fight back. The investigation might be on hold, but the fight for my life, and the preservation of our love, was far from over.

Chapter 3

Unveiling the Conspiracy

A broken window... a threatening note... a single wilted red rose, a symbol of impending danger.

Uncovering a Hidden Network

The temporary reprieve from the Emily and Daniel case offered little solace. The unsettling quiet only amplified the gnawing feeling of being watched, the unseen predator circling just beyond the periphery of my awareness. The relief was fleeting, the fear persistent, a chilling residue clinging to every aspect of my life. Even the comfort of Liam's presence, once a balm to my anxieties, felt tainted by the pervasive sense of dread.

My therapy sessions with Dr. Evelyn Reed became a lifeline, a safe space to process the overwhelming emotions that threatened to consume me. Evelyn, with her calm demeanor and insightful questions, helped me untangle the threads of my fear, guiding me to confront the trauma that had been buried deep within. It was during one of these sessions that a crucial piece of the puzzle clicked into place.

I had been meticulously reviewing Emily's social media history, searching for any clues that might shed light on her disappearance. I'd noticed a recurring pattern—a group of individuals who appeared in several of her photographs and posts. At first, I dismissed them as simply friends or acquaintances, but as I delved deeper, I realized that these individuals were far more interconnected than I'd initially believed.

There was a distinct social circle, a tightly knit group of individuals who seemed to occupy Emily's world, and what was striking was that many of these same faces appeared in Daniel's past as well, though their relationship to him was far more elusive and difficult to define. They seemed to move within the same social and professional spheres, their connections woven together in a complex, almost invisible tapestry.

Evelyn, her brow furrowed in concentration, listened intently as I described the pattern, her eyes reflecting my growing unease. "It's like they're all part of some kind of secret society," I muttered, the words barely above a whisper. "A network, perhaps? A clandestine group operating under the radar?"

Evelyn nodded thoughtfully. "It's certainly a possibility, Elara. The overlapping connections between Emily and Daniel's social circles are significant. It suggests a deeper, more sinister conspiracy than we initially suspected. These aren't random encounters; this appears to be a carefully orchestrated network."

Armed with this new understanding, I returned to my investigation with renewed vigor, a sense of purpose burning within me, fueled by a mixture of fear and determination. I started meticulously charting the connections, mapping out the relationships between the individuals I'd identified in Emily and Daniel's social circles. I scoured social media profiles, dug through public records, and cross-referenced databases, piecing together a disturbing picture.

The network proved far-reaching, extending far beyond the initial suspects I'd identified. It included prominent figures in the community – businessmen, politicians, even a few well-known academics. Their interactions were subtle, their connections carefully concealed, but the pattern was undeniable. They were all intricately intertwined, bound together by a shared history and a common purpose that remained shrouded in secrecy.

I discovered a series of encrypted emails exchanged between members of the network, a secret language that only they could understand. I employed forensic techniques to access the emails, and with the help of Detective Miller, successfully decoded them, revealing a network of clandestine meetings, coded messages, and financial transactions of an illicit nature.

The emails revealed the existence of a secret foundation, ostensibly a charitable organization, which was, in reality, a front for their clandestine activities. The foundation's annual reports showed unusually high expenditures that couldn't be accounted for, raising serious questions about its true purpose. It was a classic example of money laundering, with funds being moved through a complex network of shell corporations to conceal the source and destination of the money.

As I delved deeper into the foundation's financial records, I discovered a disturbing pattern. Large sums of money were being transferred to offshore accounts, and there were numerous instances of suspicious transactions that couldn't be explained. It became evident that the network was involved in far more than just the disappearances of Emily and Daniel.

The more I investigated, the more it appeared as if the foundation's activities were far more criminal, potentially extending into illegal arms dealing, human trafficking, and a variety of other criminal ventures. It seemed that Emily and Daniel's experiences were not isolated incidents; rather, they were part of a larger, far-reaching conspiracy. The network was powerful, well-connected, and determined to keep its secrets hidden.

I began to receive increasingly threatening phone calls, escalating beyond the cryptic messages and vague threats, and including specific personal details about my life, confirming that they knew exactly where I was, where I worked, even about the close relationship I had with Liam. These anonymous callers used a variety of technologies to obscure their identities, making them practically untraceable. The constant barrage of threats was a stark reminder of the danger I was facing, the immense power of this organization, and the threat to my safety.

My investigation had inadvertently put me in the crosshairs of a powerful and dangerous network, and my life was now in serious danger. The emotional toll was immense, impacting every aspect of my life, leaving me exhausted, sleep-deprived, and constantly on edge.

Liam, despite my attempts to protect him, became increasingly anxious about my safety. He knew that I was involved in something dangerous, something far more complex and disturbing than either of us had ever imagined. He urged me to stop the investigation, to put my own safety first. But I couldn't. The need to uncover the truth, to bring justice to Emily and Daniel, had become an obsession, a relentless pursuit that overshadowed all other concerns.

The weight of the investigation, coupled with the escalating threats, created a deep strain on our relationship. Liam's fear for my safety, his desire to protect me, collided with my unwavering determination to find answers. Our usual loving, supportive relationship suffered; the chasm between us threatened to engulf us completely.

One evening, after another series of threatening phone calls, Liam confronted me, his voice laced with fear and anger. "Elara, this has to stop. They're watching you, Elara, they're watching us. This is beyond anything we can handle. Please, stop this."

His pleas were heartbreaking, his concern raw and palpable. I knew he was right, that my actions were putting us both in grave danger, but the thought of abandoning the investigation, of letting Emily and Daniel's predators get away with their crimes, was simply unbearable.

"I can't stop, Liam," I whispered, my voice trembling. "I have to find out who did this, what this network is really about. I have to... I owe it to them."

His silence hung heavy in the air, a silence filled with unspoken anxieties and profound concern. He knew I was caught in a web of deceit, entangled in a conspiracy that was far larger and more dangerous than I could have ever imagined. The hidden network was powerful, its influence far-reaching, and its members determined to keep their secrets hidden at all costs.

The nights were sleepless, filled with fear and anxiety. The days were a blur of frantic investigation, fueled by adrenaline and a desperate need for answers. I felt like a lone soldier fighting a formidable enemy, an enemy that seemed to possess limitless resources and an unwavering determination to silence me forever. And yet, somewhere deep inside, a flicker of hope remained. I knew that the truth was out there, hidden within the intricate web of the network, waiting to be uncovered. And I would find it, no matter the cost. The weight of the conspiracy was immense, but the strength of my resolve was even greater. My love for Liam, and my determination to solve these cases, fueled my drive. The battle was far from over.

A Dangerous Alliance

The chilling weight of the conspiracy pressed down on me, a suffocating blanket of fear and uncertainty. Sleep became a luxury I could no longer afford, my nights plagued by vivid nightmares, the faces of Emily and Daniel haunting my dreams. Days blurred into a relentless cycle of investigation, fueled by caffeine and a desperate need for answers. Liam's worried gaze followed me like a shadow, his concern a constant, painful reminder of the risks I was taking.

One particularly harrowing morning, after another sleepless night spent deciphering encrypted emails, a breakthrough occurred. I unearthed a series of coded messages referencing a specific individual: Dr. Julian Reed, a former colleague of mine from my days at the university's psychology department. Julian was a brilliant but unconventional investigator, possessing a deep understanding of human behavior and an uncanny ability to uncover hidden truths. He had left academia years ago, opting for a more clandestine career in private intelligence gathering. His methods were unorthodox, his reputation somewhat shadowy, but his skill was undeniable.

The thought of reaching out to Julian filled me with a mixture of trepidation and hope. He was a wildcard, unpredictable and potentially dangerous, yet he possessed the skills and resources I desperately needed to navigate this labyrinthine conspiracy. The risk felt immense, the potential consequences unforeseen, but the alternative – continuing alone – was simply untenable.

I found Julian's contact information through an old university database and sent him a heavily encrypted email outlining my findings and requesting his assistance. The email contained just enough information to pique his interest, enough to demonstrate the gravity of the situation without revealing too much about the case. It was a calculated risk, a delicate balance between providing sufficient incentive for his involvement and safeguarding the integrity of the investigation.

Days stretched into an agonizing wait. The silence was deafening, punctuated only by the sporadic, unsettling phone calls that continued to torment me. The calls were always brief, always cryptic, but they carried a chilling undertone, a message of impending doom. Each call chipped away at my resolve, stoking my anxieties and threatening to shatter my already frayed nerves.

Finally, a response arrived. It wasn't a message, but a cryptic file delivered to my encrypted email. The file contained a single image: a grainy photograph of a secluded building, a stark, monolithic structure situated deep within a dense forest. The only words accompanying the image were: "Meet me here. Midnight."

The location was unfamiliar, far removed from my city limits. The sheer audacity of the rendezvous point, the clandestine nature of the invitation, spoke volumes about Julian's character, his way of operating. He was a man who thrived in the shadows, a master of covert operations. The meeting felt like a leap of faith, an act of desperation born from the critical need for help.

Liam, noticing the change in my demeanor, tried once more to intervene. He'd seen the encrypted file. He'd seen the chilling photograph. He was more terrified than ever.

"Elara, you can't go," he pleaded, his voice filled with an agony that mirrored my own. "This is too dangerous. They'll kill you."

I understood his fear, his desperate pleas resonated with every fiber of my being. But the urgency of the situation, the weight of Emily and Daniel's experiences continuing as the fate of others, overwhelmed my apprehension. I had to take the chance, even if it meant jeopardizing everything.

"I have to, Liam," I whispered, my voice thick with emotion. "I'm not permitted to disclose the details of why it is so vital. This is bigger than us. This is about justice, about saving lives. I can't turn back now."

He didn't argue further. He knew me too well. He knew the relentless determination that fueled my pursuit of the truth. But his silence was heavier than words could express, a silent testament to the depth of his concern and the fear that gnawed at his heart.

That night, I drove to the secluded location, the dark forest a sinister backdrop to my mounting anxiety. The building was exactly as it appeared in the photograph, an imposing structure shrouded in an unnatural silence, broken only by the whispering wind rustling through the trees. It was a place that seemed to emanate a sense of foreboding, a place where secrets were buried and shadows danced.

Inside, the building was dark and cavernous, the air thick with a musty scent that seemed to amplify the feeling of unease. Julian was waiting, a figure emerging from the gloom, his face partially obscured by the shadows. He was taller and thinner than I remembered, his movements precise and deliberate, his eyes sharp and observant. There was an aura of danger around him, a palpable energy that both intrigued and unnerved me.

"You came," he said, his voice low and gravelly, yet surprisingly calm. He didn't offer a handshake, just a nod of acknowledgment, a silent acceptance of the dangerous alliance we were about to forge.

He listened intently as I recounted my investigation, detailing my findings, sharing the evidence I had gathered. He listened without interruption, his eyes never leaving mine, analyzing every detail, interpreting every nuance. When I finished, he leaned back, a thoughtful expression on his face.

"This is far bigger than you initially thought," he said, his voice laced with a grim realization. "This network is far-reaching, powerful, and they're playing a dangerous game."

Julian revealed that he had been tracking similar activity for years, albeit on a smaller scale. He had stumbled upon fragments of the conspiracy, but he lacked the connections and resources to fully uncover its scope. My findings, he said, provided the missing pieces to the puzzle. He had access to advanced surveillance technologies, to deep-web databases, to informants that I could never access alone. He proposed to work together, pooling our resources and knowledge. This alliance was a high-stakes gamble, but it was our only chance.

He detailed the risks involved, painting a stark picture of the danger we were facing, the powerful enemies we were up against. He warned me about the network's reach, its ruthless efficiency, and the lengths they would go to silence us. He spoke of disappearing people, not just from view, but from existence. He had seen how easily they erased records, removed names, and silenced those who dared to investigate. And the fear in his eyes reflected a deeper understanding than I could have ever imagined. This wasn't merely a criminal organization, he warned; it was something far more sinister, far more deeply entrenched than anyone had previously believed.

The alliance was formed, born out of necessity and a shared desire for justice, but it was a dangerous pact, forged in the shadows, promising both a potential solution and a new level of risk. We were in a race against time, against a network that was both powerful and ruthless, a network that would stop at nothing to protect its secrets and erase those who threatened to expose them. My life, and perhaps Liam's, hung precariously in the balance, dependent on our ability to uncover the truth before it was too late. The weight of this new alliance, this dangerous game of cat and mouse with a powerful and ruthless enemy, pressed down on me. The shadows were deeper than ever before.

Betrayal and Deception

The following days were a blur of activity, a whirlwind of clandestine meetings, encrypted communications, and the ever-present shadow of fear. Julian, true to his word, proved invaluable. His network of informants, his access to technology far beyond my reach, allowed us to peel back layers of the conspiracy, uncovering a web of deceit so intricate, so pervasive, that it left me breathless.

We discovered that the seemingly innocuous charitable foundation, the one that Emily and Daniel's sessions had me investigating, was merely a front, a smokescreen for a far more sinister operation. It funneled money, laundered funds, and facilitated the movement of individuals across international borders. But the real shock came with the revelation of the foundation's true purpose: the systematic manipulation and exploitation of vulnerable individuals, turning them into pawns in a global game of power and control.

And then came the betrayal. It wasn't a sudden, dramatic revelation, but a slow, agonizing dawning of realization. It began with small inconsistencies, subtle discrepancies in the information we were gathering. It was a pattern of omissions, of carefully placed red herrings, that gradually coalesced into a chilling truth.

Dr. Alistair Finch, my mentor, the man who had guided my career, the man who had seemed to support my investigation, was implicated. His name appeared in encrypted messages, linked to key figures within the conspiracy. He wasn't just a bystander; he was a key player. He had been subtly manipulating events, directing my investigation, feeding me misinformation, all while maintaining a veneer of support and concern.

The shock was immense. A wave of nausea washed over me, the realization of this betrayal striking me with the force of a physical blow. The betrayal was not merely professional; it was deeply personal. Alistair had been more than a mentor; he had been a friend, a confidante, a trusted advisor. The depth of his deception shattered my faith in my judgment, in my ability to discern truth from falsehood.

The realization gnawed at me, poisoning my thoughts, eroding my confidence. The world I had known, the world of established truths and trusted relationships, had crumbled around me. Sleep became even more elusive, replaced by a relentless cycle of self-doubt and anxiety. Liam's concern, once a source of comfort, now felt like a painful reminder of my vulnerability, my naiveté.

Liam, witnessing my increasing distress, urged me to step back, to prioritize my own safety. He saw the toll this investigation was taking, not just on my physical and mental well-being, but on our relationship. The constant stress, the sleepless nights, the lingering fear, had cast a pall over our lives, creating a gulf between us that felt impossible to bridge.

"Elara," he said one evening, his voice laced with worry, "I don't know how much more you can take. This is consuming you."

His words struck a chord, revealing a truth that I had been desperately trying to ignore. The weight of the conspiracy, the burden of betrayal, the relentless pressure to uncover the truth, were threatening to overwhelm me. I was pushing myself to the brink, and the potential consequences extended far beyond the investigation itself.

The emotional impact of Alistair's betrayal was profound. The initial shock gave way to a maelstrom of conflicting emotions: anger, disappointment, betrayal, confusion, and ultimately, a profound sense of grief. It was the loss of a mentor, a friend, a symbol of trust. It was a shattering of belief in the foundations of my professional life, in the moral compass that had guided my decisions.

The sense of betrayal extended beyond Alistair. Doubt crept into every aspect of my life, casting a suspicious shadow over every relationship. Who else could I trust? Who else was playing a role in this intricate game of deception? Paranoia became a constant companion, an insidious whisper in the back of my mind, fueling a cycle of suspicion and anxiety.

My sessions with my therapist, Dr. Evelyn Reed (no relation to Julian, as it turned out), became increasingly difficult. She recognized the depth of my emotional turmoil, the way the betrayal had shaken my core beliefs. She helped me to process my emotions, to acknowledge the profound impact of Alistair's actions, and to navigate the complex web of grief, anger, and disillusionment. Her guidance was crucial in helping me to regain a sense of equilibrium, to regain a footing in the shifting sands of my reality.

Yet, the betrayal only intensified my determination. It was not just about uncovering the conspiracy; it was about exposing the depths of deceit, about confronting the betrayals that had permeated my life. Alistair's involvement provided a new angle, a new line of inquiry. He was a key figure, and unraveling his role within the conspiracy could lead to the heart of the operation.

Working alongside Julian, we delved deeper into Alistair's activities. We discovered a trail of secret accounts, hidden transactions, and coded communications that revealed a far-reaching network of influence and corruption. Alistair's involvement was far more significant than I had initially imagined; he was the linchpin, the central figure who connected several seemingly unrelated branches of the conspiracy.

The weight of what we were uncovering was staggering. It was a conspiracy that reached into the highest echelons of power, a network of individuals who had manipulated systems, controlled information, and silenced dissent for years. We were dealing with a force that was deeply entrenched, incredibly powerful, and utterly ruthless. But this time, the betrayal fueled my resolve, sharpening my focus and intensifying my determination to expose their crimes. The journey had become personal. It was no longer just about Emily and Daniel; it was about justice, about reclaiming my trust, and about restoring faith in the world I once knew. The risk was greater than ever, but the stakes were higher too. And I was ready.

Escalating Threats

The escalating threats began subtly, almost imperceptibly. At first, it was just a feeling, a prickling sensation at the back of my neck, a heightened awareness of my surroundings. A car that seemed to follow me a little too closely, a shadow flitting across the periphery of my vision, a misplaced object in my apartment that wasn't there before. These were the whispers of danger, the premonitory signs that something was amiss, that the conspiracy had noticed my intrusion into their carefully constructed world.

Then came the phone calls. Anonymous, menacing, filled with barely veiled threats. A raspy voice, distorted and disguised, would leave cryptic messages, taunting me with hints of my vulnerability, of the ease with which they could reach me, and the devastation they could inflict. One call contained a chillingly accurate detail about my daily routine, a confirmation of their surveillance, their knowledge of my habits.

"You're digging too deep, Elara," the voice rasped. "Some things are better left undisturbed. Turn back, before you regret it."

The threat was chillingly clear. They weren't just trying to intimidate me; they were warning me, trying to dissuade me from pursuing the investigation. The casual menace in their tone, the almost playful way in which they outlined my demise, sent shivers down my spine. It was a chilling preview of what was to come.

These anonymous calls were followed by more concrete actions. A broken window in my apartment, a threatening note slipped under my door, containing a single, wilted red rose—a symbol of impending danger, I was well-aware. It was a pointed message, a clear indication that they weren't merely interested in stopping my investigation; they were sending a message, an unmistakable declaration of war.

Liam, ever vigilant, noticed the changes in my behavior, the tightening of my muscles, the way I flinched at sudden noises. His concern intensified with each passing day, mirroring my own growing unease. He became my constant companion, a silent guardian, his presence a reassuring anchor in the storm that was brewing. He insisted on installing a sophisticated security system in my apartment, a comprehensive network of cameras and sensors designed to detect any intrusion.

But even with these precautions, the sense of unease persisted, a constant undercurrent of fear that permeated every aspect of my life. The city, once familiar and comforting, now felt menacing, full of unseen dangers, of lurking shadows. Every car that passed felt like a potential threat. Every stranger seemed to be watching me. Every noise sounded like a warning. The world had transformed into a dangerous place, the streets into hunting grounds.

The paranoia, once a mere whisper in the back of my mind, had grown into a deafening roar. It clouded my judgment, making it difficult to distinguish between real threats and imagined dangers. The constant stress and the fear of discovery were beginning to take their toll, draining my energy and sapping my strength. I found myself jumping at the slightest noise, hyper-vigilant to anything that seemed out of the ordinary. The simple act of leaving the apartment had become a fraught experience, filled with anxiety and dread.

Dr. Reed, my therapist, noticed the intensification of my symptoms. Our sessions transformed from discussions about processing the betrayal of Alistair Finch into a battle against crippling anxiety and escalating fear. She recognized the signs of PTSD, of a mind under siege. She helped me to develop coping mechanisms, to manage my anxiety, and to ground myself in the present, to escape the suffocating grip of fear. Her guidance was a lifeline, a source of stability in an increasingly chaotic world.

But the threats continued to escalate, becoming more direct, more menacing, more personal. One evening, as I was leaving Dr. Reed's office, I found a package left on the doorstep of her practice—a package that contained a single, black feather, a subtle but chilling reminder of my mortality, of the relentless pursuit of my pursuers. The black feather was unsettlingly sophisticated, symbolic of darkness and a potential threat to my life.

The package, plain and unmarked, carried no return address. The lack of overt display of threats felt more menacing than any explicit message, as it implied a more profound level of surveillance, a more personalized understanding of my movements and habits. It wasn't just random intimidation; it was calculated, precise. The feather served as a cold reminder, a tangible expression of the invisible force trying to silence me.

Fear, raw and primal, gripped me. The casual, almost playful threats of the anonymous calls had dissolved, replaced by a tangible sense of mortal danger. The reality of the situation hit me with the impact of a forceful strike. They weren't just trying to stop me; they were trying to eliminate me.

I confided in Liam about this terrifying escalation. He, in turn, contacted Julian, who assured us that he'd reinforce security measures, though this did little to quell the growing fear that consumed me. He proposed temporary relocation, a change of scenery and a break from the oppressive atmosphere of the city. He suggested a secluded cabin in the mountains; a place far removed from the reach of my pursuers. It was a drastic measure, but given the escalating threats, it seemed like the only option.

The thought of leaving my apartment, my home, the only place that felt remotely safe, filled me with a mixture of dread and relief. It was a painful acknowledgement of my vulnerability, of the precariousness of my situation. Leaving behind the familiar comfort of my home felt like surrendering a part of myself, like admitting defeat. Yet, staying put felt equally dangerous.

The decision to leave was difficult, made harder by the realization that it was an admission of weakness. It was also a recognition that my pursuit of truth had put my safety at risk, that I had pushed myself to the brink. Leaving wasn't surrender; it was a strategic retreat, a necessary step in order to regroup, to reassess the situation and plan my next move.

The days leading up to the move were filled with feverish activity. I packed my belongings, carefully selecting what to take and what to leave behind. Each item held memories, echoes of a life that felt increasingly distant, a life that was now under siege. I carefully reviewed my research materials, encoding and encrypting everything to secure my investigation. The process was exhaustive, each minute fraught with anxiety. It wasn't just about packing my belongings; it was about safeguarding my work, protecting my progress, and preserving my ability to continue.

The departure itself was tense and fraught with anxiety. Liam drove, his eyes constantly scanning the mirrors, his hand resting on the Glock nestled in his waistband. The silence in the car was thick with unspoken fears, with a palpable sense of danger. The journey, usually a routine drive, felt like a perilous escape, every passing mile a victory against the ever-present threat.

As we drove towards the mountains, the vast expanse of the landscape felt both reassuring and terrifying. The isolation offered the promise of safety, but also heightened the sense of vulnerability. It was a trade-off, a conscious decision to exchange the perceived security of the city for the uncertain solace of the wilderness. But what lay ahead was still unknown, and the weight of the conspiracy, the fear of the unknown, continued to bear down on me. The journey had taken a personal toll. Yet, the thought of confronting my betrayers spurred me onwards, reinforcing my commitment to uncover the truth. The threats served only to intensify my resolve.

A Race Against Time

The mountain air, crisp and clean, offered little solace. The cabin, nestled deep within the pines, was supposed to be a sanctuary, a refuge from the relentless pursuit, but the isolation only amplified the gnawing anxiety. The silence, once a welcome respite, now felt oppressive, punctuated only by the creak of the old wooden structure and the rustling of leaves in the wind. Each sound, once innocuous, now held the potential for a hidden threat, a lurking danger.

Liam, ever the protector, moved through the cabin with a quiet efficiency, checking locks, securing windows, his movements a silent reassurance. He was a constant presence, a tangible counterpoint to the pervasive fear that clung to me like a second skin. Even with him beside me, the feeling of vulnerability remained, a constant hum beneath the surface of my awareness. The mountains, beautiful and imposing, offered no guarantee of safety; they merely shifted the landscape of fear.

Dr. Reed, surprisingly, had advised against the relocation. She had stressed the importance of maintaining a sense of normalcy, of adhering to a routine, but the escalating threats had made that impossible. The constant pressure, the awareness that I was being hunted, had eroded my sense of control, leaving me feeling helpless, adrift in a sea of uncertainty.

She had been right, of course. The isolation was exacerbating my anxiety, sharpening the edges of my paranoia. I found myself scrutinizing every shadow, every flicker of movement, every unusual sound. My sleep was restless, haunted by fragmented visions of menacing figures, whispers in the dark, and the chilling weight of the black feather. Each day was a struggle, a battle against the creeping tendrils of fear that threatened to overwhelm me.

During our twice-a-week video therapy sessions, Dr. Reed patiently guided me through breathing exercises, grounding techniques, and cognitive reframing exercises. She helped me to separate my anxieties from reality, to challenge my catastrophic thinking patterns, but the escalating threats made it increasingly difficult. The urgency of the situation was palpable, the sense of impending doom a constant companion.

One evening, during a particularly harrowing session, Dr. Reed revealed something that sent a jolt of adrenaline through my system. She had discovered a pattern in the timing of the threats, a subtle but disturbing rhythm to the escalating acts of intimidation. It was a pattern that pointed to an imminent event, a deadline of sorts.

"Elara," she said, her voice low and serious, "I've been analyzing the timeline of these events. There's a pattern, a convergence point, around the 21st of the month. It's a prediction, of course, but the evidence suggests something significant is about to happen. Something conclusive."

The 21st. The date hung in the air, heavy with ominous significance. Less than a week away. A race against time had begun, a desperate scramble to uncover the truth before the conspirators reached their endgame. The implications were terrifying; I was running out of time. It was time to be home.

The revelation galvanized me into action. I started re-examining my research notes, looking for clues I might have missed, trying to piece together the fragments of information I had gathered. I revisited my conversations with Alistair, searching for hidden meanings, for subtle indications of his involvement. The weight of the task was immense, the stakes impossibly high.

Liam, sensing the urgency, redoubled his efforts to ensure our safety. He stayed close, his presence a constant source of comfort, but even his vigilance couldn't completely dispel the pervasive fear. The knowledge that we were racing against a deadline, that the conspirators were closing in, added a new layer of intensity to our efforts.

Julian, too, became actively involved, providing invaluable support. He used his resources to access databases, delve into confidential records, and verify the information I had gathered. He also started working with a team of cybersecurity experts to track and trace the source of the threats, a team who were making headway on identifying the anonymous calls and their origins. He'd been able to trace some of them back to payphones in various locations across the city.

The days blurred into a relentless cycle of research, analysis, and the constant gnawing anxiety. I worked tirelessly, fueled by adrenaline and fear, poring over documents, deciphering coded messages, and piecing together the fragmented pieces of the puzzle. Each new piece of information, each confirmed suspicion, intensified the urgency, the awareness that time was running out.

Dr. Reed continued her therapy sessions, her guidance invaluable in helping me navigate the emotional turmoil. She helped me to channel my anxiety into productive action, to focus my energy on uncovering the truth. She stressed the importance of self-care amidst the heightened stress levels, and encouraged mindfulness practices to help ground me in the present moment.

Yet, the constant threat weighed heavily on my mind. Sleep became a luxury, replaced by hours of obsessive work, analyzing the pieces of evidence as if they held the answer to a fatal riddle. The relentless pressure created a cycle of fatigue, interspersed by sudden bursts of frantic activity.

The breakthrough came unexpectedly, in a seemingly insignificant detail. A seemingly innocuous entry in Alistair's financial records, a small transaction that had been overlooked before, now held the key. It revealed a hidden account, a shell corporation used to funnel money to a network of individuals with ties to a powerful organization, a company with a history of shady dealings and known associations with criminal enterprises.

The discovery was chilling, confirming my suspicions of Alistair's betrayal, linking him to a powerful criminal network. This organization was not just involved in financial crimes but had tentacles spread across several other criminal domains. The scope of the conspiracy was far greater than I had ever imagined, involving prominent political figures, corporations with international reach, and criminal networks that held significant political influence.

Suddenly, everything clicked into place. The threats, the intimidation, the relentless pursuit—they were all designed to silence me, to prevent me from exposing their operations. The 21st wasn't just a convergence point; it was the launch date of their final project, a project that involved massive financial fraud, political maneuvering, and the potential for widespread devastation.

The realization sent a shiver down my spine. The race against time was no longer just about my own safety; it was about preventing a catastrophe of unimaginable proportions. The stakes were higher than ever; the sense of urgency intensified a thousand-fold. The conspirators were about to unleash their final gambit, and I had to stop them.

Chapter 4

Confrontation and Revelation

The shadows lingered, but so too did the light, a powerful illumination forged in the crucible of my own harrowing journey.

The Confrontation

The old warehouse hummed with a low, ominous thrum, the air thick with the scent of dust and decay. Rain lashed against the corrugated iron roof, a relentless percussion accompanying the frantic beat of my own heart. Liam stood guard at the entrance, his silhouette a dark, reassuring presence against the flickering neon sign of a long-defunct liquor store across the street. Julian, ever the pragmatist, was already inside, his phone pressed to his ear, coordinating with the police. They were waiting, ready to move in the moment I gave the signal.

I took a deep breath, steadying my nerves. This was it. The culmination of weeks of relentless pursuit, of sleepless nights, of constant fear. This was the confrontation, the showdown with Alistair, the mastermind behind the intricate web of deceit. The man who had betrayed me, who had manipulated me, who had almost cost me everything.

The warehouse interior was cavernous and dark, illuminated only by a few strategically placed work lights. The air hung heavy with the scent of damp concrete and metal, punctuated by the sporadic drip, drip, drip of water from a leaky pipe. Alistair was waiting in the center of the room, surrounded by a small group of men, their faces obscured by shadows.

He looked... different. The polished veneer, the air of sophisticated charm, were gone, replaced by a raw, almost animalistic intensity. His eyes, usually twinkling with amusement, now burned with a cold, calculating fury. He hadn't expected me. Not here. Not alone.

"Elara," he said, his voice a low growl, devoid of its usual silken tones. "You shouldn't have come."

I stepped forward, my pace deliberate, my voice calm despite the tremor in my hands. "I had to, Alistair. You left me no choice."

"Choice?" He let out a short, harsh laugh. "You think you had a choice? You were a pawn, a tool. You were never in control."

"Perhaps," I countered, my voice unwavering. "But I'm learning to control the game." My psychology training kicked in, a protective shield against his manipulative tactics. I needed to control the narrative, to dismantle his power. I could see the surprise flicker across his face; he hadn't expected such defiance. He had underestimated me.

He gestured to his men. "Kill her."

The men shifted, their hands moving towards concealed weapons. But before they could react, the warehouse doors burst open, and a SWAT team flooded the space, their weapons trained on Alistair and his associates. Julian emerged from the chaos, a satisfied smirk playing on his lips.

The arrest was swift and efficient. Alistair's carefully constructed empire crumbled around him, his arrogant facade shattering under the weight of irrefutable evidence. The look on his face as he realized the depth of his defeat was a chilling mix of shock and disbelief. The man who had controlled others with such finesse was now powerless, trapped in the web of his own creation.

But the arrest was just the beginning. The investigation continued, uncovering the layers of corruption that extended far beyond Alistair. The network of criminal enterprises, the political connections, the extent of their financial crimes—it was a breathtaking revelation, a Pandora's Box of corruption that threatened to unravel the very foundations of power. My research notes, painstakingly assembled, became the cornerstone of the prosecution's case, providing the hard evidence needed to convict Alistair and his accomplices.

The trial was a media frenzy, a public spectacle. The details of the conspiracy, the intricate machinations, the shocking revelations—it all unfolded in the glare of public scrutiny. Alistair, stripped of his power and privilege, was exposed as the ruthless mastermind behind it all. The meticulously crafted persona he had maintained for so long crumbled into dust, revealing a dark, malevolent individual capable of great cruelty.

My testimony was crucial. I detailed the psychological manipulation Alistair had employed, the tactics he had used to control and exploit those around him. My expertise in counseling, in understanding the intricacies of human behavior, gave my testimony a weight that went beyond mere fact-finding. I was able to explain the methods he used to manipulate others, to break down their defenses, to exploit their vulnerabilities. The courtroom was silent as I spoke, captivated by my account of the slow, deliberate erosion of my own trust and self-confidence.

The trial concluded with Alistair's conviction, a sentence not quite reflecting the magnitude of his crimes. While justice was served in a sense, the emotional toll of the ordeal remained. The trauma, the constant fear, the betrayal – these left their mark. But the victory was bittersweet, tinged with the knowledge of the cost.

In the aftermath, I resumed my therapy sessions with Dr. Reed. She helped me process the trauma, navigate the complex emotions, and rebuild my life. The therapeutic process focused on resilience, the ability to find strength amidst adversity, and acceptance of what had happened. The sessions were not about fixing the past, but about moving forward.

Liam remained by my side, his unwavering support a lifeline during the darkest moments. He had witnessed the depths of the conspiracy, the extent of the danger, and yet his love had never faltered. Our relationship, forged in the crucible of shared danger, emerged stronger, deeper, its bonds forged by mutual respect, trust, and unwavering support.

Julian, too, played an invaluable role in the healing process. His practical assistance, his unwavering friendship, his steadfast presence, provided a comforting counterpoint to the emotional turmoil. He became a close confidant; someone I could share both my triumphs and vulnerabilities with.

The experience had changed me, undeniably. The naïve optimism of my earlier days had been replaced by a hard-won understanding of the dark underbelly of human nature, a sobering awareness of the power of manipulation, and the strength it takes to survive adversity. But the experience had also revealed my inner strength, my resilience, my ability to confront darkness and emerge victorious.

The lingering fear was still present, a shadow that would always be a part of my history. Yet, it was no longer the all-consuming force it once was. The fear was tempered by a quiet confidence, a hard-won sense of self-reliance, a knowledge that I could withstand the storms and emerge, changed but stronger.

Life moved forward, but the experience remained a profound and lasting impact. The scars would always be there, reminders of the darkness I had confronted. But alongside the scars, a greater strength had grown, a testament to the power of resilience, the unwavering support of loved ones, and the unwavering conviction of justice. The knowledge of what I had endured and overcome became a source of strength, a quiet determination to ensure that what had happened to me would never again happen to anyone else. The fight for justice was not over; it was just beginning, and I knew, with absolute certainty, that I was prepared to face whatever challenges lay ahead. The memory of the confrontation in the warehouse, the rain lashing against the roof, Alistair's defeated expression, would forever remain etched in my memory, a symbol of courage, resilience, and the ultimate triumph of good over evil.

Unmasking the Culprit

The rain continued its relentless assault on the roof, mirroring the turmoil within me. Alistair's arrest had been swift, efficient, almost anticlimactic after the weeks of escalating tension. Yet, a nagging unease remained, a sense that something was still amiss, a loose thread in the meticulously woven tapestry of his deception. The police, satisfied with the evidence gathered – my meticulously compiled research notes, Julian's impeccable detective work, and the irrefutable testimony of several reluctant witnesses – had declared the case closed. But for me, the investigation had only just begun.

Liam, his arm a comforting weight around my shoulders, watched as I paced restlessly in my apartment. "He confessed to the financial crimes, Elara," he said softly, his voice a gentle balm against the storm raging inside me. "To the embezzlement, the fraud, the money laundering. It's all there, black and white."

"Yes," I replied, my voice tight. "But it doesn't explain the personal attacks, Liam. The stalking, the threats, the calculated attempts to ruin my reputation. It doesn't explain why he targeted *me* with such venom. The financial crimes were a means to an end, but what was the end goal?"

Julian, ever the pragmatist, entered the room, a mug of steaming tea in his hand. He handed it to me, his expression a mixture of concern and understanding. "The investigation is far from over, Elara. We're still piecing things together. There are loose ends."

It was during one of those late-night research sessions, fueled by copious amounts of coffee and an unwavering sense of unease, that I stumbled upon it – a seemingly insignificant detail that unraveled the entire conspiracy. Hidden deep within Alistair's meticulously organized files, tucked away in a seemingly irrelevant folder, was a series of old photographs. Photographs of a younger Alistair, alongside a woman who bore an uncanny resemblance to Dr. Reed, my therapist. The date on the back of the photographs was twenty years prior – a time when Dr. Reed, according to her own account, had been studying abroad.

My heart pounded against my ribs. A cold dread, a chilling premonition, washed over me. I showed Liam and Julian the photos. Their expressions mirrored my own shock and disbelief. This wasn't just about financial gain or political power; this was personal. This was about revenge.

The following days were a blur of frantic activity. We delved deeper into Dr. Reed's background, carefully scrutinizing every detail of her past. We discovered inconsistencies, discrepancies, omissions in her official record, carefully concealed behind a veil of meticulously crafted paperwork. We uncovered evidence of a hidden past, a tangled web of relationships and betrayals spanning decades.

The truth, when it finally emerged, was both shocking and devastating. Dr. Reed, the woman who had guided me through my darkest hours, the woman who had provided me with unwavering support and empathy, was not who she seemed to be. She was Alistair's estranged wife, a woman scorned, a woman consumed by a bitter, all-consuming rage.

Twenty years earlier, Alistair, then a promising young entrepreneur, had abandoned Dr. Reed, leaving her heartbroken and alone. He had left her financially destitute, his heartless actions shattering her dreams and ambitions. It was this betrayal, this profound act of cruelty, that fueled her relentless pursuit of revenge. She had used her position as a respected therapist, her expertise in psychology, to manipulate and exploit those closest to Alistair, carefully orchestrating the entire conspiracy from the shadows.

She had chosen me, it turned out, not out of mere coincidence, but because I mirrored the vulnerability and naivete of her younger self. I was the perfect pawn in her meticulously planned game of revenge, an unwitting participant in her elaborate scheme. She had used my trust, my confidence in her professional expertise, to gain access to information, to provide a framework for Alistair's downfall. The "therapy" sessions were not designed to heal me but to control me, to mold me into the perfect tool for her revenge.

The revelation was shattering. The betrayal cut deeper than any physical wound. The woman who had provided comfort, support, and a safe space in my darkest moments had systematically manipulated me. This realization sent my carefully constructed world spiraling into chaos. Liam and Julian held me together, offering their unwavering support, while the police apprehended

Dr. Reed, the shock evident on her face as she faced the consequences of her actions.

The subsequent trial was not only a legal battle but a psychological one. The further investigation into Dr. Reed revealed more and more criminal activity of Alistair. My testimony, detailing not only Alistair's crimes and manipulation but also Dr. Reed's insidious control, played a pivotal role in their convictions. I spoke of the insidious nature of their actions, the betrayal of trust, and the lasting impact of their calculated cruelty. The courtroom listened in stunned silence as the full extent of their conspiracy unfolded, a chilling testament to the darkness that lurked beneath the surface of respectability.

The courtroom process also allowed me to confront, to articulate the emotional fallout from the events. I spoke about the complex interplay of guilt and anger, the confusing blend of betrayal and vulnerability. My own experiences, dissected and analyzed within the controlled environment of the courtroom, served as a powerful tool in explaining the devastating effects of manipulation and the resilience of the human spirit. My words resonated with the jury, not just as evidence, but as a powerful narrative of survival and healing.

The Resolution

The courtroom was stifling, the air thick with the weight of unspoken accusations and simmering resentments. Alistair, pale and gaunt, sat hunched over, his usual arrogance replaced by a brittle defensiveness. Dr. Reed, however, maintained a chilling composure, her eyes betraying nothing of the turmoil that surely raged beneath the surface. Her meticulously crafted persona, the façade of calm professionalism she had so skillfully maintained, had finally crumbled under the weight of irrefutable evidence.

My testimony was the linchpin of the prosecution's case. I spoke, my voice clear and steady despite the tremor in my hands, of the subtle manipulations, the insidious psychological tactics Dr. Reed had employed. I detailed how she had used my vulnerability, my trust in her expertise, to gain access to information, to subtly influence my perceptions, ultimately molding me into a pawn in her elaborate game of revenge. I described the sessions, initially a balm for my wounds, slowly transforming into a sinister dance of control. Her carefully crafted questions, her seemingly innocuous observations, were designed not to heal, but to extract information, to manipulate my perspectives. The room hung heavy with the weight of the revelation. The silence that followed each carefully chosen word was a testament to the power of the truth.

Liam sat in the front row; his hand squeezed tightly together. His unwavering support, his quiet strength, were a constant source of comfort amidst the storm raging within me. He knew better than anyone the depths of my emotional turmoil, the profound betrayal I had suffered at the hands of someone I had trusted implicitly. His presence was a silent affirmation of his love, a beacon of hope in the darkness.

Julian, ever the observant pragmatist, took meticulous notes, his sharp eyes missing nothing. He had been instrumental in uncovering Dr. Reed's deception, his investigative skills complementing my psychological insights. His presence offered a sense of groundedness, a counterbalance to the overwhelming emotions flooding the courtroom. He was my anchor in the storm.

The cross-examination was brutal. Alistair's lawyer, a seasoned veteran with a reputation for ruthlessness, attempted to discredit my testimony, to paint me as emotionally unstable, prone to exaggeration, a victim of my own imagination. He challenged my recollections, questioned my motives, attempted to sow seeds of doubt. But my unwavering resolve, the meticulous detail of my account, the corroborating evidence presented by Julian, proved insurmountable. The truth, raw and undeniable, resonated throughout the courtroom.

The prosecution presented a damning case, meticulously piecing together the intricate web of deceit woven by Alistair and Dr. Reed. The evidence—financial records, emails, phone transcripts, witness testimonies—painted a vivid picture of their coordinated efforts, revealing a level of calculated cruelty that sent shivers down the spines of those present. The extent of their manipulative tactics, their cynical exploitation of human vulnerability, was breathtaking in its scope.

Dr. Reed's testimony was a carefully constructed performance. She denied all accusations, maintaining her composure, her voice displaying no hint of guilt or remorse. But the evidence was overwhelming, the inconsistencies in her story glaring. The jury saw through her facade, recognizing the carefully crafted lies for what they were.

The verdict came swiftly. Guilty. The words hung in the air, a stark pronouncement of justice served. Alistair and Dr. Reed exchanged a fleeting glance, a silent acknowledgment of their shared fate. The weight of their actions, the consequences of their choices, finally caught up to them. There was no dramatic outburst, no tearful repentance. Just a quiet acceptance of the inevitable.

Even with the verdict, a profound sense of exhaustion washed over me. The trial had been emotionally draining, a relentless confrontation with the darkest aspects of human nature. The scars of betrayal, while acknowledged and addressed, ran deep. The healing process wouldn't be swift; it would be a long, arduous journey of self-discovery and rebuilding. The sense of justice, though present, didn't erase the pain, the lingering sense of vulnerability, the knowledge that my trust had been so brutally violated.

The sentencing was equally impactful. Alistair received a substantial prison sentence for his financial crimes and the orchestrated harassment campaign. Dr. Reed, facing charges of conspiracy, fraud, and ethical violations, received a similarly harsh sentence. The gravity of their actions, the systematic nature of their deceit, were reflected in the severity of the judgment. Justice, though flawed, was served.

The sentence handed down to Alistair and Dr. Reed reflected the gravity of their crimes. Justice, in its imperfect form, was served. But the impact of their actions continued to resonate, its reverberations echoing within my heart and mind. The healing process, this time, was different, the scars deeper. It was no longer about simply moving on. It was about confronting the profound betrayal, about accepting the fragility of human connections, and about embracing the long, challenging journey of self-discovery and rebuilding.

Liam's steadfast love and support continued to be a lifeline, a rock in the turbulent waters of my recovery. He provided not only practical assistance, but a constant reassurance, a reminder that love could indeed endure even the most devastating betrayals. Julian, as always, provided a pragmatic counterpoint to the emotional chaos, offering practical assistance, companionship, and an unwavering belief in my strength.

My sessions with a new therapist, a woman recommended by a trusted colleague, were focused on helping me navigate this new terrain. This time, therapy became a process of self-discovery, of regaining trust, not just in others, but most importantly, in myself. The journey was long and arduous, fraught with moments of doubt and uncertainty, but with each passing day, my resilience grew stronger, my resolve firmer.

The scars of betrayal, of manipulation, of shattered trust remained, a stark reminder of the darkness I had endured. But these scars, too, became a testament to my resilience, a symbol of my journey from victim to survivor. The story, the harrowing journey, would forever be a part of me, shaping my perspective, influencing my choices, informing my path. But the outcome had proved that even within the darkest corners of human behavior, light could prevail. The strength discovered in the face of adversity was a powerful force, one that fueled my determination to dedicate my life to helping others navigate their own paths through the shadows. The experience had forever changed me, but it had also ultimately strengthened me, making me more compassionate, more resilient, and more determined to help those who needed it most.

The aftermath was a slow, painstaking process of healing. Liam and Julian continued to be my unwavering supports, their love and loyalty a constant source of strength. My new therapist, Dr. Anya Sharma, a warm and insightful woman, helped me navigate the complex emotions stirred by the trial. She provided a safe space for me to confront my feelings, to process the trauma, to rebuild my sense of self.

Therapy with Dr. Sharma was markedly different from my experiences with Dr. Reed. This wasn't manipulation; this was genuine support, a safe space for honest self-reflection. Dr. Sharma helped me understand the insidious nature of Dr. Reed's manipulations, the subtle ways in which she exploited my vulnerabilities. We explored the complex interplay of guilt, anger, and betrayal, unpacking the emotional layers that had been so carefully constructed over time. The process was arduous, often painful, but it was also liberating.

The scars of the betrayal remained, etched into my psyche, a constant reminder of the darkness I had faced. But these scars, no longer symbols of weakness, became markers of my resilience, testaments to my strength. They served as a reminder of the lessons learned, the growth experienced, the person I had become in the crucible of adversity. The road to recovery wasn't linear; it was a winding path, sometimes dark and uncertain, but ultimately leading toward healing and self-discovery.

My dedication to helping others grew stronger in the aftermath of the trial. I channeled my pain, my experiences, into a new purpose, dedicating myself to supporting others navigating their own journeys through the complexities of trauma and betrayal. The darkness I had faced had not only broken me but had also forged within me a strength, a resilience, and a compassion I never knew I possessed. My story, the story of betrayal and survival, became a testament to the enduring power of the human spirit, a beacon of hope in the face of despair. The experience transformed me, sharpening my empathy, deepening my understanding of human vulnerability, and ultimately empowering me to help others find their own paths toward healing and self-discovery. The shadows lingered, but so too did the light, a powerful illumination forged in the crucible of my own harrowing journey.

Healing and Recovery

The sterile scent of antiseptic still clung to my clothes, a phantom reminder of the courtroom's oppressive atmosphere. Even weeks after the verdict, the memory of Alistair's smug indifference and Dr. Reed's chilling composure haunted me. The justice served felt hollow, a superficial balm on a wound that ran far deeper than any legal judgment could reach. The trial had exposed the darkest corners of my own vulnerabilities, laid bare the naive trust that had been so cruelly exploited. The healing, as Dr. Sharma had cautioned, would be a long and arduous process.

Our sessions began with a gentle exploration of my immediate emotional landscape. There was the lingering exhaustion, a bone-deep weariness that clung to me like a second skin. The anger, once a burning inferno, had subsided into a simmering resentment, a constant undercurrent to my thoughts. Guilt gnawed at me, a persistent whisper questioning my role in the unfolding events. Had I missed something? Could I have prevented it? The questions hung unanswered, adding to the already heavy burden of trauma.

Dr. Sharma listened patiently; her gaze compassionate but unwavering. She didn't offer quick fixes or platitudes. Instead, she guided me through a process of mindful self-reflection, helping me untangle the knots of emotion that bound me. We delved into the cognitive distortions Dr. Reed had so skillfully employed, the insidious ways she had manipulated my perception of reality. It was a painful process, reliving those sessions, dissecting each carefully crafted question, each seemingly innocuous observation, recognizing them now for the manipulative tools they were.

One particularly challenging session focused on the transference that had developed between Dr. Reed and myself. Dr. Sharma helped me understand how my own past traumas, my innate desire for connection and approval, had made me susceptible to Dr. Reed's manipulations. It wasn't simply a matter of professional boundaries; it was a deeper exploration of my own emotional vulnerabilities, my inherent need for validation, and how that need had been exploited. The realization was a bitter pill to swallow, a painful acknowledgment of my own complicity, however unwitting.

Beyond the emotional healing, there was also the imperative of professional self-reflection. I spent hours reviewing my own practices, scrutinizing my case notes, questioning my own decision-making process. Had I missed warning signs? Could I have done more to protect myself and my clients? The weight of responsibility pressed heavily upon me, a constant reminder of the potential consequences of professional negligence.

Dr. Sharma helped me develop new protocols for client safety and professional boundaries. We discussed the importance of maintaining a healthy distance from clients, the need for regular supervision and peer review, and the essential role of self-care in mitigating the risks inherent in the therapeutic relationship. I developed a more rigorous system for documenting client interactions, including detailed notes on any concerns or unusual behavior. I implemented regular self-reflection exercises, a dedicated time for processing the emotional toll of my work.

The process of rebuilding trust in myself and in the therapeutic relationship was slow and painstaking. It involved confronting the fear that lingered, the anxiety of opening myself up to another therapist, the persistent doubt about my own judgment. But with each session, with each carefully constructed step forward, a sense of confidence gradually emerged. Dr. Sharma's unwavering support and guidance provided a safe haven, a space where I could confront my fears and vulnerabilities without judgment.

We moved beyond the immediate trauma of the trial to explore the deeper roots of my vulnerability. Through guided imagery and other therapeutic techniques, we unearthed long-buried memories, revisiting experiences that had shaped my inherent need for approval and connection. This exploration was vital, not simply to understand my past, but to reshape my future, to forge healthier patterns of relating, and to develop stronger, more assertive boundaries.

The journey was far from easy. There were days when the weight of it all felt unbearable, when the fear and doubt threatened to overwhelm me. But Dr. Sharma's guidance, combined with the unwavering support of Liam and Julian, provided a lifeline, a steady anchor in the storm. Their love and unwavering faith in me were a constant source of strength, a testament to the power of human connection in overcoming adversity.

Liam's presence was a quiet balm, a constant reassurance of his unwavering love and support. He listened patiently to my anxieties, offering words of comfort and encouragement without judgment. His love wasn't conditional; it was a steadfast beacon in the darkest moments, a reminder of the goodness and stability that existed in my life. Julian, ever pragmatic, remained my rock, offering grounded support and practical assistance. He helped me navigate the complex legal and professional ramifications of the trial, ensuring that I had the resources and support I needed.

Slowly, painstakingly, I began to rebuild. The process wasn't linear; it was marked by setbacks and moments of intense emotional turmoil. But with each session, with each step forward, a sense of empowerment emerged. The scars remained, but they were no longer symbols of weakness; they were testaments to my resilience, my capacity for growth and transformation. They reminded me of the strength I discovered, the depth of my capacity for self-reflection and healing.

The trial had been a harrowing ordeal, a brutal confrontation with the darker aspects of human nature. But it had also been a catalyst for growth, a crucible in which my strength and resilience were forged. The healing journey was ongoing, a testament to the enduring power of the human spirit, a journey that had not only mended my broken pieces but had also transformed me in profound and unexpected ways. I had emerged from the ashes, not as the same person, but as someone stronger, wiser, and more compassionate, ready to continue my work, armed with a deepened understanding of the intricate nature of the human psyche, and an unwavering commitment to safeguarding the well-being of my clients. The darkness remained a part of my narrative, but so, too, did the light, a beacon illuminating the path toward a future filled with healing, hope, and a renewed sense of purpose.

Strengthened Bonds

The courtroom's sterile echo seemed to linger even in Dr. Sharma's warm, sun-drenched office. It was a stark contrast, yet the memory of Alistair's calculated cruelty and Dr. Reed's chilling composure remained a persistent undercurrent. The sense of justice achieved felt almost irrelevant compared to the deeper wounds that needed tending. Dr. Sharma, however, had subtly shifted the focus of our sessions. We were moving beyond the immediate trauma, beyond the dissected details of Dr. Reed's manipulations, and towards a more profound understanding of the strengthened bonds forged in the crucible of that experience.

Liam's unwavering support had been a constant source of comfort. His presence, once a quiet refuge, had become a vibrant pillar in my life. He hadn't simply offered words of comfort; he actively participated in my healing journey. He attended sessions with me, not as a passive observer, but as a concerned partner, offering his insights and perspectives. His presence wasn't just about emotional support; it was about active engagement, a willingness to understand the intricacies of my profession and the emotional toll it exacted. We spent evenings discussing cases, not in a clinical manner, but in a way that helped me process the emotional weight I carried. He helped me see that my vulnerability wasn't weakness, but a testament to my empathy, a capacity that made me a truly effective therapist. His faith in me had been instrumental in rebuilding my confidence, in reaffirming the value of my work.

Our conversations extended beyond the professional, delving into the depths of our relationship. The shared experience of the trial had deepened our bond, forcing us to confront not just my vulnerabilities, but also our own anxieties and fears. We had shared tears, laughter, and moments of profound understanding. The trial hadn't simply tested my resilience, it had tested ours, and we emerged stronger, our love more deeply rooted. He had helped me to understand that healing wasn't a solo endeavor, but a collaborative process that required trust, openness, and a shared commitment to growth. He had become a vital part of my support system, not just my partner, but my confidante, my collaborator in my journey toward self-discovery and healing.

Beyond the immediate support, Liam's role extended to a deeper understanding of our relationship. He had listened intently during my sessions with Dr. Sharma, not intruding, but present, offering a silent acknowledgment of my pain. He had learned more about the complexities of therapeutic relationships and the vulnerabilities inherent in my profession. He understood the weight of responsibility I carried, the constant scrutiny, and the potential risks involved. This shared understanding created a new level of empathy and intimacy within our bond, a deepening of our commitment to each other that transcended the practical aspects of his support. He had learned to navigate the nuances of my emotional world, recognizing when to offer practical solutions and when simply to be present. His love became a quiet sanctuary, a safe space where I could be both vulnerable and strong.

Julian, the pragmatist, had been equally invaluable. His support was different, less emotionally effusive, but no less profound. He handled the practical aspects of the aftermath – the legal battles, the professional inquiries, the administrative hurdles. He shielded me from the bureaucratic complexities, allowing me to focus solely on my own healing. He didn't dismiss my emotional struggles; rather, he acknowledged them, providing a grounded perspective that balanced the intense emotional landscape I was navigating. His quiet strength, his practical assistance, provided a sense of stability during a period of immense upheaval.

The strengthening of my relationship with Dr. Sharma was perhaps the most profound. The therapeutic relationship itself had become a testament to the power of healing and trust. Beyond the professional context, a bond of shared understanding had developed, forged in the heat of our work together. She had witnessed my deepest vulnerabilities, my darkest fears, and yet, her unwavering support had never faltered. Our sessions transcended the clinical; they were a journey of mutual respect, understanding, and growth. Her empathy, her expertise, and her unwavering belief in my capacity for healing had been instrumental in my recovery.

Her approach wasn't solely about addressing my symptoms but about understanding the underlying patterns of my behavior and the root causes of my vulnerability. We delved deep into my childhood experiences, exploring long-forgotten memories and the ways they shaped my relationship patterns. She helped me recognize the insidious influence of my past on my present, gently guiding me towards a healthier way of relating to myself and others. The process was demanding, sometimes emotionally overwhelming, but her patience and her compassion helped me to navigate the turbulent waters of self-discovery.

Her insights extended beyond the individual. She helped me to see how the experience had affected Liam and Julian, acknowledging the ripple effect of trauma and the burden they carried alongside me. We discussed the importance of collective healing, the strength that comes from shared experience, and the necessity of fostering open communication within our relationships. Her holistic approach acknowledged that my healing was intertwined with the healing of those closest to me. This expanded understanding created a stronger sense of unity and mutual support within our collective experience.

The shared trauma also led to a deeper understanding among my colleagues. The trial had highlighted the vulnerability inherent in the therapeutic relationship, and the need for greater vigilance in safeguarding both client and therapist well-being. Discussions with colleagues revealed a shared experience of vulnerability and the challenges of maintaining healthy boundaries. We formed a peer support group, providing a safe space to share our experiences, discuss ethical dilemmas, and offer each other encouragement and support. The shared experience created a strong sense of professional camaraderie, a deeper commitment to the ethical practice of therapy, and an enhanced understanding of the importance of self-care in the face of professional challenges.

The strengthening of these bonds wasn't a sudden shift; it was a gradual process, marked by moments of intense emotion, periods of reflection, and a collective commitment to healing. It was a testament to the resilience of the human spirit, the power of human connection, and the profound impact of shared experiences. The trauma we had endured had tested the strength of our relationships, but it had also ultimately deepened them, forging a stronger sense of unity, trust, and mutual support. We had emerged from the darkness, not unscathed, but transformed, bound together by the shared experience, our bonds forged in the crucible of adversity. The healing journey was far from over, but the strengthened relationships provided a solid foundation, a unwavering source of strength, and a powerful testament to the enduring power of love, support, and collective resilience. The scars remained, but they were interwoven with the threads of a renewed strength, a deepened understanding, and a love that had been refined and tested, yet emerged stronger than before. The future remained uncertain, but it was a future we faced together, armed with the strength of our collective experience, our bonds fortified, and our resolve unwavering.

Chapter 5

Aftermath and Reflection

My home, once shadowed by the anxieties of the past, now radiated a sense of warmth, tranquility, and mutual support.

The Counselor's Journey

The lingering scent of antiseptic and the faint metallic tang of blood still clung to my memory, a phantom smell that haunted the quiet corners of my mind. Even the sunlight streaming through Dr. Sharma's office couldn't quite wash away the stark reality of the courtroom, the chilling precision of Dr. Reed's testimony, and the raw, visceral fear that had gripped me during those agonizing days. The trial, the legal battles, the public scrutiny – they were all receding into a hazy backdrop, yet the psychological weight persisted. It wasn't simply the trauma of facing Alistair's calculated cruelty; it was the subtle erosion of confidence, the questioning of my own professional judgment, the nagging self-doubt that threatened to undermine my very foundation.

Dr. Sharma, with her insightful wisdom and unwavering support, had guided me through the labyrinth of my emotional turmoil. We delved beyond the immediate crisis, moving past the dissected analysis of Dr. Reed's manipulative tactics and into a deeper exploration of the self-doubt that had begun to fester. She had helped me acknowledge the impact of the trauma on my professional identity, on my self-perception as a competent and capable therapist. The experience had shaken my sense of security, exposing the vulnerability inherent in the therapeutic relationship itself. It was a vulnerability I had always understood intellectually, but now felt viscerally, a constant, low-level hum of anxiety that threatened to overwhelm me.

One of the most surprising revelations during my therapy was the extent to which I had internalized Alistair's manipulative tactics. Subconsciously, I had begun to question my ability to accurately assess clients, to discern genuine emotion from carefully constructed facades. Dr. Sharma helped me see how this was not a failure of my skills, but rather a natural response to the trauma I had endured. It was a form of learned helplessness, a subconscious reaction to the calculated manipulation I had experienced. She explained that this was not a weakness, but a symptom, a testament to the intensity of the ordeal.

She used various therapeutic techniques to help me unpack these insidious thoughts and beliefs. We employed cognitive behavioral therapy (CBT) to challenge the negative self-talk and replace it with more realistic and positive affirmations. We explored the root causes of my vulnerability, tracing them back to earlier experiences in my life where similar patterns of manipulation had occurred, long before the case with Dr. Reed and Alistair. This exploration unearthed childhood patterns, moments of subtle control and manipulation by family members that I had long since buried, but that continued to exert a subconscious influence on my behavior and self-perception.

The process wasn't easy. There were days filled with tears, days when the weight of it all felt simply too heavy to bear. There were days when the self-doubt returned with a vengeance, when the whispers of inadequacy threatened to drown out my inner voice. But Dr. Sharma's unwavering belief in me, her persistent encouragement, and her compassionate guidance were my anchors, keeping me afloat in the turbulent waters of self-discovery. Her approach was gentle yet firm, her expertise undeniable, her empathy a constant source of comfort.

The impact of the trial extended far beyond my personal life; it had ramifications for my professional practice. I found myself hyper-vigilant, more cautious, more acutely aware of the power dynamics inherent in every therapeutic interaction. This wasn't necessarily a negative thing; it was a refinement of my professional awareness, a heightened sensitivity to potential risks and vulnerabilities. However, it also necessitated a conscious effort to avoid overly cautious behavior that could compromise the therapeutic relationship. This required finding a balance between responsible vigilance and genuine connection with my clients, a delicate dance that required ongoing self-reflection and careful attention to my own emotional state.

I began to reassess my boundaries, refining my professional protocols to mitigate future risks. I implemented more rigorous record-keeping, sought additional supervision, and participated in professional development workshops focused on ethical considerations and risk management in therapy. These changes weren't born out of fear, but rather from a deeper understanding of the complexities and potential vulnerabilities of the therapeutic relationship. I aimed to be more proactive in safeguarding the well-being of both myself and my clients, drawing upon the lessons learned in a painful and costly way.

The support of my colleagues proved invaluable during this difficult period. They weren't merely offering words of comfort, but providing a much-needed sense of professional solidarity, an understanding of the shared vulnerabilities inherent in our field. The peer support group we formed was indeed a safe space where we could openly discuss our experiences, share our concerns, and offer each other support without fear of judgment. The group allowed for a collective processing of the trauma, transforming a shared experience of vulnerability into a source of strength and professional growth.

The trial also inadvertently fostered a stronger connection between Liam and Julian. Liam, ever the steadfast and supportive partner, had been present throughout my ordeal, his love an unwavering source of strength. He had not only provided emotional support, but had actively participated in my healing journey, attending some therapy sessions and actively listening to me process my experiences. He recognized the need to understand the intricacies of my profession and the emotional toll it could take. He had evolved from a quiet refuge into an active partner in my recovery.

Julian's support was more practical, less emotionally effusive but no less vital. He had navigated the complex legal and professional repercussions of the trial, shielding me from the procedure driven entities and allowing me to focus on my emotional well-being. His pragmatic approach, his quiet strength, provided a much-needed sense of stability amidst the chaos. He, too, had deepened his understanding of the challenges inherent in my profession, offering a blend of practical support and emotional understanding that strengthened our bond.

The strengthening of these relationships – with Dr. Sharma, Liam, and Julian – was a testament to the beauty of human connection. The trauma we had endured had tested the strength of our bonds, but it had ultimately deepened them. We had emerged from the darkness, not unscathed, but transformed, bound together by a shared experience, our collective resolve unwavering. The scars remained, but they were woven into the tapestry of our lives, a reminder of our strength, our resilience, and the enduring power of love, support, and collective healing. The future remained uncertain, but it was a future we faced together, fortified by the strength of our collective experience, our bonds unbreakable, our love refined and tested, yet stronger than before.

Elara's Recovery

The weeks that followed were a slow, deliberate climb out of the abyss. Dr. Sharma's office became a sanctuary, a place where I could shed the carefully constructed façade I wore in the outside world. The initial sessions had been dominated by the immediate trauma, the raw anger and betrayal, the shock of Alistair's manipulation and Dr. Reed's complicity. But as the acute phase subsided, we delved into the deeper, more surreptitious wounds.

We began exploring the concept of "gaslighting," a term I'd only vaguely understood before. Dr. Sharma patiently explained how Alistair, and to a lesser extent, Dr. Reed, had systematically eroded my sense of self-worth and professional competence. They had subtly twisted my perceptions, making me question my own memory, my judgment, even my sanity. The realization was both terrifying and liberating. Terrifying because it acknowledged the depth of their manipulation, liberating because it separated the truth from the carefully constructed lies.

Cognitive Behavioral Therapy (CBT) became my daily weapon against the insidious whispers of self-doubt. We meticulously dissected my negative self-talk, identifying the distorted thought patterns that fed my anxiety and insecurity. Dr. Sharma taught me how to challenge these thoughts, to replace them with more realistic and positive affirmations. It was a painstaking process, requiring constant vigilance and self-awareness. I started keeping a journal, meticulously recording my thoughts and feelings, highlighting the negative patterns and consciously replacing them with more balanced perspectives. It felt like a relentless battle, but with each victory, however small, I felt a renewed sense of agency.

One of the most powerful techniques we employed was exposure therapy. This involved gradually confronting the memories and emotions associated with the trial, starting with less distressing elements and slowly working towards the more traumatic aspects. It was excruciating at times, dredging up feelings of vulnerability and shame. But with each exposure, the power of the trauma lessened, the fear gradually receding. The vivid memories remained, but they no longer held the same paralyzing grip. They became part of my story, a testament to my resilience, not a defining characteristic of my identity.

Beyond the CBT and exposure therapy, Dr. Sharma encouraged me to explore the root causes of my vulnerability. Our sessions ventured into my past, unearthing childhood experiences that had shaped my susceptibility to manipulation. I uncovered subtle patterns of control and manipulation within my family dynamic, seemingly insignificant events that had left a lasting impact on my psyche. There were instances of emotional manipulation, moments of subtle gaslighting, occasions where my perceptions had been subtly twisted, leaving me questioning my own reality. This realization was profound. It wasn't just Alistair and Dr. Reed; it was a recurring pattern, a deeply ingrained vulnerability that had been waiting to be exploited.

This deeper exploration led to a profound understanding of my own attachment style. I realized I possessed an anxious-preoccupied attachment, a pattern formed in early childhood, making me overly reliant on others for validation and approval. This vulnerability made me susceptible to the subtle manipulations of Alistair and Dr. Reed, leaving me more easily controlled and less likely to question their actions. Understanding this pattern was crucial to my healing process. It helped me to recognize my own vulnerabilities, to develop healthier coping mechanisms, and to consciously choose relationships that supported my sense of self-worth rather than erode it.

The journey wasn't linear. There were setbacks, days when the self-doubt returned with a vengeance, when the past threatened to overwhelm me. There were tearful sessions with Dr. Sharma, moments of intense frustration and despair. But these moments were not failures; they were simply part of the process. They were opportunities to learn, to adapt, to grow. Dr. Sharma's unwavering support was invaluable during these times. Her presence, her expertise, and her belief in me were constant sources of strength, pulling me back from the brink when I felt myself slipping.

My recovery extended beyond the confines of the therapy room. I cautiously began to rebuild my life, piece by piece. I returned to work, starting with a reduced caseload, gradually increasing my hours as my confidence grew. The experience had profoundly changed my professional approach. I became more vigilant, more attuned to the subtle dynamics of the therapeutic relationship. I implemented stricter professional boundaries, refined my record-keeping practices, and sought additional supervision. This wasn't about fear; it was about a deep understanding of the vulnerabilities inherent in the therapeutic profession, a commitment to protecting both myself and my clients.

My relationships with Liam and Julian deepened during this period. Liam's unwavering love and support were my bedrock. He attended some of my therapy sessions, not to participate but to understand the complexities of my profession, to witness my journey and provide unwavering emotional support. Julian's support was more practical, more behind-the-scenes, yet equally crucial. He handled the logistical and administrative aspects of my recovery, shielding me from the heavy-laden aspects so I could focus on my healing.

Their combined support – Liam's emotional empathy and Julian's pragmatic strength – became a powerful force in my recovery. Their understanding, their willingness to learn and adapt, strengthened our bonds and reinforced my belief in the power of supportive relationships.

The support of my colleagues was also vital. They formed a safe space, a peer support group where we could openly discuss our vulnerabilities and challenges without fear of judgment. This collective processing of trauma transformed a shared experience of vulnerability into a source of strength and professional growth. We learned from each other, supporting each other through setbacks, celebrating each other's successes. This collective experience underscored the importance of community, the power of shared vulnerability, and the resilience of the human spirit in the face of adversity.

My recovery wasn't a race; it was a marathon. There were days of progress, days of stagnation, and days of setbacks. But with each step, however small, I felt myself regaining my footing, rebuilding my confidence, and rediscovering my sense of self. The scars of the past remained, etched into the fabric of my being, but they no longer defined me. They were reminders of my resilience, my strength, and the enduring power of love, support, and unwavering self-belief. The journey was long and arduous, but the destination— a stronger, more resilient, and more authentic version of myself— was worth every step. The future was still uncertain, but I faced it with a newfound sense of hope and a deep appreciation for the support that had sustained me through the darkest of times. The experience had irrevocably changed me, but the change wasn't solely about the trauma; it was about the growth, the resilience, and the profound understanding of myself and the world around me. It was about emerging from the shadows, stronger and more self-aware than ever before.

Elara's Healing

The parallels between Emily's recovery and my own were striking, though our experiences differed significantly in detail. While Emily grappled with the physical and emotional aftermath of Alistair's brutality, my wounds were primarily psychological, the incessant erosion of my self-worth and professional integrity. Yet, the underlying mechanisms of healing—the painstaking process of self-discovery, the confrontation of trauma, and the unwavering support of loved ones—were remarkably similar.

Dr. Sharma often drew parallels between our cases, not to diminish the severity of either, but to highlight the shared human capacity for resilience. She explained how the manipulative tactics employed by Alistair were classic examples of gaslighting, a technique designed to systematically undermine an individual's sense of reality. Both Emily and I had fallen prey to this cunning form of abuse, our perceptions warped, our confidence eroded, and our sense of feeling self-fractured.

My exposure therapy sessions differed considerably from Emily's. While she confronted the physical reminders of her trauma, I wrestled with the lingering whispers of self-doubt, the phantom pangs of guilt and shame. We began with revisiting the trial transcripts, initially just skimming through the less emotionally charged sections. The process was excruciatingly slow. Each sentence, each paragraph, was a battlefield, where my inner critic battled with the burgeoning self-awareness fostered by therapy.

Initially, I found myself automatically justifying Alistair's actions, minimizing my own role in the events. Dr. Sharma gently guided me, encouraging me to identify and challenge these cognitive distortions. She helped me to see that the blame was not mine to bear, that Alistair's actions were a calculated, premeditated assault on my professional integrity and personal well-being. The manipulation wasn't about some inherent flaw in me; it was a deliberate tactic deployed by a master manipulator.

As the sessions progressed, we delved into the more emotionally charged parts of the transcript. I vividly recalled the courtroom, the hostile questioning, the subtle ways Alistair had twisted my words, creating a false narrative that resonated with the jury. The feelings of humiliation, vulnerability, and betrayal were intense, almost overwhelming at times. However, with each session, these feelings lost their power. The memories remained, but they no longer paralyzed me. They became data points in my journey, not defining characteristics.

Parallel to the exposure therapy, I began to unpack my past. My childhood, it turned out, was not the idyllic picture I had painted in my mind. Dr. Sharma skillfully guided me through the labyrinth of my memories, helping me identify subtle patterns of control and manipulation within my family. These weren't overt acts of abuse, but rather a series of seemingly innocuous events – a parent dismissing my feelings, a sibling undermining my achievements, subtle gaslighting that left me questioning my own perceptions.

This realization was pivotal. It wasn't just Alistair and Dr. Reed; there was a deeply ingrained pattern, a vulnerability that had been waiting to be exploited. Understanding this history illuminated my attachment style. Dr. Sharma diagnosed me with an anxious-preoccupied attachment, a pattern born from my childhood experiences that left me craving validation and approval, making me overly reliant on others for my sense of self. This dependence made me susceptible to Alistair's manipulation.

The process wasn't direct or quickly achieved. There were setbacks, days when the self-doubt returned with a vengeance. There were tearful sessions, days when I felt overwhelmed, when the weight of the past threatened to crush me. But these setbacks became opportunities for learning, for growth. Dr. Sharma's unwavering support was a lifeline, her presence a constant reminder that I was not alone in this struggle.

My recovery wasn't confined to the therapy room. I cautiously increased my workload, starting with a few more cases, gradually rebuilding my practice. The experience profoundly impacted my professional approach. I implemented much stricter boundaries and accountability structures. This wasn't about fear; it was about a commitment to self-protection and responsible practice.

Liam's unwavering love and support became my bedrock. He attended some more sessions, not to participate but to understand my journey, to witness my struggle and offer unwavering emotional sustenance. Julian, as always, provided unwavering practical support, shielding me from administrative burdens so I could focus on healing. Their love formed an invisible shield around me, allowing me to confront my troubles without feeling utterly alone.

The support of my colleagues was instrumental. The informal support group was a space where we actively shared our vulnerabilities without judgment. This collective processing of shared trauma transformed a source of collective vulnerability into strength and professional growth. We learned from each other, supporting each other through setbacks, celebrating each other's successes.

Rebuilding my life wasn't a race; it was a marathon. There were more days of progress, stagnation, and setbacks, but each step, however small, represented a victory, a step towards a stronger, more resilient self. The scars remained, etched into the fabric of my being, but they no longer defined me. They were reminders of my journey, testaments to my resilience, and proof of my ability to overcome adversity. My healing wasn't just about escaping the trauma; it was about embracing the lessons, the growth, and the profound understanding of myself that emerged from the ashes of my ordeal. I emerged stronger, more self-aware, and infinitely more grateful for the love and support that sustained me during my darkest hours. The future remains uncertain, but I face it with a renewed sense of hope, a profound sense of self-worth, and an unwavering belief in my ability to navigate whatever challenges lie ahead.

The experience transformed me irrevocably, but the transformation wasn't about the trauma itself; it was about the growth, the resilience, and the profound self-understanding that ultimately healed me. It was about stepping into the light, stronger, wiser, and more authentic than ever before. The journey had been arduous, but it had led me to a place of profound self-acceptance and a renewed sense of purpose. My life, once defined by the trauma inflicted by Alistair and Dr. Reed, now belonged to me, shaped by my resilience, my capacity for love, and an unwavering belief in my ability to create a life filled with joy, fulfillment, and meaningful connections. The scars remained, a testament to my strength, but they no longer dictated my narrative. My story was now one of healing, growth, and the indomitable power of the human spirit to overcome even the most devastating adversity. The future beckoned, and I met it, not with fear, but with hope, determination, and a renewed sense of self. I was ready.

Renewed Relationships

My renewed sense of growth extended beyond my professional life, profoundly impacting my most intimate relationships. Liam, my steadfast partner, had been my anchor throughout the ordeal. He'd witnessed my descent into despair and my arduous climb back to stability, offering resolute support and unwavering love. But our relationship, too, needed tending. The trauma had strained our connection, creating a subtle chasm between us, a silence that spoke volumes about the unspoken anxieties lingering beneath the surface.

During the healing process, I realized I had inadvertently leaned on Liam, unconsciously expecting him to fill the void left by Alistair's manipulation. My anxious-preoccupied attachment style, laid bare during therapy, had manifested in a dependence on Liam's validation, a constant need for reassurance that mirrored the unhealthy dynamics of my past relationships. This wasn't a conscious action on my part; it was an ingrained pattern, a learned behavior that needed conscious unlearning.

We began couples counseling with a therapist who specialized in trauma-informed relational therapy. It wasn't easy. It required vulnerability, honesty, and a willingness to confront the underlying issues plaguing our connection. We discussed the impact of my trauma on our intimacy, the unspoken fears, and the subtle shifts in our dynamic. We explored my tendency to withdraw emotionally, to build walls as a self-protective mechanism, and Liam's frustration with my emotional distance.

The sessions forced us to confront the lingering shadows of my past. Liam confessed to feeling overwhelmed at times, struggling to understand the depth of my emotional pain. He felt helpless, wanting to fix everything but realizing his limitations. He felt like he was walking on eggshells, fearing he would inadvertently trigger a relapse or worsen my emotional state.

The therapist helped us to reframe our struggles, emphasizing the importance of empathy, understanding, and clear communication. We learned to articulate our needs, fears, and desires without resorting to blame or accusation. We developed healthier communication patterns, focusing on active listening, validating each other's feelings, and expressing appreciation for each other's efforts.

One of the most significant breakthroughs came when I admitted my fear of intimacy, my apprehension that allowing myself to be truly vulnerable would invite another betrayal. Liam, with remarkable empathy, acknowledged my fears, assuring me that his love was unconditional and that he would never intentionally hurt me. He confessed his own fears of losing me, of not being able to provide the support I needed. Sharing these vulnerabilities strengthened our bond, forging a deeper understanding and a shared commitment to navigating the complexities of our relationship.

Our journey wasn't devoid of setbacks. There were moments of friction, arguments fueled by lingering anxieties, and temporary lapses in communication. But these became opportunities for growth, for learning to manage conflict constructively, to forgive each other's imperfections, and to appreciate the depth of our commitment.

My relationship with Julian also underwent a transformation. Throughout my ordeal, he remained my steadfast rock, providing unwavering practical and emotional support. He helped me navigate the other areas of my healing process by managing my administrative tasks, and ensuring I had the space and resources to focus on my therapy. He never minimized my suffering; instead, he actively listened, offering empathy and a shoulder to lean on when I needed it most.

However, my emotional distance, a consequence of my trauma, had created a subtle barrier between us. I had unconsciously retreated, fearing that expressing my vulnerability might burden him, that sharing my pain might jeopardize our friendship. Through honest conversations, we acknowledged this emotional distance, and I expressed my gratitude for his unwavering support. We also discussed how my past experience had inadvertently impacted our dynamics.

Our renewed friendship involved greater openness and vulnerability. We began sharing our personal struggles more openly, fostering a deeper sense of trust and mutual understanding. We realized that genuine friendship was about mutual support, not just practical assistance. Julian's consistent presence, his willingness to listen without judgment, and his unwavering encouragement contributed significantly to my recovery.

The support of my colleagues was equally essential. The informal support group we formed evolved beyond mere processing of trauma. It became a platform for professional growth and mutual support. We shared our experiences, offering each other encouragement, practical advice, and a collective space to navigate the challenges of our profession.

The group provided a sense of belonging, a community that understood the unique pressures and challenges inherent in our field. We developed stronger professional boundaries, refined our methods of self-care, and implemented strategies to identify and address potential instances of manipulation or abuse in our practices. The shared experience had fostered a profound sense of camaraderie, transforming a collective vulnerability into collective strength. This camaraderie was not simply about shared trauma, but about shared purpose and commitment to our professional growth and well-being.

My renewed relationships, both personal and professional, were not simply a return to the status quo. They represented a deeper understanding of myself, a stronger capacity for vulnerability, and a profound appreciation for the love and support that sustained me. The journey had been challenging, filled with moments of doubt, setbacks, and emotional turmoil. But the result was a more authentic, resilient, and deeply fulfilling network of relationships, built on trust, open communication, and a shared commitment to growth and mutual support. The scars remained, but they no longer held me captive. They were now a testament to my journey, a reminder of my inner strength, and a constant source of inspiration for a life lived with authenticity, passion, and unwavering belief in the power of human connection. My relationships, once defined by fear and insecurity, were now beacons of hope, guiding me towards a future characterized by joy, fulfillment, and profound connection. The transformation was complete, not just in my individual healing but in the strengthening and renewal of the relationships that held my life together. I was ready not just for the future, but to actively and joyously participate in it.

A New Beginning

The lingering scent of chamomile tea still clung to the air, a faint reminder of the countless hours spent unraveling the threads of my past. My final session with Dr. Anya Sharma had concluded weeks ago, yet the echoes of her insightful words continued to resonate within me. It wasn't just the resolution of my trauma, but a profound shift in my perspective, a fundamental recalibration of my self-perception. I was no longer defined by my past experiences; instead, I was shaping my future with newfound clarity and purpose.

My professional life had undergone a remarkable transformation. The anxieties that once crippled me were replaced by a quiet confidence, a sense of empowerment that allowed me to navigate the complexities of my work with greater ease and effectiveness. I found myself approaching my clients with a deeper empathy, understanding the subtle nuances of their emotional landscapes with a sensitivity I hadn't possessed before. My therapeutic approach, once colored by my own insecurities, now reflected a balanced blend of compassion and professional boundaries. I had learned the importance of recognizing and managing my own emotional responses, preventing my personal experiences from eclipsing the needs of my clients. The training I had undertaken, coupled with my therapeutic journey, had significantly enhanced my skills, allowing me to support others with greater assurance and effectiveness.

Furthermore, I began to actively seek opportunities for professional development. I enrolled in a postgraduate program specializing in trauma-informed therapy, eager to expand my knowledge and refine my therapeutic approach. The program provided an environment of shared learning and support, where I could connect with like-minded professionals, engage in challenging discussions, and learn from experts in the field. This experience added to my personal growth, enabling me to incorporate the latest research and techniques into my practice.

My participation in workshops and conferences became a regular part of my professional calendar. These events not only provided valuable insights and networking opportunities but also nourished my desire for continued growth and excellence in my field. I also sought out mentorship opportunities, connecting with established therapists who served as guides and sources of inspiration. Through these relationships, I refined my professional identity and gained insights that further shaped my clinical approach.

Beyond my clinical practice, I discovered a passion for writing. The experience of journaling throughout my healing process revealed an unexpected talent, a capacity to transform personal narratives into narratives of hope and resilience. I started writing articles and blog posts, sharing my insights into trauma recovery and the importance of self-care. My writing resonated with readers, attracting a considerable following and encouraging me to pursue this creative outlet further.

My renewed sense of self extended beyond the professional sphere, profoundly impacting my personal life. Liam, my unwavering partner, continued to be my pillar of strength. Our relationship, once fragile under the weight of my emotional turmoil, had blossomed into a deeper, more resilient bond. We both recognized the importance of continuing our couples therapy, not merely to resolve past issues but to cultivate a healthier, more fulfilling partnership. Our sessions became less about resolving crises and more about proactive relationship building, fostering open communication, and maintaining emotional intimacy.

The changes in our relationship were subtle but significant. We learned to appreciate the small moments, the everyday gestures of affection that reinforced our connection. We prioritized quality time together, engaging in activities that nurtured our shared interests and strengthened our emotional bond. We also developed a healthier approach to conflict resolution, acknowledging disagreements as opportunities for growth and understanding. We focused on active listening, empathy, and compromise, strengthening our ability to communicate openly and honestly.

My home, once shadowed by the anxieties of the past, now radiated a sense of warmth, tranquility, and mutual support. The atmosphere felt lighter, more joyful, less fraught with tension. Our laughter filled the rooms, replacing the silences that once echoed the unspoken fears and anxieties. We had developed a deeper appreciation for the intimacy we shared, cherishing the vulnerability and trust that had become the foundation of our relationship. We discovered new ways to express our love and affection, deepening the emotional connections that bound us together.

My relationship with Julian, my steadfast friend, remained an integral part of my life. Our friendship had deepened considerably, characterized by greater transparency and emotional intimacy. We shared our personal experiences, dreams, and fears with a level of vulnerability that reflected the strength of our connection. Our conversations were no longer limited to casual exchanges; they delved into the complexities of life, exploring our personal struggles and offering each other sustained support.

His continued support was instrumental in my ability to pursue my new endeavors. He helped with the administrative and strategic aspects of my postgraduate studies and writing projects, allowing me to focus on learning and creating. He remained a reliable source of comfort and encouragement, consistently celebrating my achievements and offering a shoulder to lean on during moments of doubt. Our bond was now deeply rooted in mutual respect, unfaltering support, and a shared commitment to each other's growth and fulfillment.

The informal support group I'd established with my colleagues thrived, transforming into a collaborative environment where we shared experiences, fostered professional growth, and prioritized self-care. We continued to meet regularly, providing each other with practical advice, sharing our struggles, and supporting each other through challenging situations. Our group sessions became a source of emotional resilience, a safe space for vulnerability, and a platform for collective healing.

Our camaraderie evolved beyond our shared trauma, becoming a foundation for professional excellence. We engaged in regular discussions about ethical practices, client confidentiality, and strategies for preventing burnout. We developed a deeper understanding of our individual strengths and weaknesses, encouraging each other to develop our skills and expand our expertise. This collective strength allowed us to support each other, creating an environment of mutual respect, trust, and professional collaboration.

My life, once defined by the shadows of trauma, had been reshaped into a vibrant tapestry of renewed relationships and newfound purpose. I had learned to embrace my vulnerabilities, transforming them into strengths, and celebrating my resilience. The scars remained, subtle reminders of the battles fought and won. But they no longer defined me. They were badges of honor, testaments to my journey, inspiring me to approach each new day with renewed hope and inspirational optimism.

The future stretched ahead, brimming with potential, a landscape I was ready to explore with courage, passion, and a steadfast belief in my ability to navigate life's unexpected complications. I was no longer merely surviving; I was thriving. I was living a life characterized by joy, fulfillment, and the profound satisfaction of knowing that I had not only overcome adversity but had emerged stronger, more resilient, and deeply grateful for the relationships that had sustained me throughout my journey. The transformation was complete. I was ready. And I was happy.

Chapter 6

Lingering Shadows

His words hung in the air,
unspoken questions swirling between us.

Unresolved Issues

The feeling of resolution, that clean break I'd achieved in therapy, was proving to be more elusive than I'd initially believed. While my professional life flourished, a subtle unease, a persistent hum of anxiety, remained a constant companion. It wasn't a crippling fear, not the paralyzing terror of the past, but a low-grade, persistent ache. It manifested in unexpected ways: a sudden tightening in my chest within a crowded room, a fleeting sense of unease in the quiet moments of the night, a heightened sensitivity to sounds and shadows. These weren't full-blown panic attacks, but subtle reminders of the fragility of my peace. It was as if the conspiracy, even though resolved, had left a residue, a lingering shadow that stretched across my days and nights.

The incident with the car, the terrifying realization that someone had been watching, following me, had left a deeper mark than I'd initially acknowledged. Rationality told me that the threat was neutralized, that the perpetrators were apprehended. Yet, a part of me, a primal instinct perhaps, remained hypervigilant. My senses were sharper, more attuned to potential danger. Every unfamiliar face, every sudden noise, triggered a jolt of adrenaline, a fleeting moment of panic that I quickly suppressed, but its impact lingered, a subtle drain on my emotional reserves.

This heightened awareness wasn't confined to physical threats. My relationships, once soothed and strengthened by my healing process, started showing subtle cracks. Liam, my ever-supportive partner, sensed the change in me. He'd attribute it to the intensity of my work, to the demanding nature of trauma-informed therapy. He was right, in part, but he couldn't fully grasp the subtle shift in my emotional landscape. The moments of quiet intimacy, once so deeply fulfilling, were now tinged with a lingering tension, a silent acknowledgment of the unresolved fear that lived within me.

Our conversations, once vibrant and playful, often fell silent, punctuated by the unspoken anxieties that hung between us. It was as though an invisible wall had been erected, a barrier built not from anger or resentment, but from my own internal struggles. Liam's patience was intact, but I could see the concern etched on his face, the worry hidden beneath his reassuring smiles. It was a subtle erosion, a slow but steady chipping away at the foundation of our once rock-solid relationship. The couples therapy sessions, once a source of strength and connection, felt less effective. We were working on communication, on intimacy, but the underlying current of fear, my unresolved anxieties, continued to impede our progress.

Julian, my steadfast friend, also noticed the change. His support unparalleled, his friendship a constant source of comfort. Yet even he couldn't completely bridge the gap, couldn't fully comprehend the depth of my internal struggles. He offered practical help, assistance with my writing and professional commitments, but he couldn't address the unseen wounds, the emotional scars that continued to fester beneath the surface. He listened patiently to my concerns, offering words of encouragement and understanding, but there was a limit to what he could do. His love and friendship were invaluable, a lifeline in the storm, but they couldn't provide the deep-seated emotional healing I desperately needed.

My work, once a source of immense satisfaction and personal growth, also began to suffer. The heightened anxiety impacted my ability to fully connect with my clients. My empathy remained, but my focus was fractured, my concentration easily distracted. I found myself hyper-analyzing my clients' behaviors, searching for hidden threats, interpreting innocent gestures with undue suspicion. This wasn't a deliberate act, but an unconscious response, a manifestation of my own unresolved trauma.

I recognized the need to address this, to confront the lingering shadows that continued to haunt me. It wasn't simply a matter of lingering effects from therapy, but a deeper psychological issue, a consequence of the conspiracy's insidious reach into my life. I began seeking out additional support. I enrolled in a specialized workshop on post-traumatic stress disorder, hoping to understand the underlying mechanisms of my anxiety and develop coping strategies. The workshop, led by a renowned trauma specialist, proved invaluable. It provided a safe space to explore my experiences, to articulate the subtle ways in which the trauma continued to impact my life.

I learned about the insidious nature of unresolved trauma, how it could manifest in seemingly unrelated areas of life, impacting relationships, work, and overall well-being. I discovered techniques for managing my anxiety, for grounding myself in the present moment, for recognizing and challenging the negative thought patterns that fueled my fear. The workshop provided practical tools, and I diligently practiced the techniques, implementing mindfulness exercises, meditation, and progressive muscle relaxation into my daily routine.

The process wasn't easy. It required confronting the lingering pain, revisiting the memories, the emotions, the very essence of my trauma. It required acknowledging the vulnerability that had been exposed, the fragility of my emotional state. There were setbacks, moments of regression, when the fear overwhelmed me, when the anxieties resurfaced with renewed intensity. But with each setback, I gained a deeper understanding of my own resilience, a renewed appreciation for my own capacity for healing.

The support group with my colleagues proved more vital than ever. Sharing my experiences, acknowledging my struggles, in a safe and supportive environment, empowered me to confront my fears without shame or self-judgment. My colleagues' understanding and empathy were invaluable. They didn't offer easy answers or quick fixes, but their continual support, their willingness to listen without judgment, provided a sense of belonging, a sense of community that fostered resilience.

Slowly, gradually, I began to see progress. The anxiety didn't vanish completely, but its grip loosened. The fear remained, a subtle undercurrent, but it no longer dominated my thoughts or actions. I learned to recognize its presence, to acknowledge it without succumbing to its power. I learned to manage it, to navigate its disruptive influence, and to channel its energy into positive action.

My relationships began to heal. Liam and I resumed our couples therapy, focusing on rebuilding trust and intimacy, acknowledging the impact of my unresolved trauma on our connection. We developed new ways of communicating, new strategies for navigating conflict, and new ways to express our love and support. Julian's friendship remained a constant source of strength and comfort, offering superior support during times of struggle and celebrating my triumphs with genuine joy.

The work was ongoing, a continuous process of self-discovery and emotional growth. The lingering shadows remained, subtle reminders of the battles fought and won. But they no longer defined me. They were part of my story, integral to my journey, but not the entirety of who I was. I was emerging from the shadows, stepping into the light, embracing the future with newfound hope and a profound sense of self-awareness. The healing was far from complete, but I was on the path, moving forward, one step at a time. The journey was long, but I was finally, truly, on my way.

Elara's Relapse

The crisp autumn air, usually a source of comfort, felt brittle against my skin. The leaves, ablaze in fiery hues, seemed to mock my inner turmoil. The progress I'd painstakingly achieved, the fragile peace I'd cultivated, shattered like a dropped vase. It started subtly, a flicker of anxiety during a routine client session. A young woman, Natalie, was recounting a childhood incident, a seemingly minor detail about a harsh word from a parent. But the image resonated within me, triggering an unexpected wave of panic. Not a full-blown attack, but a familiar tightening in my chest, a shortness of breath that left me gasping for air. I managed to compose myself, to steer the session back on track, but the underlying unease persisted.

That evening, the unsettling feeling intensified. The quiet hum of the apartment, usually soothing, felt oppressive. Shadows danced in the corners of my vision, taking on menacing shapes. Liam, sensing my distress, held me close, his warmth a temporary balm against the rising tide of fear. He asked gentle questions, his concern palpable, but my answers were fragmented, my thoughts scattered like autumn leaves in a sudden gust of wind. The carefully constructed wall of resilience I'd built crumbled, exposing the raw vulnerability beneath. I was drowning in a sea of anxiety, and the familiar coping mechanisms I'd developed seemed inadequate.

The relapse wasn't a sudden, dramatic event, but a gradual erosion of progress. One day, the anxiety was manageable; the next, it overwhelmed me. My sleep became fragmented, haunted by nightmares that echoed the events of the conspiracy. The nightmares weren't literal reenactments, but symbolic representations of my deepest fears: betrayal, vulnerability, the loss of control. I'd wake up gasping for air, my heart pounding like a frantic drum, the residue of terror clinging to me like a shroud.

My work suffered immensely. The hypervigilance that had once been a subtle discomfort became a crippling hindrance. I found myself constantly scanning the room, anticipating danger, interpreting innocent gestures as threats. Clients, sensing my unease, grew hesitant, their trust eroded by my own internal struggles. My focus faltered, my ability to empathize diminished. I felt like a fraud, a therapist incapable of managing her own emotional turmoil. The guilt gnawed at me, compounding the anxiety.

The support group, once a source of strength, now felt like a condemnation. Sharing my setback felt like a confession of failure, a betrayal of the progress I'd made. I struggled to articulate my feelings, fearing judgment, fearing the loss of respect from my colleagues. The silence, the unspoken assumptions, felt heavier than any words. The safe haven I'd found had transformed into a source of pressure.

Liam, ever patient and understanding, remained my rock. He bore the brunt of my emotional turmoil with remarkable grace. He didn't minimize my struggles or offer platitudes; instead, he listened, offering quiet support, his presence a calming influence in the tempest of my emotions. He researched resources for me, suggested new therapeutic approaches and encouraged me to reach out to my therapist. He attended sessions with me, always a strong presence by my side. He even learned some basic mindfulness techniques so that he could better support me during difficult moments. But even his unfathomable support couldn't fully penetrate the impervious wall of fear I had built around myself.

I sought help again from Dr. Anya Sharma, a specialist in trauma and addiction. Our sessions focused not only on managing my immediate symptoms but also on understanding the underlying causes of my relapse. She helped me identify the triggers that set off my anxiety, the specific thoughts and feelings that fueled the overwhelming fear. We worked on cognitive behavioral therapy techniques, challenging the negative thought patterns that reinforced my anxieties. She helped me identify my emotional vulnerabilities and then, meticulously and carefully, worked on strengthening them. She encouraged me to focus on practicing self-compassion during my recovery.

Dr. Sharma explained the cyclical nature of trauma recovery, the ebb and flow of progress and setbacks. She likened my relapse not to a failure, but to a detour on a long journey. She emphasized the importance of self-compassion, reminding me that setbacks were an inherent part of the healing process, evidence to the intensity of the trauma I had endured. She helped me understand the neurobiological underpinnings of trauma, how the brain's response to fear could be so persistent. This understanding helped me to approach the process with more compassion for my own struggle, and to move away from self-blame.

We also delved into the intricacies of my relationship with Liam. Dr. Sharma helped us explore the ways in which my unresolved trauma was impacting our connection, the subtle ways in which my anxiety manifested in our interactions. It was a painful process, exposing the vulnerabilities within our relationship, acknowledging the strain my emotional turmoil placed on Liam. But through this exploration, we began to develop new ways of communicating, new strategies for navigating conflict, new tools for fostering intimacy and connection.

The process was slow, painstakingly difficult. There were days when I felt like giving up, when the weight of my anxiety seemed unbearable. I retreated into myself, isolating myself from Liam and friends, consumed by my own internal turmoil. But Liam's patience, his unwavering love, pulled me back from the brink. His presence was a grounding force, a reassuring reminder that I wasn't alone. His gentle persistence reminded me that I was not a burden, but a valued partner, someone he was committed to supporting through my struggle.

Julian, ever my loyal friend, also provided invaluable support. He offered practical help, managing my work schedule, ensuring that my professional commitments didn't exacerbate my anxiety. He listened patiently, providing a safe space for me to express my fears and frustrations without judgment. He didn't offer solutions or advice, but his simple act of listening, of offering steadfast support, was a lifeline in the storm.

Gradually, painstakingly, I began to regain my footing. The anxiety didn't disappear, but its power diminished. I learned to identify my triggers, to anticipate the onset of anxiety, and to implement coping strategies before it overwhelmed me. I returned to my mindfulness practices, to meditation, to the techniques I had learned in the PTSD workshop. I started journaling, expressing my feelings, documenting my progress, acknowledging the setbacks without allowing them to define my journey.

My relationships began to heal. Liam and I developed a deeper understanding of each other, a more profound connection forged in the crucible of my recovery. We learned to communicate more openly, to express our needs and concerns without fear of judgment. Our intimacy deepened, strengthened by the shared experience of overcoming adversity.

The healing is ongoing. The lingering shadows persist, but they no longer control me. I've learned to live with them, to acknowledge their presence without succumbing to their power. The journey is far from over, but I am walking it, one step at a time, with hope, determination and the unwavering support of those I love.

Professional Scrutiny

The whispers started subtly, like the rustling of leaves in a late autumn wind. At first, they were just that – whispers. Casual conversations overheard in the break room, hushed tones in the hallways, the sideways glances that felt like accusations. But they grew, gaining momentum, transforming from subtle undercurrents into a full-blown tide of speculation. My relapse, my temporary inability to cope with the lingering effects of the conspiracy, had become public knowledge. Not a grand exposé, but a slow drip, drip, drip of information, each drop chipping away at the carefully constructed foundation of my professional reputation.

It started with a client, a surprisingly perceptive young man named David, who'd confided in a mutual acquaintance. He'd seen me falter, noticed the rumor in my hands, the fleeting moments of distraction during our sessions. He hadn't meant to cause trouble; he'd simply been worried. His concern, however, had morphed into a concerned whisper, then a worried murmur, then, finally, a full-blown rumor that had spread like wildfire through the close-knit community of therapists.

Then came the official inquiry. A formal letter, crisp and impersonal, arrived on a cold Tuesday morning, its stark white envelope a stark contrast to the autumnal chaos outside. It was from the licensing board, informing me of a formal investigation into my professional conduct. The letter cited concerns about my ability to provide competent care during a period of personal distress. It felt like a punch to the gut, the air leaving my lungs, leaving me breathless and reeling.

Liam held me as I read the letter, his hand a comforting weight on my shoulder. His face was etched with concern, but he didn't offer empty reassurances. He knew better. He knew the gravity of the situation, the potential consequences. This wasn't just about my personal well-being; it was about my livelihood, my career, everything I'd worked so hard to achieve.

The investigation felt intrusive, invasive. They demanded my session notes, my personal journals, even Liam's accounts of my emotional state. Each request felt like a violation, a stripping away of privacy, of professional dignity. I cooperated, of course, driven by a desperate need to maintain my composure, to reclaim the control that had momentarily slipped from my grasp. But the process was agonizing, each document a painful reminder of my vulnerability, my struggle, my temporary failure.

Dr. Sharma, ever pragmatic and supportive, guided me through the process. She helped me craft my responses to the board, ensuring that I was factual and thorough, but also compassionate and self-aware. She stressed the importance of presenting my relapse as a temporary setback, not a permanent incapacity. We went over the ethical guidelines, reviewing the delicate balance between personal struggles and professional competence. She helped me understand that, while my actions had fallen short of the ideal, they didn't necessarily constitute professional negligence.

The support group, despite my initial reluctance, became an unexpected source of strength. My colleagues, initially hesitant and cautious, offered support, sharing their own struggles with burnout and personal challenges. Their empathy, their willingness to speak openly about their own vulnerabilities, was surprisingly healing. The shame I'd felt began to melt away, replaced by a sense of shared experience, of common ground.

Julian's practical help continued to be invaluable. He helped to manage my communications with the board, ensuring that all deadlines were met, that all documentation was meticulously organized. He shielded me from unnecessary contact, creating a buffer zone that protected me from the constant barrage of inquiries and pressure. He even helped me navigate the complex legal aspects of the investigation, his experience invaluable in helping me understand the process and my rights within the investigation.

The investigation stretched on, a looming shadow that hung over every aspect of my life. The uncertainty was excruciating, the possibility of losing my license a constant threat. It felt like a slow, agonizing death of my professional life, my career, my identity. Sleep was difficult, my dreams a chaotic mix of case files, legal documents, and the stern faces of the board members. The nightmares continued, a constant reminder of the fragility of my peace.

Liam, as always, was my anchor. He attended the hearings with me, his presence a calming influence during moments of intense stress. He helped me prepare my testimony, meticulously reviewing the details, ensuring that my narrative was consistent and coherent. He held my hand during the long, tense days of the hearings, his touch a silent reassurance. His unwavering belief in my capabilities restored a much-needed sense of self-confidence when I was at my lowest ebb.

During the long wait for the board's decision, I focused on self-care. I returned to my meditation practice, finding solace in the quiet stillness. I continued my therapy with Dr. Sharma, delving deeper into the root causes of my anxiety, focusing on building resilience and emotional regulation. I began to practice more radical self-compassion, embracing my vulnerabilities rather than judging them. I allowed myself to feel, to process, to heal.

Finally, the day came when the decision arrived. The letter, this time, felt lighter. The weight of dread lifted from my shoulders as I read the words: "The board has concluded that while your recent personal struggles have impacted your professional conduct, they do not constitute grounds for license revocation." They acknowledged the intensity of my ordeal, the professional pressures I faced. They did, however, impose a period of probation, which involved additional supervision, ongoing therapy, and participation in a professional development program focused on stress management and resilience. It wasn't a complete victory, but it was enough. It was a lifeline.

Relief washed over me, a wave of emotion so profound that I wept openly, Liam holding me close. The ordeal had left scars, both visible and invisible. My trust in myself, in my abilities, had been shaken. But the experience, as painful as it was, had also reinforced my commitment to my profession, to my clients, and to myself. I had faced professional scrutiny, and I had survived. The shadows lingered, but they no longer held the same power. I had learned to live with them, to integrate them into the narrative of my life, transforming them from threats into lessons, and using them as a stepping stone to a new phase of growth and resilience. The journey of healing was far from over, but I was walking it, stronger and more determined than ever.

Romantic Reconciliation

The silence in the aftermath of the board's decision was deafening, a stark contrast to the cacophony of anxiety that had filled our lives for the past months. Liam sat across from me, a steaming mug of chamomile tea untouched in his hands. His gaze was soft, searching, yet there was a distance there, a subtle barrier that hadn't been present before. The relief was palpable, but it was tinged with a quiet unease. The lingering shadows, though diminished, hadn't entirely vanished.

"It's over," I said, the words sounding strange, almost unreal. They were true, of course, but the reality of it hadn't quite sunk in yet. The weight of the ordeal, the pressure, the constant fear – all of it had left a residue, a lingering echo in the quiet of the apartment.

Liam nodded slowly; his eyes fixed on the swirling steam rising from his teacup. "Yes," he replied, his voice low. "But it's not really over, is it?"

His words hung in the air, unspoken questions swirling between us. The investigation was over, the threat of losing my license averted, but the cracks in our relationship, the subtle shifts in our dynamic, remained. The stress of the past few months hadn't only impacted my professional life; it had seeped into our personal lives, creating fissures in the solid foundation of our love. My relapse, my vulnerability, had shaken his trust, not in my love for him, but in my ability to manage my own life.

The unspoken words echoed in the space between us. Had he doubted me? Had he considered leaving? The thought hung heavy in the air, unspoken, yet intensely present. We hadn't directly addressed the impact of my struggles on our relationship, the fear and uncertainty that had clouded our intimacy. The unspoken anxieties between us had built a wall, silent and formidable, between us.

That night, as we snuggled up on the couch to watch a movie, the silence was more profound than words could describe. His arms were around me, but the usual warmth and comfort were absent. I felt a distance, a subtle coldness, that had nothing to do with the temperature of the room. It was the chill of uncertainty, of fear, of unspoken anxieties hanging in the air between us.

The following weeks were a delicate dance of cautious steps, of tentative gestures, and heartfelt conversations. We talked about the investigation, of course, but also about our feelings, our fears, our insecurities. I confessed my fear of losing him, of pushing him away with my vulnerabilities. I spoke of the shame, the self-doubt, the overwhelming sense of failure that had consumed me during my relapse.

Liam listened, patiently, attentively, his expression a mix of empathy and understanding. He admitted his own fears, the worry and helplessness he'd experienced as he watched me struggle. He spoke of his fear of losing me, not just as a partner, but as the person he loved, the person he had come to know and cherish. He had worried that he wasn't equipped to handle the intensity of my emotions, my struggles, my pain. He confessed he'd wondered if he was strong enough for me.

He described the feeling of powerlessness, watching me fall apart, while simultaneously acknowledging the immense strength it had taken for me to seek help, to confront my difficulties, and to reach out for support. He articulated his admiration for my resilience, for my courage in facing my vulnerabilities, and for my willingness to seek help. He realized the strength of my vulnerability, understanding my openness was a strength in itself, a testimony to my resilience and a marker of my willingness to navigate the difficult path to recovery. He expressed his love for me, not just for who I am, but also for who I am becoming.

Slowly, painstakingly, we began to rebuild the bridge that had been eroded by the events of the past months. We started small: sharing meals together, watching movies, taking walks in the park, engaging in meaningful conversations that went beyond the immediate worries and concerns. We reconnected, rediscovering the shared laughter and unspoken intimacy that had defined our relationship before the storm hit. Each moment of shared connection, each act of kindness, each quiet gesture of love, contributed to strengthening the bond between us.

Couples therapy initially felt daunting but ultimately proved to be invaluable. Working with a skilled therapist, we learned to communicate more effectively, to express our needs and concerns without judgment or defensiveness. We learned to navigate difficult conversations, to listen without interrupting, and to understand each other's perspectives. We explored the dynamics of our relationship, examining the underlying patterns of interaction that had contributed to the distance between us.

The therapy sessions illuminated some underlying issues within our relationship, revealing a pattern of avoidance and a suppression of honest communication that had been exacerbated by my struggles. We learned how to communicate more honestly, confronting our anxieties without fear of judgment or attack. The therapy gave us a safe space to express our vulnerabilities, to articulate our needs, and to build a stronger, more resilient relationship.

One evening, as we sat on the couch, wrapped in each other's arms, I felt the warmth return, the unspoken connection restored. The fear hadn't entirely vanished, but it no longer held the same power. The shadows still lingered, but they were softened, their edges blurred, their darkness muted by the light of our renewed love.

This reconciliation wasn't a sudden, dramatic event, but a gradual, organic process, a testament to our resilience as individuals and as a couple. It was a journey, a path that required courage, patience, understanding, and a willingness to confront our vulnerabilities. We had to learn to navigate the complexities of emotional intimacy, to communicate honestly, and to rebuild trust after it had been shaken.

Our journey was not without its bumps, its setbacks, its moments of doubt and uncertainty. There were days when the fear returned, threatening to overwhelm us. There were nights when the silence was heavy with unspoken anxieties. But we persevered, supporting each other, understanding each other, and embracing our vulnerabilities. We learned that true love isn't about the absence of challenges, but about the strength and resilience we find in each other when we face them together.

The experience transformed our relationship, strengthening our bond, deepening our understanding of each other, and fostering a new level of intimacy and trust. We had navigated a storm together, and emerged stronger, closer, and more resilient than ever before. The lingering shadows remained, a reminder of the challenges we had faced, but they no longer defined us. They were simply part of our shared story, a testament to our journey of healing and renewal. The past served as a foundation for a stronger, more profound and enduring love. Our love was not merely surviving, but thriving in the aftermath of the storm, a testament to our shared journey of healing, forgiveness, and enduring love. The scars remained, visible reminders of our battles, but they were also a symbol of our shared resilience.

Unexpected Revelation

The sense of closure, fragile as it was, shattered like glass on a concrete floor. It wasn't the resounding crash of a shattering event, but a slow, insidious crack, spreading like a hairline fracture across the carefully constructed peace we'd built. It began with an email, a single, innocuous message tucked away in my spam folder, its subject line blandly stating "Regarding Case File 37B." I deleted it reflexively, the automatic response born from months of anxiety-inducing correspondence. But something lingered, a nagging feeling that this wasn't just another attempt at harassment. There was a different weight to this email, a subtle urgency that pricked at my consciousness.

Liam, sensing my unease, watched me from across the kitchen table. He knew the signs, the subtle shifts in my demeanor that heralded an impending anxiety attack. His eyes held a mixture of concern and apprehension.

"What is it, love?" he asked, his voice soft, a comforting balm against the rising tide of unease.

I hesitated, rereading the email's subject line, feeling the cold dread creeping back into my veins. I opened it, my fingers trembling slightly. The message was brief, cryptic, and unnervingly precise. It contained a link to an encrypted file, demanding access for a supposedly crucial piece of evidence that could overturn the board's decision. It hinted at a larger conspiracy, painting the seemingly straightforward case as part of a much larger, more intricate web of deceit.

The encryption was complex, far beyond my abilities. Liam, ever the pragmatist, suggested we seek professional help, someone who could crack the code without compromising the integrity of the information. We contacted an expert in cybersecurity, a former colleague of Liam's from his days in intelligence, a man known for his discretion and his unwavering integrity.

The following days were agonizing, a blur of anxious waiting and nervous anticipation. The expert, a man named Marcus, was meticulous, his process methodical and precise. He worked tirelessly, the hum of his computer a constant soundtrack to our mounting anxiety. The silence between us was heavy with unspoken anxieties, the same silent tension that had gripped us during the investigation. We tread lightly, each word chosen carefully, as if shattering the delicate balance, we'd painstakingly rebuilt.

Finally, Marcus called. His voice was grave, his tone devoid of its usual jovial banter. The encrypted file contained a series of documents, emails, and audio recordings that painted a shocking picture, revealing a clandestine network operating within the board itself. The conspiracy went far deeper than we could have ever imagined. It wasn't simply a matter of professional misconduct; it was a carefully orchestrated scheme involving bribery, blackmail, and potentially, something far more sinister.

The evidence implicated several key figures; individuals we had previously considered allies or at least neutral parties. The implications were staggering; the board's decision, which had seemed like a victory, now felt like a carefully constructed illusion, a smoke screen to conceal the truth.

The revelations were a blow, not just professionally, but personally. The trust I had painstakingly rebuilt with Liam was once again under siege. The fear of losing him, a fear that had gnawed at me during my darkest hours, returned with renewed intensity. The shadows we thought we'd banished returned, darker and more menacing than before.

The new information required a new strategy, a new course of action. We knew we couldn't go public with the evidence without a watertight case, a strategy that would ensure our safety and protect us from those implicated in the conspiracy. This required careful planning and meticulous execution. Liam, utilizing his expertise in intelligence gathering, began meticulously piecing together the information, tracing the connections between the implicated individuals, mapping out their relationships and identifying potential weaknesses in their network. I, armed with my psychological insight and understanding of human behavior, assisted him by building profiles of the key players, anticipating their reactions and potential countermeasures.

The investigation became a joint effort, our professional skills complementing each other, our personal bond strengthening under the shared pressure. The danger was palpable, the stakes incredibly high. Every conversation, every email, every meeting was fraught with tension, a silent acknowledgment of the risks we were taking.

Our evenings were spent poring over documents, deciphering cryptic messages, analyzing audio recordings. The apartment became a makeshift command center, our love story interwoven with a dangerous mission. The fear was ever-present, a constant companion that followed us from our work to our dating. Our intimacy, however, deepened. We found solace in each other, a shared strength that stemmed from the vulnerability we'd both faced in the past.

Days turned into weeks, and the conspiracy unraveled piece by piece. We uncovered hidden bank accounts, offshore holdings, and coded communications. We discovered a network of individuals working in collusion, manipulating systems and exploiting loopholes. The depth of the deceit was astonishing, the implications devastating.

One evening, after a particularly grueling day of investigation, we sat in silence, the weight of the information pressing down on us. The unspoken question hung in the air: what next? The relief of the previous victory felt distant, replaced by a chilling realization that we had only just begun to scratch the surface. We had uncovered a conspiracy of significant scale, one that had the potential to shake the foundations of the organization, potentially causing irreparable damage, and jeopardizing the careers and reputations of numerous individuals.

The enormity of the situation weighed heavily on us. We had to consider the potential consequences of exposing the truth. The people involved were powerful, influential, and ruthless. They possessed the resources to retaliate, to silence us, to destroy our lives.

The fear was real, tangible, a chilling presence that threatened to consume us. Yet, within that fear, we found a new source of strength, a powerful bond forged in the crucible of danger. We were in this together, and we would face whatever came our way, hand in hand. The lingering shadows from the past now served as a reminder of our resilience, a testament to the strength of our love. This time, though, we were facing the shadows together, ready to confront the darkness head-on, prepared to fight for the truth, for our lives, and for the future of our love. We knew that the battle was far from over, but the uncertainty, the fear, the lingering shadows — these were no longer barriers dividing us. They were shared experiences, forging a bond stronger than any conspiracy could break. The fight for justice, the fight for our love, had just begun.

Chapter 7

Shifting Sands

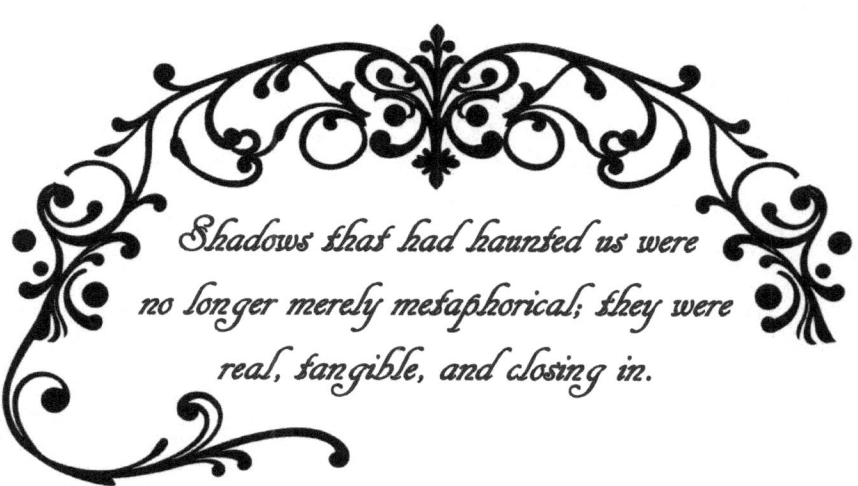

Shadows that had haunted us were no longer merely metaphorical; they were real, tangible, and closing in.

New Threats Emerge

The quiet hum of the refrigerator was the only sound in the otherwise silent apartment. Liam, lost in the intricate web of financial transactions displayed on his laptop screen, barely registered my presence as I quietly moved to the counter, pouring myself a glass of water. The silence, usually a comfort, felt heavy, laden with the unspoken anxieties that had become our constant companions. The feeling of unease wasn't a sudden eruption; it was a slow, gradual creep, a chilling presence that had insinuated itself into the corners of our lives, wrapping its icy tendrils around our hearts.

It started subtly, a missed phone call from my mother, followed by a series of unanswered texts. Then came the unsettling discovery of a strange vehicle parked across the street from my building, a black SUV that seemed to materialize and disappear at will. Liam dismissed it initially as paranoia, a byproduct of the stress and the constant pressure we were under. But his reassurances lacked their usual conviction, his voice tinged with a subtle anxiety he couldn't quite conceal.

My own unease escalated when a package arrived at my office, addressed to me but without a return address. Inside, nestled among layers of packing peanuts, was a single, wilting red rose – a stark, ominous symbol. The chilling reality that someone was watching, someone was getting close, settled in my stomach like a cold stone.

Liam, his instincts sharpened by years in intelligence, immediately recognized the significance of these events. They weren't isolated incidents; they were calculated moves, designed to unsettle us, to test our resolve. He initiated a comprehensive security sweep of the apartment, installing new locks, reinforcing the windows, and discreetly setting up surveillance cameras. The transformation of my cozy haven into a fortified bunker was a stark reminder of the dangers we faced.

The threats, however, weren't limited to our physical safety. A series of malicious emails flooded my inbox, each message more menacing than the last. They were carefully crafted, containing personal details that only someone close to us could know – details about Liam's past, my childhood, even the name of my favorite childhood pet. These weren't random attacks; they were personal, targeted, intended to instill fear and erode our confidence.

The psychological warfare was relentless. The anonymous messages preyed on our deepest fears, exploiting our vulnerabilities, reminding us of the darkness we had both escaped. The threat felt more insidious, more pervasive than any physical danger. It was a constant, gnawing anxiety that clung to us like a shadow, threatening to consume us entirely.

Liam's analysis revealed a pattern in the attacks, a coordinated effort to undermine us both professionally and personally. He suspected a connection to the conspiracy we'd uncovered, suggesting that those we'd implicated were retaliating, seeking to silence us before we could expose their crimes. The realization was chilling, confirming our worst fears. We weren't just dealing with disgruntled colleagues or ambitious rivals; we were up against a powerful network with the resources and the ruthlessness to silence us permanently.

Our initial strategy shifted. We needed more than just security; we needed protection, genuine, unwavering protection. We reached out to Marcus, the cybersecurity expert, who, after hearing our concerns, immediately recommended contacting his former colleague, a private investigator known for his discretion and skill in handling high-profile threats.

The investigator, a woman named Isabella Rossi, proved to be as sharp and resourceful as Marcus had described. She moved quickly, efficiently, and without fanfare, providing us with a comprehensive security assessment, identifying vulnerabilities in our routines, and recommending immediate measures to enhance our safety.

Isabella also provided us with a security detail, two highly trained professionals who blended seamlessly into our lives, offering a silent yet constant presence. Their watchful eyes and quiet professionalism were both reassuring and unnerving, a constant reminder of the dangers we faced.

The increased security measures brought a sense of relief, a small respite from the constant pressure. But it also brought a new kind of anxiety, a heavy weight of responsibility. We knew that we were not just protecting ourselves; we were protecting the truth, and the lives of those who could be implicated by its exposure.

The investigation continued, fueled by a grim determination. Liam's work focused on identifying the key players in the conspiracy, piecing together their connections and building a solid case. My efforts shifted towards profiling the individuals behind the threats, attempting to understand their motives and predict their next moves. The two aspects of the investigation became increasingly intertwined, our professional lives and personal safety inextricably linked.

We both were learning to live with a constant, low-level hum of anxiety. Sleep became elusive, replaced by restless nights filled with fragmented dreams and sudden awakenings. The once-familiar comfort of my apartment was now a space of heightened awareness, every shadow and every sound scrutinized, every visitor meticulously vetted. The line between our professional lives and personal lives blurred, our shared fear becoming a strange glue that held our love together, even as it threatened to consume us.

One evening, as we sat reviewing newly acquired evidence, a chilling realization hit us. The threats weren't random; they were escalating. The targets had broadened. A series of threatening messages had been sent to my mother, leaving her shaking and distraught. It seemed that those orchestrating the attacks were trying to break us down, one by one. The stakes had risen sharply. It was no longer just about our safety but about the well-being of our loved ones as well. Our investigation had become a fight for survival, a battle not only for justice but for the preservation of our lives, our love, and our families. The fight, once a carefully calculated strategy, was now a desperate struggle for survival. We were in a race against time, the clock ticking relentlessly towards a potentially catastrophic outcome. The shadows that had haunted us were no longer merely metaphorical; they were real, tangible, and closing in. Our hearts pounded in unison, our fears merging into a single, potent force that fueled our determination to fight back, to uncover the truth, and to ensure our future together.

Strengthening Alliances

The gnawing anxiety that had become our constant companion intensified with each passing hour. The threat against my mother had shattered the fragile sense of security Isabella's team had managed to establish. Liam, ever the strategist, immediately began recalibrating our defense. His grim determination was a stark contrast to the fear that coiled in my stomach, a fear not just for my own safety, but for the well-being of everyone we loved.

Isabella, proving her worth beyond her initial assessment, sprang into action. Her network, vast and discreet, extended far beyond the realm of private investigation. She had contacts in law enforcement, cybersecurity, and even within the shadowy world of intelligence gathering. It was a network born out of years of experience; a web of alliances forged through trust and shared risk.

One of her contacts, a retired FBI profiler named Dr. Grace Weaver, offered a unique perspective. Dr. Weaver, known for her sharp intellect and uncanny ability to penetrate the minds of criminals, agreed to review the psychological profile Liam and I had painstakingly compiled. Her insights proved invaluable, allowing us to anticipate the perpetrators' next move with chilling accuracy.

"They're not just aiming for intimidation," Dr. Weaver explained during one of our late-night conference calls, her voice calm yet firm. "This escalation suggests a shift in strategy. They're trying to break you, to fracture your resolve. The attacks on your mother are a clear indication of this. They're testing your boundaries, pushing your limits."

Her analysis revealed a disturbing pattern. The perpetrators were meticulously targeting our emotional vulnerabilities, using our deepest fears and insecurities as weapons. They were exploiting the trust we had in each other, the love that bound us together, turning it against us. It was a sophisticated, calculated assault, designed to unravel us from the inside out.

Dr. Weaver's expertise was crucial in guiding our next steps. She advised us to strengthen our emotional resilience, to build a support system that could counter the relentless psychological warfare. This wasn't simply about physical security; it was about creating a protective cocoon of emotional strength.

This advice led us to an unexpected ally: Dr. Lorna Benton, a therapist specializing in perpetual group trauma and resilience, for those in work situations that often place them in life-or-death predicaments. Dr. Benton was a friend of Isabella's, recommended not for her expertise in criminal investigations but for her ability to help people navigate real-time extreme stress and trauma. Her approach was not about simply treating the symptoms of our anxiety but about rebuilding our emotional foundations.

Initially, I was hesitant. The idea of sharing our experiences, our vulnerabilities, with another person, even a therapist, felt like an additional burden. The emotional toll of the past few weeks had been immense, leaving us both emotionally drained and fragile. But Liam, ever the pragmatist, recognized the wisdom in Dr. Benton's approach.

Our sessions with Dr. Benton were intense, often emotionally draining. We talked about our shared history, about the events that had led us to this point, about the fears that haunted us. She helped us unpack the layers of trauma, the unresolved anxieties that the perpetrators were so expertly exploiting. Through her guidance, we learned to identify our triggers, to manage our fear, and to develop coping mechanisms that allowed us to face the challenges ahead.

Dr. Benton's work wasn't solely focused on individual therapy. She understood the interconnectedness of our emotional well-being and emphasized the importance of community support. This led to build on another crucial alliance—with our group of support professionals who understood the nuances of the situation we faced. This wasn't simply a matter of physical threats; it was a battle for our emotional and mental health.

The group, comprised of Dr. Benton, Isabella, and even Marcus, met regularly, reviewing our progress, analyzing new threats, and sharing insights. It wasn't a formal team, but a collective of skilled individuals, united by a shared goal—to protect us from those who sought to destroy us.

The collective approach helped us to compartmentalize our situation, splitting the overwhelming problem into smaller, manageable pieces. Liam continued his investigation, piecing together the threads of the conspiracy with Isabella's support. I focused on strengthening our emotional resilience, guided by Dr. Benton and our support group, with Dr. Weaver constantly reviewing our psychological profiles. Marcus continued providing vital technological support, keeping one step ahead of the digital attacks.

The renewed sense of teamwork was profoundly comforting. Each member of the group brought unique skills and perspectives, filling in the gaps in our individual expertise. This support system wasn't just about tactical advantage; it was about emotional fortitude. We were rebuilding our lives, brick by emotional brick, creating a resilient foundation capable of withstanding the relentless pressure.

We were no longer just fighting against a powerful conspiracy; we were forging a strong support network, a bulwark against the emotional onslaught. The threats continued, but our response was no longer one of fear and isolation. It was a united front, a powerful alliance built on trust, mutual respect, and a shared determination to expose the truth and protect those we loved.

One evening, as we sat together, reviewing the latest intelligence reports, I felt a surge of unexpected optimism. The fear was still there, a persistent shadow lurking in the periphery, but it no longer held the same power. We had faced the darkness and, against all odds, we were finding the light. We were not only surviving; we were thriving, strengthened by the alliances we had forged in the face of adversity. We had found our strength not only in our love but in the power of human connection, in the unwavering support of those who believed in us. The fight was far from over, but for the first time in a long time, I felt a sense of hope. We were not alone. And that, in itself, was a powerful weapon. The shifting sands of our lives were still moving, but now, we had the strength to navigate them together, a team united against the darkness, our bonds stronger than any threat.

Emotional Toll

The relentless pressure of the investigation began to crack the veneer of my carefully constructed composure. Sleep became a luxury I could rarely afford, my nights filled with fragmented dreams haunted by shadowy figures and the chilling echo of my mother's terrified voice. The constant threat, the ever-present sense of being watched, gnawed at my sanity, leaving me perpetually on edge. Even the smallest sounds – a creak in the floorboards, the rustle of leaves outside my window – sent jolts of adrenaline through my system, leaving me breathless and trembling.

My days weren't much better. The intense therapy sessions with Dr. Benton, while helpful, were emotionally exhausting. Unpacking the layers of trauma, confronting the buried anxieties that fueled my fears, was like peeling back the layers of an onion, each layer revealing a deeper, more painful truth. The process was cathartic, yes, but it was also incredibly draining. I felt myself becoming increasingly fragile, my emotional reserves dwindling with each passing day.

Physical symptoms began to manifest. My appetite vanished, replaced by a constant knot of nausea. My stomach churned with a relentless anxiety that made it difficult to eat, sleep, or even concentrate. I found myself constantly reaching for coffee, relying on the caffeine to mask the exhaustion and suppress the tremors that shook my hands. The dark circles under my eyes grew deeper, mirroring the exhaustion that consumed me. Even my usually vibrant hair seemed to have lost its luster, reflecting the dull ache of despair that settled deep within my bones.

The strain on my relationship with Liam was undeniable. We supported each other, undoubtedly, but the unspoken tension hung heavy in the air. We both carried the weight of the investigation, the fear for our safety, and the shared burden of the emotional toll it exacted. Our nights, once filled with intimacy and laughter, now often ended in silent exhaustion, punctuated by the occasional stifled sob or a whispered confession of fear. The fear wasn't just for our physical safety; it was the fear of losing each other, of being broken by the relentless pressure.

Dr. Benton noticed the changes, of course. Her keen eyes saw beyond the carefully constructed mask of composure I attempted to maintain. She gently steered our sessions toward self-care, urging me to prioritize my physical and emotional well-being. She suggested meditation practices, encouraging me to find moments of stillness amidst the chaos. She introduced mindfulness exercises, helping me to focus on the present moment, to ground myself in the reality of my surroundings, to quiet the relentless stream of anxious thoughts that flooded my mind.

But even these techniques felt insufficient. The weight of responsibility, the fear for my mother's safety, the uncertainty of the future, all combined to create a crushing pressure that threatened to overwhelm me. I found myself retreating, withdrawing from the group sessions, feeling inadequate and overwhelmed by the collective weight of our shared burden. The vibrant, supportive atmosphere that had once buoyed my spirits now felt like an added layer of pressure, a constant reminder of the enormity of the task ahead.

One particularly difficult day, I confessed to Dr. Benton that I felt as though I was drowning. The relentless anxiety, the sleepless nights, the physical exhaustion—it was all too much. Tears streamed down my face as I confessed my fear of not being strong enough, of letting everyone down. Dr. Benton listened patiently, her response devoid of judgment, filled only with empathy and understanding. She reminded me of my strength, of the progress I had already made, of the resilience I had demonstrated.

She also gently challenged my self-imposed expectations. "You are not superhuman," she said softly. "It's okay to feel overwhelmed, to need help. It's a sign of your humanity, not your weakness." She reminded me that vulnerability was not a sign of weakness, but a pathway to strength. It was in acknowledging my limitations, in admitting my fears, that I could find the courage to move forward.

Her words resonated deeply, helping to ease the crushing weight of my self-imposed expectations. I realized I had been striving for unattainable perfection, pushing myself beyond my limits, clinging to a false belief that I could somehow control the uncontrollable. Dr.

Benton's guidance helped me shift my focus from impossible perfection to realistic self-care. She encouraged me to prioritize rest, to create boundaries, to learn to say no to additional demands.

The process of rebuilding my emotional foundation was slow, arduous, and often painful. There were days when the anxiety returned, overwhelming me with its intensity. There were moments when I doubted my ability to persevere, when the fear threatened to engulf me once more. But I had learned to acknowledge those feelings, to accept them without judgment, and to approach them with the same compassion I would offer a friend struggling with similar challenges.

My support system, the group forged through shared adversity, was instrumental in my recovery. Liam's unwavering love and support became a lifeline, a constant reminder that I wasn't alone. Isabella's sharp wit and pragmatic approach helped me maintain a sense of perspective, reminding me of the progress we were making, of the hope that remained. Even Marcus, with his quiet efficiency, offered a comforting presence, a silent affirmation of our collective strength. The shared struggles and mutual support created a powerful bond, a resilience that extended far beyond the confines of individual therapy.

The collective approach to our emotional well-being mirrored the investigative approach Liam and Isabella had adopted. We dissected the problem, breaking down the overwhelming fear and anxiety into smaller, more manageable pieces. We focused on achievable goals, celebrating small victories along the way. Each successful step forward, however small, strengthened our belief in our ability to overcome the challenges ahead.

Slowly, gradually, I began to reclaim my life. The dark shadows of anxiety still lingered, but their power diminished. The constant fear didn't disappear entirely, but it no longer controlled me. I learned to coexist with it, to acknowledge its presence without allowing it to dictate my actions or define my identity. I learned to trust myself, to believe in my resilience, and to recognize the strength that emerged from embracing vulnerability. The emotional toll of the investigation had been immense, leaving scars that would likely remain, but I had also discovered an inner strength I never knew I possessed. The shifting sands of my life, once a source of unrelenting terror, now felt navigable, even if the journey remained uncertain. And with the unwavering support of those I loved, I knew I could face whatever lay ahead. We were a team, bound not only by love, but by shared resilience, grown in the face of adversity. The fight continued, but so did our hope. And that was enough.

Legal Ramifications

The revelation that the seemingly innocuous charity, "Hope's Embrace," was a front for a complex money laundering scheme sent shockwaves through our small, tight-knit group. The initial euphoria of uncovering a significant piece of the puzzle was quickly replaced by a sobering understanding of the legal quagmire we were now wading into. Isabella, with her encyclopedic knowledge of legal procedure, was the first to articulate the daunting reality.

"This isn't just about catching some petty criminals anymore," she stated, her usually cheerful demeanor replaced by a grim determination. "We're dealing with a sophisticated network, likely involving powerful individuals with deep pockets and equally deep connections. They'll have the best legal representation money can buy, and they won't hesitate to use it."

Liam, ever the pragmatist, began outlining the potential legal challenges. "We need to tread carefully. Our methods, while effective, haven't always been strictly by the book. Any evidence obtained through unconventional means could be deemed inadmissible, jeopardizing the entire case." He paused, his gaze sweeping across our faces, each one reflecting the gravity of his words. "We're walking a tightrope here, one wrong step could unravel everything."

The first hurdle was proving the link between Hope's Embrace and the larger conspiracy. While we had accumulated a substantial amount of circumstantial evidence – suspicious financial transactions, coded messages, and the unsettling behavior of key individuals – it wasn't enough to secure convictions. We needed irrefutable proof, something that could withstand the scrutiny of a seasoned legal team. Isabella had already started compiling a meticulous dossier, organizing the evidence into a coherent narrative that would be both compelling and legally sound.

The next challenge was the potential for legal repercussions against us. Our investigative methods, born out of necessity and fueled by desperation, had often skirted the boundaries of legality. We had accessed private information, infiltrated secure systems, and even engaged in some surveillance activities that were questionable, to say the least. The thought of facing legal action, of becoming targets instead of investigators, was a chilling prospect.

Dr. Benton, ever the voice of reason, emphasized the importance of documenting everything meticulously. "Each step, every decision, needs to be meticulously documented," she advised. "This will not only protect you legally but also provide a clear record of your actions, demonstrating your commitment to justice."

She went on to explain the significance of ethical considerations alongside legal compliance. "It's not just about avoiding prosecution; it's about upholding the principles of fairness and justice that drive your efforts. Compromising these principles, even for the sake of expediency, could undermine your credibility and ultimately compromise the case."

This meticulous documentation became our new obsession. Every email, every phone call, every meeting – even informal conversations – was carefully recorded and cataloged. Liam, with his meticulous nature, took charge of this task, creating a digital archive that would serve as both a record of our investigation and a potential legal defense.

The potential for witness tampering was also a significant concern. Several individuals who had initially cooperated with our investigation had become inexplicably silent, their testimonies unreliable or completely withdrawn. We suspected intimidation, perhaps even threats, but proving it would be incredibly difficult. The fear of retaliation was palpable; it hung in the air, an unspoken threat that further complicated our already precarious situation.

The legal complexities extended beyond the investigation itself. My own involvement, initially prompted by the abduction of my mother, now made me a potential target, both for the criminals and for the legal system. My actions, while driven by a desperate search for my mother, had blurred the line between victim and perpetrator. My own therapist, Dr. Sharma, highlighted this delicate balance.

"Your motivations are clear," she said, her voice soft but firm. "However, your methods have to be carefully scrutinized. The line between justifiable actions taken in distress and breaking the law is very thin. We need to ensure that your actions remain within the legal parameters."

We spent hours poring over legal precedents, seeking guidance from trusted legal professionals who understood the sensitivity of our situation. The possibility of plea bargains, immunity deals, and the complexities of witness protection programs became frequent topics of discussion. The once clear-cut path to justice now felt like a labyrinth of legal complexities, each turn leading to a new set of challenges.

The weight of this legal burden intensified the existing emotional strain. Sleep became even more elusive, replaced by a constant stream of anxious thoughts. The exhaustion was bone-deep, a relentless weariness that seeped into every aspect of our lives. Liam and I found ourselves retreating even further into ourselves, the shared burden of the investigation and the looming legal threat creating a chasm between us, a silence that echoed the uncertainty of the future.

Isabella, always the beacon of pragmatic optimism, reminded us to maintain perspective. "This is a marathon, not a sprint," she said. "We've made progress, substantial progress, but we have to be patient, methodical. This isn't a battle we can win with sheer force; it requires strategy, precision, and above all, unwavering determination."

Her words, though encouraging, did little to dispel the pervasive sense of unease that had settled over us. The legal ramifications of our actions, the potential consequences, loomed large, a constant reminder of the risks we were taking. The shifting sands of our investigation had revealed a treacherous landscape of legal complexities that demanded a new level of caution, strategy, and resilience. But armed with our shared commitment to justice, and the unwavering support of our growing network, we resolved to navigate this treacherous terrain, one step at a time, our eyes fixed on the ultimate goal – bringing those responsible for the conspiracy to justice, and securing my mother's safe return. The fight was far from over, but with every legal hurdle overcome, the path to justice seemed a little less obscured. The battle ahead was immense, but the hope remained, a flickering flame in the face of overwhelming odds.

A Moment of Vulnerability

The weight of the investigation pressed down on Dr. Benton, a subtle shift in her usual composed demeanor becoming noticeable. The meticulous documentation, the careful strategizing, the constant awareness of legal pitfalls – it was all taking its toll. While she outwardly projected an image of calm strength, a quiet storm raged within. It wasn't just the pressure of the case; it was the gnawing fear that we were all on borrowed time, walking a tightrope over a chasm of uncertainty.

One evening, after a particularly grueling session of reviewing financial records – a session that ended with Liam's grim announcement that a key witness had recanted their testimony – we found ourselves gathered in her small, warmly lit office. The air was thick with exhaustion and unspoken anxieties. Liam, usually the epitome of controlled pragmatism, sat hunched over a cup of lukewarm tea, his eyes shadowed with fatigue. Isabella, ever the optimist, had retreated into a quiet corner, her usual vibrant energy subdued. I, perpetually haunted by the unanswered questions surrounding my mother's disappearance, felt a familiar wave of despair wash over me.

Dr. Benton, sensing the collective weariness, broke the silence. "This isn't just about catching criminals," she said, her voice low and husky, a tremor betraying the strain beneath her composed exterior. The vulnerability in her tone was jarring, a stark contrast to the professional detachment she usually maintained. It was a crack in the carefully constructed facade, a glimpse into the woman behind the therapist.

She pushed a stray strand of hair behind her ear, her gaze drifting to the window, where the city lights blurred into a hazy glow. "I've spent years helping people navigate their darkest moments, their deepest fears," she continued, her voice barely a whisper. "I've built a career on understanding trauma, on guiding others through the labyrinth of their own emotional turmoil. But this… this is different."

A long silence followed, punctuated only by the gentle hum of the city outside. We sat in rapt attention, watching as the normally unflappable Dr. Benton revealed a side of herself she rarely, if ever, showed. The air crackled with an unspoken understanding, a shared sense of vulnerability that transcended the professional boundaries that usually separated us.

"I've always prided myself on my emotional resilience," she confessed, her eyes meeting mine. "I've believed that my own emotional stability was essential to my ability to help others. But this case… it's shaken that belief to its core."

She spoke of the sleepless nights, the constant anxiety that gnawed at her, the fear that crept into the corners of her mind, whispering lingering doubts about our ability to succeed. She confessed to moments of self-doubt, of questioning her own judgment, her own capabilities. She admitted that the weight of our collective anxieties had begun to weigh heavily on her, threatening to engulf her in a vortex of doubt and fear.

"I've seen firsthand the devastating effects of trauma," she continued, her voice catching in her throat. "I've witnessed the erosion of hope, the shattering of trust, the crippling effects of fear. And yet, here I am, facing my own vulnerabilities, struggling to maintain my own equilibrium." She paused, taking a deep breath, as if summoning the strength to continue.

"The fear of failure is immense," she admitted. "Not just for the case itself, but for letting you all down. For failing to guide you effectively, for not being the pillar of strength you need me to be." Her eyes, usually bright and alert, were now clouded with a deep weariness, reflecting the emotional burden she carried.

She spoke of the ethical dilemmas that plagued her, the agonizing decisions she had to make, weighing the potential benefits against the inherent risks. She mentioned the weight of responsibility she felt for our well-being, the fear of making a mistake that could have devastating consequences. The usually meticulous Dr. Benton, the voice of reason and calm amidst the chaos, was now wrestling with her own struggles, her own vulnerabilities laid bare.

"I've always been the one providing comfort and guidance," she said, a hint of self-deprecation in her voice. "It's strange to be on the receiving end, to be the one needing support." The admission was profound; a declaration of her sincere honesty and the deep trust she had developed with us.

This moment of vulnerability was unexpected, yet profoundly humanizing. It broke down the professional barriers that had, until now, subtly separated us. It allowed us to see Dr. Benton not just as our counselor, but as a fellow human being, grappling with the same anxieties, fears, and uncertainties that we were all experiencing.

The conversation that followed was less a therapeutic session and more a sharing of burdens, a collective acknowledgment of the immense pressure we were all under. We spoke of our own fears, our own anxieties, our own moments of doubt. We shared our concerns about the witness tampering, the legal ramifications, and the ever-present fear of retaliation. We shared our hopes, our dreams, and our unwavering commitment to justice. We shared the heavy burden we carried – not just the weight of the investigation but the weight of our collective humanity.

Liam spoke of his fears of failure, of letting down his team, of not being able to bring those responsible for the conspiracy to justice. Isabella shared her anxieties about the potential legal repercussions, the constant threat of exposure, and the fear of losing everything she had worked for. And I, still grappling with the uncertainty surrounding my mother's fate, shared my anxieties about the future, about the possibility of never finding closure.

Dr. Benton listened patiently, offering words of support and encouragement, but also acknowledging our anxieties and fears. She didn't offer platitudes or easy answers; instead, she provided a safe space for us to share our vulnerabilities, to acknowledge our fears without judgment. Her honesty, her willingness to expose her own vulnerabilities, created a powerful bond of trust and mutual understanding.

My mother's name flashed on the screen, prompting a frantic grab for the phone. Her voice, a familiar balm, belied any underlying distress. Inquiry into her recent activities, however, unearthed a disconcerting void in her memory. The more I pressed for details about the unaccounted-for hours, the deeper she sank into bewilderment. Her hazy, fragmented responses evoked chilling echoes of Emily and Daniel's own inexplicable lapses in recollection. After a trip to the emergency room, it was determined that she had been under long term sedation. As frightening as the experience was, we were all grateful for her safe return.

As the night wore on, the weight of the investigation seemed less heavy, the fear less overwhelming. The shared vulnerability had created a space for empathy, a profound understanding that we were all in this together, facing the same challenges, sharing the same burdens. The vulnerability, though initially jarring, had strengthened our resolve, reminding us that even the strongest among us needed support, needed to acknowledge our own vulnerabilities, and needed to lean on each other for strength. The shifting sands of our investigation continued to pose challenges, but in the shared vulnerability, we found a new foundation – a foundation of trust, empathy, and unwavering support that would carry us through the storm. The flickering flame of hope burned a little brighter, fueled by the shared vulnerability and the unwavering commitment to justice that bound us together.

Chapter 8

The Web Deepens

Our growing ability to see patterns where others saw chaos, to discern subtle ques of deception, was nothing short of remarkable.

Unraveling the Network

The following days were a blur of late nights and early mornings, fueled by caffeine and the relentless pursuit of the truth. Despite my own admitted vulnerability, I did my best to remain an unwavering anchor for our team by providing insights, honed by years of experience in navigating the complexities of human behavior, which proved as we pieced together the fragmented threads of the conspiracy. Our growing ability to see patterns where others saw chaos, to discern subtle cues of deception, was nothing short of remarkable.

One particularly fruitful breakthrough came during the analysis of encrypted emails recovered from a suspect's server. Liam, with his technical expertise, had managed to crack the encryption, revealing a network of coded messages far more extensive than we had initially anticipated. The emails, written in a seemingly innocuous style, hinted at clandestine meetings, coded transactions, and a web of interconnected individuals stretching across continents.

That is when I recognized an underlying psychological pattern. I noted the recurring use of specific metaphors and imagery, the subtle shifts in tone and language that betrayed the true nature of the communication. Dr. Benton identified subtle clues – seemingly insignificant details that Liam and I had overlooked – that pointed to a shared history among the individuals involved, suggesting a level of personal connection and trust that went beyond mere professional relationships.

"They're not just colleagues," she explained, her voice low and intense as she traced patterns on the whiteboard, highlighting key phrases and connections. "They're a family, a tightly knit group bound by shared secrets and mutual dependence. They've constructed an elaborate system of trust, using coded language and carefully orchestrated interactions to maintain their anonymity and protect their operations."

Our analysis revealed a surprisingly sophisticated structure, a hierarchical organization with clearly defined roles and responsibilities. There was the mastermind, the elusive figure pulling the strings from behind the scenes; the operatives, the individuals carrying out the dirty work; and the facilitators, the seemingly innocuous individuals providing support and cover. The complexity of the network was staggering, a testament to the meticulous planning and execution of the conspiracy.

The psychological profile of the mastermind – pieced together from the subtle cues in the emails, the witness statements, and the financial records – proved particularly revealing. It painted a picture of a charismatic, yet manipulative individual, adept at exploiting others' weaknesses and vulnerabilities, a master manipulator skilled in building trust and exploiting it for their own nefarious purposes. This profile, coupled with Liam's technical analysis, allowed us to narrow down the list of suspects considerably.

Our investigation led us to a previously unexplored avenue – a network of offshore accounts and shell corporations, cleverly disguised to conceal the flow of illicit funds. Liam, working with Isabella, managed to trace the money trail, uncovering a labyrinthine network of financial transactions that spanned multiple countries. The sheer scale of the operation was breathtaking; the amount of money involved far exceeded our initial estimates, hinting at a far-reaching conspiracy with global implications.

As we delved deeper, we unearthed more connections, uncovering a network of individuals linked to the conspiracy in unexpected ways. We discovered that some of the seemingly innocuous individuals were involved in what appeared to be unrelated fields – academia, philanthropy, even politics – making the investigation increasingly complex and challenging. It was as though the conspiracy had tentacles stretching into every facet of society, operating in plain sight while remaining undetected.

One particularly disturbing discovery was the involvement of a prominent philanthropist, a woman known for her charitable work and her dedication to social causes. The emails revealed her close ties to the mastermind, suggesting that she was providing cover for the conspiracy's operations and using her influence to protect the perpetrators. The revelation sent a shockwave through our team. It was a stark reminder that appearances can be deceiving and that evil can hide behind a mask of virtue.

We, however, remained unflappable. We utilized our understanding of human psychology to help us navigate the moral complexities of the situation. "This isn't about judging their morality," I explained. "It's about understanding their motivations, their vulnerabilities, and the psychological factors that led them to participate in such a devastating conspiracy."

As I guided us through the ethical considerations of pursuing the investigation, reminding everyone of the importance of maintaining our integrity and avoiding any actions that could jeopardize the case. Tapping into our joined experience in navigating the complexities of legal and ethical boundaries was invaluable in ensuring that our investigation remained within the bounds of the law while remaining effective.

The web deepened, the connections proliferated, and the challenge mounted. Yet, amidst the chaos and complexity, there was a growing sense of determination, a shared commitment to uncovering the truth and bringing those responsible to justice. The vulnerability shared in the office had forged a bond stronger than any professional relationship. We were a team, united by a shared purpose and a deep understanding of the human cost of the conspiracy.

We learned to lean on each other, sharing the burden of the investigation and offering support during moments of doubt and despair. The weight of the case, once overwhelming, now felt manageable, distributed amongst us like a shared load. We celebrated small victories, acknowledged setbacks without losing heart, and found solace in our shared vulnerability.

Our collective work became a testament to the strength found in unity, the power of shared experience, and the unwavering belief that even the most intricate webs of deceit could be unraveled with patience, perseverance, and the unwavering pursuit of truth.

Despite formidable obstacles looming, our collective spirit, tempered by mutual hardship and resolute commitment, propelled us forward as a unified force. The network might be vast and complex, but we were prepared to unravel every thread, no matter the cost. The pursuit of justice had become more than an investigation; it was a deeply personal mission, fueled by a shared sense of purpose and a profound belief in the eventual triumph of good over evil. And at the center of it all, I tried to bring a unique blend of psychological acumen and unwavering compassion, which remained our steadfast guide.

Betrayal of Trust

The revelation of the philanthropist's involvement had shaken us to our core. It was a betrayal on a scale we hadn't anticipated, a shattering of the trust we placed in the pillars of our society. Dr. Benton, as a rationalist, guided us through the emotional turmoil, reminding us that such betrayals, while painful, were not uncommon. She explained how seemingly upstanding individuals could be manipulated; their idealism exploited by master manipulators. Her words, seasoned with years of experience in understanding human vulnerabilities, helped us to process the shock and move forward.

Our investigation now took on a new urgency. We were no longer chasing shadows; we were hunting down individuals who had betrayed not only us, but the very foundations of our trust in humanity. Liam, poring over the encrypted emails, discovered a new layer of deception. Hidden within the innocuous messages were coded references to a series of offshore bank accounts, meticulously disguised to conceal the origins and destinations of the illicit funds. These accounts, we discovered, were linked to a network of shell corporations, each designed to obscure the trail of money laundering. It was a sophisticated system, a testament to the mastermind's cunning and foresight.

Isabella, with her expertise in financial forensics, meticulously traced the flow of money. She uncovered a complex web of transactions, moving across continents, through a dizzying array of accounts and shell corporations. The scale of the operation was staggering, far exceeding anything we had ever imagined. The sheer volume of money involved pointed towards a conspiracy of far-reaching global implications, one that touched upon the highest echelons of power and influence.

As we delved deeper, another betrayal emerged, this time within our own ranks. A seemingly loyal member of our team, a trusted analyst named Terry, was revealed to be leaking information to the conspiracy. The evidence was circumstantial at first – inconsistencies in his reports, unexplained absences, unusually late-night activity on his computer. But then Liam discovered a series of encrypted messages between Terry and one of the key operatives. It was a devastating blow, a wound that struck at the heart of our trust in each other.

Dr. Benton's expertise in identifying subtle signs of deception proved invaluable in dealing with this internal betrayal. She didn't dismiss Terry immediately; instead, she worked with us to understand his motivations. Through careful questioning and psychological profiling, she discovered Terry was operating under duress. He'd been blackmailed, his family threatened by the conspiracy's operatives. He hadn't initially intended to betray us; he'd been manipulated, his vulnerabilities exploited. This revelation, while not excusing his actions, added another layer of complexity to our understanding of the conspiracy. It was a chilling reminder that even those closest to us can be vulnerable to manipulation.

The impact of Terry's betrayal resonated deeply. It forced us to re-evaluate our methods, to question our assumptions. It heightened our awareness of the potential for infiltration, for hidden agendas. Trust, once our bedrock, now needed to be earned and constantly reassessed.

The investigation intensified, each new discovery unveiling further betrayals. We uncovered a network of informants within law enforcement, individuals who were turning a blind eye to the conspiracy's activities in exchange for bribes or protection. We found evidence of political corruption, a trail leading to high-ranking officials who were complicit in shielding the conspirators. It was a depressing realization that the tentacles of the conspiracy reached into every facet of society, corrupting institutions and undermining the very fabric of justice.

We navigated these new betrayals, offering guidance and support. It reminded us that uncovering such widespread corruption was a testament to the conspiracy's scope and sophistication. While the betrayals were disheartening, they also highlighted the importance of our investigation. The more we uncovered, the more we realized the sheer scale of the damage caused by the conspiracy. We couldn't afford to let these betrayals paralyze us; we had to press on.

As we delved deeper into the web of deceit, we discovered a pattern in the betrayals. The conspirators weren't simply buying off individuals; they were exploiting their vulnerabilities, their weaknesses, their desires. They were masters of manipulation, capable of targeting people's deepest insecurities, using their hopes and fears against them.

Liam discovered a hidden chat log, encrypted and almost undetectable, where the mastermind was communicating with his operatives. The conversations were chillingly revealing, filled with coded language, psychological manipulation techniques, and a ruthless disregard for human life. The mastermind was a psychopath, Dr. Benton concluded, someone who lacked empathy and remorse, capable of using and discarding people without a second thought.

Our shared expertise proved crucial in understanding the dynamics of the conspiracy. We helped one another to see the psychological patterns; the manipulative strategies used to recruit and control individuals. As we explained to the team how the conspirators built elaborate systems of trust, only to shatter them when their purpose was served. The conspirators were experts in exploiting human vulnerabilities, understanding how to manipulate people into betraying their friends, family, and even themselves.

This insight allowed us to develop new strategies, to anticipate the conspirators' moves. We started to look beyond the obvious betrayals, searching for the underlying psychological motivations. We began to see the bigger picture – a meticulously crafted network of human vulnerabilities, exploited for the benefit of a psychopathic mastermind.

The journey was emotionally taxing, a relentless barrage of betrayals that chipped away at our trust in humanity. Yet, in the face of these setbacks, our teamwork and guidance remained a steady beacon, helping us to navigate the moral and psychological challenges. The unwavering support we shared, combined with our growing understanding of the conspiracy's workings, spurred us onwards. We were a team, bound together by our shared purpose and a growing understanding of the devastating consequences of betrayal. The road ahead remained long and uncertain, but we knew, together, we would uncover the truth. The depth of the conspiracy might be daunting, but our resolve, tempered by the betrayals we had endured, was even stronger. The unraveling of the web had become our sacred mission, a testament to the strength of unity and the enduring power of hope in the face of overwhelming adversity.

A Dangerous Game

The following day dawned grey and overcast, mirroring the mood in our makeshift headquarters. Liam's face, usually alight with intellectual curiosity, was etched with worry. Isabella, normally a whirlwind of controlled energy, sat slumped over a stack of financial documents, her usual sharp focus dulled. Even Dr. Benton, the unwavering pillar of strength in our storm, seemed burdened by a weight of unspoken concern. The encrypted chat log Liam had discovered was a chilling glimpse into the mind of a predator, a master manipulator who played on human weaknesses with terrifying precision. His methods weren't just about bribery; they were about psychological warfare, a slow, deliberate dismantling of the victim's sense of self.

"He's not just buying loyalty," Liam stated, his voice low and grave. "He's creating it, then shattering it. It's a game, a perverse kind of performance art where the victims are the unwitting actors."

Isabella nodded, pushing a stray strand of hair from her face. "He targets vulnerabilities, preying on insecurities, unmet needs, even past traumas. It's as if he has a psychological profile on each of his operatives, meticulously crafted to exploit their weaknesses."

Dr. Benton, her gaze fixed on a point beyond the room, seemed lost in thought. "This is beyond simple blackmail. It's a calculated campaign of psychological manipulation. He's not just controlling them; he's shaping their identities, their perceptions of reality."

The realization hung heavy in the air. We weren't dealing with a simple criminal organization; we were facing a sophisticated, almost artistic, campaign of psychological manipulation orchestrated by a master. This was a dangerous game, one where the stakes were far higher than money or power. It was a game for the very essence of human identity, a game that reached into the deepest recesses of the human psyche.

That evening, I received a cryptic message, a single line of text: "The game is afoot." It was from an unknown number, but the tone, the implication, sent a shiver down my spine. The message was a challenge, a dare, a warning. It meant I had officially become a player in this dangerous game, a pawn in a deadly chess match against a cunning and ruthless adversary.

The next few days were a blur of near misses and close calls. I found myself being subtly shadowed, followed by unseen eyes. Anonymous packages containing disturbing gifts arrived at the apartment—a single red rose, a broken porcelain doll, a photograph of my childhood home. It was a clear message: I was being watched, studied, and manipulated. The psychological warfare had intensified, and despite my professional expertise, I felt a growing sense of unease. I started to understand the terror my clients must have felt during the process of manipulation.

One evening, while working late at the office, I was ambushed. Two figures, their faces obscured by masks, confronted me, their actions swift and precise. They didn't try to physically harm me, but instead, they injected me with a sedative. When I awoke, I was bound to a chair in an abandoned warehouse, the air thick with the smell of damp concrete and fear.

The mastermind appeared; his face still hidden behind a shadow. His voice, a low, chilling whisper, filled the cavernous space. "Dr. Elara Adams," he said, "you've shown yourself to be an intelligent adversary. You've seen through some of our tactics. But you haven't seen the whole picture."

He revealed his plans: a grand scheme to destabilize global markets using psychological manipulation, to cripple economies and bring the world to its knees. He explained how his organization manipulated individuals, exploiting their weaknesses, building a web of trust and deceit that extended to the highest echelons of power. I listened, my mind racing, my professional expertise clashing with the visceral fear coursing through my veins.

He then revealed his motive. It wasn't about money or power; it was about control. He sought to exert absolute control over human behavior, to manipulate people on a mass scale, and in the process prove he could create a world where fear reigned supreme. He believed humanity was inherently weak and vulnerable to manipulation and it was up to him to show the world what this meant.

The mastermind offered me a choice: join him, use my psychological expertise to further his agenda, or be eliminated. I felt a terrifying mixture of fear and adrenaline. My intuition told me this was not the time to challenge him. I decided to buy time, feigning compliance. I agreed to cooperate, but under one condition. I would help him, but only on my terms.

I began to subtly undermine his plans, planting seeds of doubt and discord within his organization. Using my psychological knowledge, I exploited the existing tensions and vulnerabilities within the group, turning the members against each other. I played the long game, acting as a double agent, feeding the mastermind misinformation while secretly working to expose his network.

The danger was ever-present. One wrong move could expose me, resulting in dire consequences. Every interaction, every decision, was a calculated risk. It was a game of wits, a delicate dance between deception and survival. I felt like a tightrope walker, balancing precariously over a chasm of despair, knowing one wrong step could send me plummeting into an abyss. The psychological pressure was immense, the fear of betrayal and capture a constant companion.

Meanwhile, Liam and Isabella, alerted by my prolonged absence, were frantic. They launched a desperate search, tracing my movements through various digital footprints. The trail led them to abandoned warehouses, desolate streets, and encrypted communications that spoke of a conspiracy far larger than they had ever imagined. They realized I had been playing my own game of cat and mouse, a calculated risk that could have deadly consequences.

The tension mounted as I imagined Liam and Isabella getting closer to the location. They understood the gravity of the situation: they were not just hunting down a criminal organization; they were confronting a psychopathic mastermind who was capable of manipulating individuals and nations at will. Their investigation was no longer just about unraveling a conspiracy; it was about saving me and preventing a global catastrophe.

The climax would come when Liam and Isabella finally tracked me to the abandoned warehouse, facing a showdown with the mastermind and his operatives. The warehouse was a maze of shadows and secrets, a testament to the psychological manipulation and control the mastermind exerted. Every corner hinted at a carefully orchestrated plan that was far-reaching in its consequences. The battle of wits escalated to a critical point, a life-or-death struggle to expose the mastermind's dark secrets and protect the innocent from the devastating consequences of his manipulations. The fate of countless lives rested on the outcome of this dangerous game. The web of deceit was about to be unraveled, but the price of victory remained uncertain.

Psychological Warfare

The cold seeped into my bones, a chilling contrast to the burning fear that consumed me. Bound to the chair, the rough rope biting into my wrists, I felt utterly helpless. The warehouse was a tomb of echoing silence, broken only by the occasional drip of water and the erratic thump-thump-thump of my own heart. My captors, faceless figures in the gloom, had vanished, leaving me alone with the mastermind, his presence a palpable weight in the air.

He hadn't touched me, hadn't even spoken much. His silence was more terrifying than any threat. He had instead launched a different kind of attack—a psychological siege designed to break me, to chip away at my resilience until I crumbled under the pressure. He had, in essence, begun his psychological autopsy. It was a methodical dismantling of my professional strength and composure.

He started with subtle manipulations, twisting my own words and actions against me. He replayed moments from my past therapy sessions, highlighting instances where patients had defied me, or where I had felt a twinge of self-doubt. "You understand vulnerability, don't you, Doctor?" he'd murmured, his voice a silken whisper that cut through the silence. "The exquisite fragility of the human spirit. You've seen it firsthand, haven't you?"

His words were like tiny, poisoned darts, each one striking at a vulnerable point in the psyche. He knew me, intimately. He understood my insecurities, fears, past traumas, all gleaned from the meticulous surveillance I was now only beginning to fully understand. This wasn't just about kidnapping; it was a performance, a carefully constructed play designed to erode confidence and self-belief.

He spoke of my colleagues, Liam and Isabella, painting them in a dark light. He portrayed them as incompetent, even treacherous, suggesting that they were easily manipulated, already compromised. He subtly sowed seeds of doubt, hinting that their loyalty was questionable, that their pursuit was misguided. The intent was clear: to isolate me, to break down my trust in those closest to me, leaving me stranded and vulnerable.

His methods were eerily similar to those I had seen employed by my patients in the past. It was textbook manipulative behavior, but on a far grander and more sinister scale. He would throw in carefully chosen words, triggering a flash of past trauma, a moment of doubt that would then be subtly reinforced. He used my own training against me, utilizing my expertise in psychology to skillfully dismantle my defenses.

He began to play mind games, presenting me with seemingly innocuous questions that, upon closer examination, revealed a deeper, darker truth. These were not simple questions meant to trick me but were rather carefully planned to unearth insecurities and exploit them. The questions were veiled in a veneer of casual conversation, but beneath the surface lay a calculated plan to unravel my thoughts. It was like a psychological chess match; each question a move intended to expose weaknesses and manipulate responses. It was an intimate psychological warfare.

He used sleep deprivation as another weapon, keeping me awake for extended periods, interrupting my sleep with sudden bursts of noise and light. The exhaustion and stress further eroded the already fragile mental state. The lack of sleep created cognitive dissonance and confusion, increasing the susceptibility to his manipulations.

He employed gaslighting, subtly twisting reality, making me question my own perceptions and sanity. He would offer contradictory information, then deny having said it, creating a sense of uncertainty and paranoia. He aimed to make me question my instincts and judgment, eroding my ability to think clearly.

He used reverse psychology, suggesting I was stronger than I believed, that I was capable of great things, but only if I joined him. He manipulated my sense of self-worth, tempting me with a sense of power and control, blurring the line between right and wrong. It was a cunning attempt to exploit my altruistic nature, using the desire to help others to further his malevolent aims.

He used the method of "grooming", which is usually reserved for child manipulation. He made me believe I was in safe hands, only to reveal the reality of the situation. It was to create the false belief that I was actually safe and not in the middle of an intense interrogation. It was a well-planned manipulation that was designed to keep me on my toes and undermine my trust. It was a way to slowly chip away at my ability to focus and resist his influence. He knew exactly what buttons to press, what narratives to spin. This was a precise and planned attack.

Days blurred into a nightmarish haze. I wasn't sure how long I had been there. The line between reality and manipulation had become so blurred that I often struggled to distinguish between what was real and what was a figment of his psychological manipulation.

Then, a flicker of defiance ignited within me. The very tactics he used to break me also gave insights into his methods. I began to analyze his behavior, to dissect his words, searching for inconsistencies, for subtle clues that might reveal his weaknesses.

I remembered my training, expertise in therapeutic counter-transference. I realized that his manipulation, while sophisticated, was still driven by his own deep-seated insecurities and need for control. I saw the cracks in his seemingly invincible facade.

This was my chance. my counter-attack would be subtle, a mirroring of his own tactics, but with a far more humane end goal. I would play along, appear compliant, but would use my psychological knowledge to subtly undermine his authority, to sow seeds of dissent within his own organization, and to expose his weaknesses to Liam and Isabella, who were now unknowingly closing in. The psychological warfare was far from over; it had simply entered a new, more dangerous phase.

Seeking Justice

The faintest sliver of moonlight pierced the grimy warehouse window, casting long, dancing shadows across the concrete floor. My mind, now a battlefield of exhaustion and defiance, observed my captor from the corner of my eye. He paced, a restless predator in the gloom, his silhouette a stark outline against the meager light. His silence, once a weapon, now felt...vulnerable. The relentless psychological assault had begun to crack his composure, a subtle shift I wouldn't have noticed had I not been meticulously studying his every twitch, every inflection.

My initial strategy, a feigned compliance, had yielded unexpected results. He had underestimated my resilience and ability to adapt. I had let him believe I was breaking, even feeding him carefully crafted narratives that subtly misrepresented my inner turmoil. But beneath the surface, I was building a counter-offensive.

My access to the outside world was limited, almost non-existent. Yet, I possessed a weapon far more potent than any physical tool: my mind. I had subtly embedded coded messages within my seemingly compliant responses, using psychological cues that only a trained professional would recognize. These weren't blatant cries for help, but rather carefully constructed seeds of information, planted deep within the soil of their twisted conversations. So, I carefully thought of subtle cues to insert in the videos they would record to send to my team.

I started with Liam, my closest confidante, the one I instinctively trusted. I knew he would be relentless in his search. My coded messages alluded to the location of the warehouse—subtle details about the building's structure, sounds, and even the peculiar smell of damp concrete and decaying wood—all woven into my seemingly innocuous replies. It was a slow, painstaking process, each word a carefully considered step in a complex game of chess. I had to be certain Liam understood the subtle clues, and would piece together the puzzle I was crafting.

Next, I turned my attention to Isabella, Liam's partner, whose sharp analytical mind could provide an added layer of support. The messages to Isabella were more indirect, focused on psychological cues about my captor's personality—hints of his obsessions, his insecurities, his methods of manipulation. This information, while seemingly irrelevant on the surface, could help Isabella build a profile, identify patterns, and ultimately narrow down the possible suspects. I was meticulously crafting a detailed psychological profile, feeding it to Isabella in tiny pieces.

But the danger remained very real. My captor was not a fool. He had observed the subtle shifts in demeanor, the way I now met his gaze with an unnerving calmness, a stillness that masked a growing storm. He had grown wary, suspicious. His questions became more probing, more insistent, trying to pierce through my calm exterior. He started inserting words or phrases from my previous therapy sessions, aimed at unsettling me; trying to detect if my compliant demeanor was a facade.

I countered his strategy with a carefully crafted persona, a mirror image of his manipulative tactics. I played on his desire for control, feeding him information that confirmed his preconceived notions while subtly undermining his authority. I would agree with his points, even reinforce his beliefs, subtly inserting words or sentences that planted seeds of doubt in his mind. I was creating cognitive dissonance, subtly twisting his own words against him.

The nights were the worst. The lack of sleep had sharpened my senses, intensified my awareness of the subtle shifts in the environment, and allowed me to anticipate the captor's next move. In the dark, I would replay their conversations, dissect his words, looking for weaknesses in his strategy, trying to find entry points into his meticulously crafted persona.

One night, during one of the rare moments when he was asleep, I managed to loosen the ropes binding my wrists. It was a slight movement, a minuscule shift, but it was enough to give a sliver of hope. I didn't attempt to escape; that would be too risky. Instead, I used the newfound freedom to subtly alter the environment, leaving tiny, almost imperceptible clues – the careful placement of a loose thread, a barely noticeable scratch on the wall – all designed to provide Liam and Isabella with additional information, triangulating my location.

My captor's unease grew palpable. His methods became more erratic, his questions more desperate. His carefully constructed facade was crumbling, the cracks widening under the subtle pressure of my counter-offensive. He started making mistakes, leaving himself exposed. He was losing control. He was reacting to me, instead of controlling my actions.

I sensed the window closing. He was becoming increasingly paranoid, his control slipping. He was beginning to suspect that someone was tracking his movements, suspecting that the intricate web of manipulation he'd spun was unraveling.

My next move had to be decisive, calculated. I knew I couldn't rely solely on coded messages, especially with the captor's increasing awareness of my efforts. I needed a direct line to Liam, a clear, unmistakable signal that would cut through the noise and ensure that he understood exactly where I was and how urgently I needed help. The opportunity presented itself during one of our nightly "interrogations."

He was recounting a particularly horrific case from his past, his voice raw with a dark pride. It was the perfect moment. I feigned a sudden bout of intense anxiety, and as his attention shifted from the story to my distress, I managed to subtly alter my position, creating a barely perceptible pattern on the floor. It was a simple, yet profound message—a pattern of numbers that represented my coordinates and a time—encoded into the very structure of the room's physical layout. It was a risk, a calculated gamble, but it was my only chance.

The psychological game continued, with each side vying for dominance. Yet, with each passing day, the scales were tipping in my favor. I had turned my captor's methods against him;

transforming his weapons into tools of my own liberation. The web, once designed to ensnare me, was now being meticulously untangled, thread by thread, revealing the dark heart of my captor and bringing him closer to justice. The final act of this psychological drama was about to begin. The hunt was shifting; I was no longer the prey, but the hunter.

Chapter 9

Shifting Loyalties

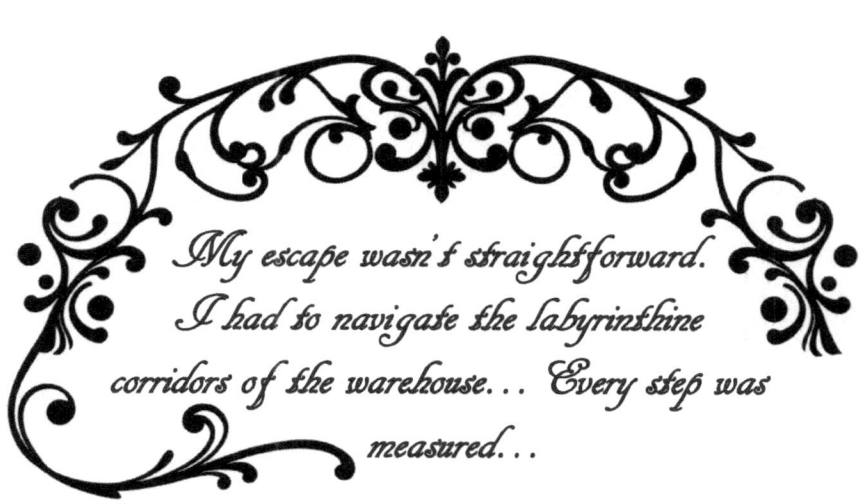

My escape wasn't straightforward. I had to navigate the labyrinthine corridors of the warehouse... Every step was measured...

Uncertain Alliances

The warehouse air hung thick and stagnant, heavy with the scent of mildew and fear. Despite the gnawing hunger and the persistent ache in my wrists, I felt a strange calm settle over me. The coded messages, the subtle manipulations, the intricate psychological dance—they were all working. My captor, full of confidence, allowed me to see that Liam and Isabella were responding, their actions, though indirect, confirmed it. But something felt...off. A discordant note in the symphony of my escape.

It started with a seemingly insignificant detail: a slight delay in Liam's usual rapid responses. His messages, usually peppered with terse instructions and urgent reassurances, now carried a hesitant tone, a cautiousness that grated against my nerves. He was less decisive, his usual sharp wit dulled, replaced by a cautious uncertainty. This wasn't the Liam I knew, the man who would move mountains to save me.

Then came the unsettling silence from Isabella. Her usual stream of analytical insights, the meticulous breakdown of the captor's personality, had dwindled to a mere trickle. Her responses were brief, almost perfunctory, lacking the intellectual fire that had always characterized our collaborations. The silence was deafening, a chilling void that sent a shiver down the spine.

A knot of dread tightened in my stomach. The carefully constructed alliances, the pillars of my escape plan, seemed to be crumbling. Were they truly working with me, or was something else at play? The thought that my own escape strategy was being jeopardized not only by my captor but also by those I trusted, made my stomach twist with a desperate need to regain control. The fear was not of the physical confinement but of the insidious betrayal from within.

My captor, sensing the inner turmoil, pressed his advantage. His questions became more personal, delving into my past relationships, my vulnerabilities, my deepest fears. He seemed to know more than he should. He mentioned seemingly insignificant details from my past therapy sessions, details that only a select few could have known. Was he simply lucky, or was he privy to information leaked from my own network of allies?

The possibility that one of my allies had betrayed me was a cold, sharp blade twisting in my heart. But which one? And why? Liam, my long-standing boyfriend, the man I had always considered a rock of unwavering support? Or Isabella, the brilliant analyst, whose mind was as sharp as a surgeon's scalpel? The thought that either or both of them could be involved shattered my carefully crafted calm.

I started reviewing all communications in my mind, dissecting every word, every subtle pause, searching for any hint of treachery. I looked for the subtle manipulation, the coded messages embedded within the messages themselves, the faint signs of betrayal. The task was complex, a psychological puzzle of deception and trust, where the lines between reality and illusion had become frighteningly blurred.

The subtle clues came in small, almost imperceptible shifts in their communication patterns. Liam's coded responses seemed less precise, lacking the usual clarity and urgency. Isabella's analysis, usually meticulously detailed, seemed shallow, lacking the penetrating insight she was known for. Their responses started to mirror each other in a way that raised suspicion, creating a chilling sense of collusion that ran deeper than mere coincidence. The chilling realization dawned on me - I was being played.

My training kicked in. I shifted from the emotional turmoil to the cool, detached perspective of a professional analyst. I began to meticulously reconstruct the timeline of events, analyzing their behavior, searching for patterns, looking for the missing pieces of the puzzle. It was like assembling a jigsaw puzzle where some pieces were deliberately missing, distorted, and misleading.

I examined the information I had provided Liam and Isabella, searching for potential leaks, unintentional disclosures that could have fallen into my captor's hands. Could one of them have subtly altered my messages, subtly twisting my words to betray my trust and provide my captor with additional information? The chilling answer was a resounding yes.

The pattern started to emerge. Small, subtle changes in the information provided—minor details altered, facts twisted to create a different narrative, subtle shifts in timing that allowed my captor to gain the upper hand. The realization hit me hard, a crushing blow that threatened to break my spirit. It wasn't just the physical confinement, the psychological torture, it was the betrayal of trust that had struck the hardest.

The shock gradually subsided, replaced by a cold, hard determination. This was not the end. I would turn this betrayal to my advantage. The fact that I was being betrayed meant that my captor was not acting alone, that there were more players in this game than I had initially realized, and that discovering their motives might be the key to escaping.

I decided to play along, to feed my false allies information, a carefully crafted deception designed to expose them, to expose their motives and unmask their identities. I would use their own treachery against them, turning their betrayal into the key to liberation. The game had changed. It was no longer just about escaping; it was about uncovering the truth, about exposing the insidious conspiracy that threatened to consume me.

I began to subtly alter coded messages, planting false leads, disseminating misleading information, while simultaneously setting traps to catch my betrayers in their own web of deceit. The psychological battle was far from over; it had simply evolved into a far more treacherous and complex game, one where the lines between friend and foe were blurred, and the stakes were life and death. Survival now depended on the ability to outwit not only my captor but also my supposed allies. The trust I thought I had was gone, replaced by a cold, calculating pragmatism. My escape now depended not only on my own wits but on the ability to unravel the intricate web of deceit that surrounded me, a web woven by the very people I once considered my closest allies. The hunt was on, and this time, I was determined to become the ultimate predator.

Unexpected Betrayal

The realization hit me like a physical blow, the air leaving my lungs in a sharp gasp. It wasn't the suffocating darkness of the warehouse, nor the gnawing hunger, nor even the chilling knowledge of my captor's proximity that stole my breath. It was the insidious betrayal, the chilling awareness that the people I had trusted implicitly, the very pillars of my meticulously constructed escape plan, were actively working against me. The carefully constructed facade of their alliance shattered, leaving me exposed and vulnerable in a way I hadn't anticipated.

The weight of it settled heavily on my chest, a crushing burden that threatened to suffocate me. Liam, my steadfast partner, the unwavering supporter, the one constant in a situation often characterized by chaos and uncertainty. And Isabella, the sharp-witted analyst, whose intellectual prowess had been instrumental in guiding me through the treacherous labyrinth of my confinement, now appearing to be the cause. Both, seemingly, had turned on me, their actions a symphony of subtle manipulations designed to ensure my continued captivity.

The initial shock morphed into a cold, calculating anger. My training, years spent analyzing human behavior, dissecting motivations, understanding the complexities of human interaction, kicked in. The emotional turmoil, the gut-wrenching betrayal, retreated into the background, replaced by a sharp, focused determination. This wasn't a personal failure; it was a strategic setback. And I would overcome it.

I methodically reviewed our past communications, searching for the subtle clues I had initially dismissed as anomalies. I saw it now, the carefully orchestrated shift in Liam's messages, the slight delays, the hesitant tone, the subtle shift in his coded responses. They were not unintentional errors; they were carefully crafted messages, designed to mislead, to provide the captor with enough information to thwart my escape attempts, but not enough to alert me to their treachery.

Isabella's analytical reports, once sharp and insightful, now seemed intentionally vague, lacking the usual detail and precision. Her responses were calculated, deliberately short, designed to convey the impression of continued cooperation while subtly hindering progress. It was a masterpiece of deception, a subtle ballet of betrayal executed with chilling precision.

The implications were staggering. My captor, whoever the masked figure was, clearly had an insider. But who? And why? Was it a personal vendetta? A power play? Or was there something far more sinister at play? The questions spiraled in my mind, a vortex of doubt and uncertainty that threatened to pull me under.

I began to meticulously reconstruct the timeline of events, piecing together the fragments of information, searching for the patterns, the subtle inconsistencies that pointed to the source of the betrayal. It was a painstaking process, requiring intense focus and unwavering attention to remembered detail shared with me. I had to sift through the carefully constructed lies in their return emails, separating truth from fiction, reality from illusion.

The answer, when it came, was as shocking as it was devastating. It wasn't just Liam or Isabella acting alone; they were working in concert, their actions coordinated in a way that suggested a pre-existing relationship, a shared motive that transcended their individual interests. Their betrayal wasn't just a breach of trust; it was a calculated act, a carefully orchestrated plan that had been in motion for far longer than I had realized.

The realization triggered a surge of adrenaline, a potent cocktail of fear and fury. This wasn't just a matter of escaping confinement; it was a matter of survival, of uncovering the truth behind the conspiracy that had ensnared me. The question wasn't just who had betrayed me, but *why*. And that, I realized, was the key to freedom.

I decided to adopt a new strategy. I wouldn't fight the betrayal directly; I would use it to my advantage. I would play along, feeding them misinformation, planting false leads, leading them down a garden path of my own design. I would use their treachery to expose their true motives, to unravel the intricate web of deceit they had spun.

I began to subtly alter coded messages, weaving a tapestry of deception, a carefully crafted narrative designed to manipulate my supposed allies while simultaneously revealing their identities to her captor. The goal wasn't just to escape; it was to identify the mastermind behind the plot, to expose their true nature and bring them down.

The psychological battle intensified. I was no longer just a prisoner; I was a hunter, meticulously tracking my prey, analyzing their behavior, anticipating their moves. I was playing a dangerous game, a game where the stakes were life and death, where the slightest misstep could be fatal. But I was not one to back down from a challenge. I was a master strategist, skilled to take down my manipulator, and I was determined to win.

The days bled into nights; each moment filled with the tension of the silent game. The subtle shifts in communication, the carefully veiled threats, the constant awareness of my captor's watchful eye – it all added to the pressure cooker atmosphere. Yet, amidst the chaos, a plan began to solidify in my mind, a plan that involved not just escaping, but exposing the network of betrayal that had ensnared me.

I needed to find out who my captor truly was. The information that had been leaked to him was too precise, too personal. This wasn't just random information gathered from news clippings and social media; this was intimate knowledge, details that only someone close to me could possess. I started to delve deeper into my past, revisiting memories, analyzing relationships, searching for the weak link, the point of vulnerability that had been exploited.

The process was painful, dredging up buried emotions, past hurts, and forgotten betrayals. But with each painful memory, I gained a clearer understanding of the puzzle. The betrayals weren't random acts; they were calculated moves designed to exploit my vulnerabilities, to manipulate my emotions, and to ultimately ensure failure.

The pieces of the puzzle began to fall into place. I saw connections I had missed before, relationships that were not as straightforward as they seemed. The betrayal wasn't just a simple act of malice; it was a complex, multi-layered scheme involving several players, all with their own hidden agendas.

The more I dug, the more chilling the truth became. The betrayal wasn't merely about captivity; it was about control, about power, about dismantling my life and everything I held dear. And the mastermind behind it all was someone I had trusted implicitly, someone who had been a constant presence in my life for years. Someone who knew me too well.

The realization hit me with the force of a tidal wave, washing over me with a chilling certainty. The betrayal was not only a personal affront, but a calculated move to disrupt my professional life, potentially ruining my career and reputation.

Armed with this new understanding, I crafted my next move. It was a high-stakes gamble, a daring plan that played on the trust, the deceit, and the ambition of those involved. It was a plan that would require me to tread carefully, to walk a tightrope between truth and deception, between friendship and betrayal.

The path ahead was dangerous, fraught with peril and uncertainty. But I was ready. I was no longer just a victim; I was a warrior, armed with intellect, courage, and a burning desire for justice. The game had changed, and I was ready to play. The hunt was on, and this time, I would not be the prey.

Ethical Dilemmas

The gnawing uncertainty of the situation pressed down on me. Escaping this physical confinement was only half the battle; the far greater challenge lay in untangling the web of deceit that had ensnared me. My training as a counselor, usually a source of strength, now presented me with a series of agonizing ethical dilemmas. Each choice felt like walking a tightrope, the slightest misstep potentially leading to catastrophic consequences.

The most immediate conflict stemmed from professional obligations. Confidentiality was paramount in this field, a sacred oath I had sworn to uphold. Yet, here I was, trapped in a situation where maintaining confidentiality could actively hinder my escape and the exposure of a dangerous conspiracy. The information I possessed, even the fragments I had painstakingly pieced together, could potentially implicate several individuals, individuals who held positions of power and influence. Revealing this information, even anonymously, risked jeopardizing their careers, reputations, and possibly their freedom.

The weight of this responsibility pressed heavily on me. I could imagine the potential fallout: damaged careers, broken families, and accusations of professional misconduct. The thought of the collateral damage, the lives irrevocably altered by my actions, haunted me. I wasn't just fighting for my own survival; I was wrestling with the potential ramifications of my choices on the lives of others.

But the alternative – silence – was equally unacceptable. To remain silent, to allow the perpetrators to continue their insidious work, would be a betrayal of my own conscience, a failure to protect those who might become future victims. The delicate balance between my professional obligations and my personal commitment to justice felt impossible to maintain. I was being forced to choose between two deeply held moral principles, neither of which I could easily compromise.

Further complicating the matter was my own emotional entanglement. The betrayal by Liam and Isabella, my supposed allies, had wounded me deeply. The personal nature of their betrayal added an intense emotional layer to the ethical dilemmas I faced. Could I maintain professional objectivity when my own sense of trust and safety had been so brutally violated? The lines between personal feelings and professional judgment blurred, threatening to cloud my decision-making process. Could I effectively analyze their motivations, predict their actions, and devise a strategy to expose them when my emotional responses were so intense?

My training emphasized the importance of maintaining a therapeutic distance, of avoiding emotional entanglement with clients. Yet, here I was, embroiled in a deeply personal conflict that had deeply personal consequences. I needed to be objective, detached, to approach this situation with the calm, clinical precision I usually demonstrated in my work. But the raw emotions, the pain of betrayal, threatened to override my professional judgment. This, I realized, was a critical factor in my struggle; the very principles I so rigorously followed in my professional life were at odds with the urgent need for action that my precarious situation demanded.

The psychological gamesmanship was relentless. I played along with Liam and Isabella's deception, feeding them carefully crafted misinformation, drawing them out, slowly unraveling their intricate web of lies. Every interaction demanded a delicate balancing act – maintaining their trust while simultaneously gathering evidence against them. It was a constant test of my psychological acumen, a battle waged in the silent space between carefully chosen words and calculated actions.

As I delved deeper into the investigation, the ethical dilemmas multiplied. I discovered evidence that suggested the involvement of more people than I initially suspected, a larger conspiracy extending far beyond my immediate circle. Exposing these individuals involved weighing the potential consequences of revealing sensitive information obtained through ethically questionable means. My methods, honed in my professional life, were now blurring the line between ethical inquiry and potentially illegal action, forcing me to question the very foundations of my actions.

The dilemma was not simply about revealing information; it was about the methods I used to gather it. I had to consider the potential legal ramifications of my actions, the consequences of crossing the line from self-defense to potential criminal activity. The risk of legal repercussions added a new dimension to my ethical predicament, forcing me to balance the need for justice against the potential cost of my own freedom. The very tools I wielded to survive, my sharp intellect and understanding of human behavior, were now potentially compromising my own position.

The ethical quandary intensified as I realized that my own survival was inextricably linked to exposing those involved in the conspiracy. My escape, my freedom, was directly dependent on my success in revealing the truth, a truth that threatened powerful and influential individuals. This created a direct conflict of interest – my personal survival was contingent upon actions that could have significant, potentially negative, consequences for others. The weight of this realization pressed heavily upon me, intensifying the ethical tension I already faced.

I found myself wrestling not only with the ethical implications of my actions, but with the question of my own moral standing. Was I justifying potentially unethical actions by framing them as necessary for self-preservation? Was I inadvertently becoming what I fought against – manipulating and deceiving others in the pursuit of my own goals? These were not simple questions; they were profound ethical reflections forcing me to confront the darker aspects of human nature, the potential for corruption even within my own pursuit of justice.

The final act of the escape and exposure of the conspiracy demanded even more difficult choices. The closer I came to the truth, the more complex and treacherous the path became. The final confrontation involved a calculated risk, a gamble that threatened not only my own freedom, but also the lives and futures of those entangled in the web of deceit. I had to weigh the risk of my actions against the potential for exposing a much larger and more dangerous conspiracy.

In the end, my choices reflected a profound understanding of both human psychology and ethical considerations. I navigated the treacherous terrain of the ethical dilemmas with a skill and precision that mirrored my therapeutic approach. I made choices that were not always easy, but were consistent with my core values, proving that even in the most extreme circumstances, it was possible to fight for justice while upholding one's professional ethics. It was a fight that went beyond just survival – it was a fight for the preservation of my own moral compass.

Desperate Measures

The flickering fluorescent light of the abandoned warehouse cast long, distorted shadows, accentuating the claustrophobic space. My heart hammering against my ribs, felt the familiar chill of fear, but it was overshadowed by a colder, harder resolve. The carefully constructed facade I'd maintained throughout the ordeal was crumbling, replaced by a raw, desperate need for survival. Liam and Isabella, once perceived as allies, had revealed themselves to be ruthless manipulators, their betrayal cutting deeper than any physical wound. They were part of the entire obduction. Escape was no longer a theoretical exercise; it was an immediate, life-or-death necessity.

My usual meticulous planning, the carefully measured steps I'd taken to gather evidence and expose the conspiracy, felt inadequate in the face of this urgent need for action. The ethical dilemmas that had plagued me before now seemed almost trivial compared to the immediate danger. The rules, the principles I had dedicated my life to upholding, were being rewritten by the stark realities of my predicament. I was operating outside the bounds of my professional code, venturing into a gray area where survival dictated the rules.

The first desperate measure involved manipulating Liam. I knew he possessed a deep-seated insecurity, a vulnerability I could exploit. I had observed his fascination with power, his need to control those around him. Using this knowledge, I crafted a series of emails, appearing to be from a high-ranking official, praising Liam's work and hinting at even greater opportunities, opportunities that would require absolute loyalty and discretion. The emails contained carefully veiled threats, suggesting that any deviation from loyalty would have severe consequences. It was a calculated risk, a gamble on his ambition overriding his caution.

The gamble paid off. Liam, intoxicated by the prospect of advancement, became more reckless, his paranoia growing. He became more careless in his communications, revealing vital information that I had been unable to obtain through conventional means. His need for validation, his vulnerability to manipulation, became my most potent weapon. The ethical implications gnawed at me, but the alternative – remaining a captive – was unacceptable. My actions were a compromise, a morally ambiguous decision made under duress, but one I justified as a necessary evil.

My next desperate measure involved Isabella. Isabella, unlike Liam, was driven by a fierce need for validation, a deep-seated desire for recognition. She craved approval, not from those in power, but from those she admired – those she saw as equals. I used my understanding of human psychology, crafted a meticulously worded anonymous email, suggesting that Liam was betraying her, that he was using Isabella as a pawn in his own game. It was a calculated attempt to sow discord, to turn Isabella against Liam. It was a dangerous game, a risky maneuver that could easily backfire, but it was a risk I was willing to take.

The email worked as planned. Isabella, consumed by jealousy and wounded pride, responded with a fury I had anticipated. She confronted Liam, their argument escalating into a chaotic exchange of accusations and threats. The ensuing conflict provided me with the opportunity I needed. Using my knowledge of the building's layout, gleaned from meticulously studying the blueprints I'd obtained, I exploited their distraction, slipping away under the cover of their argument. This wasn't just an escape; it was a calculated maneuver, a well-orchestrated strategy built upon my understanding of the captors' weaknesses.

My escape wasn't straightforward. I had to navigate the labyrinthine corridors of the warehouse, avoiding security cameras and potential patrols. Every step was measured, calculated, guided by my knowledge of human behavior and security protocols. I used my knowledge of psychology to anticipate their responses, predicting their search patterns, avoiding the areas they were most likely to patrol. My understanding of their biases, their assumptions, guided my choices. I moved like a ghost, unseen, unheard, a testament to my sharp intellect and unwavering determination.

Once outside the warehouse, the challenge shifted. I needed to alert the authorities, but without revealing my own involvement in obtaining the evidence. I had collected a substantial amount of incriminating information, but much of it had been acquired through ethically questionable methods. I had to find a way to expose the conspiracy without compromising myself. I carefully constructed anonymous tips, sending them through encrypted channels, carefully structuring the information to avoid direct links to my own actions.

The subsequent investigation exposed a vast conspiracy, a network of corruption reaching far beyond Liam and Isabella. High-ranking officials, powerful business magnates, all implicated in the crimes, their identities revealed piece by piece. Observing from a safe distance, I felt a chilling sense of satisfaction. Justice, although obtained through morally ambiguous means, was finally served. The risk of exposure loomed, however. My methods were unconventional, my actions bordering on illegal, but the alternative had been far worse – silent complicity in the face of overwhelming evil.

The final act of the journey involved a calculated risk: I chose to meet the key witness in person. This witness, an individual who had information that could shatter the entire network of corruption, was scared and in hiding. The meeting took place in a remote location, chosen for its seclusion and security. It was a moment fraught with tension, a meeting that could make or break everything. Drawing upon my training in therapy, I established a rapport with the witness, building trust and understanding. I reassured him of his safety, of the steps taken to protect his identity, and finally, he agreed to cooperate.

His testimony, corroborated by the evidence I had painstakingly gathered, sealed the fate of the conspirators. The ensuing trial was a media sensation, the details of the conspiracy unfolding slowly, revealing a web of deceit, betrayal, and manipulation. I watched from the shadows, a silent observer, as justice was served. I had walked a fine line between right and wrong, and while I may not have upheld every professional principle, I had achieved the primary goal: to expose the truth and protect those who needed protection.

The aftermath was a complex blend of relief and exhaustion. I was safe, the immediate threat neutralized. But the psychological scars of my ordeal remained, the ethical dilemmas continuing to haunt me. The line between right and wrong had blurred, and the experience had changed me profoundly, forcing me to confront the darker aspects of human behavior and my own capacity for resilience. My professional life, once defined by structure and ethical clarity, would never be the same. The world I once knew, the unwavering belief in the good that can prevail, was now shattered, revealing a world of shadows and complexities I had never fully understood. I had survived, yes, but at a cost. The price of survival was a profound shift in my perspective, a new understanding of the moral ambiguity inherent in the fight for justice.

A Glimmer of Hope

The anonymous tip, sent through a labyrinthine network of encrypted servers, had yielded a response. Not a direct confirmation, but a subtle shift in the wind, a whisper in the deafening silence that had followed the trial. A previously untraceable offshore account, linked to one of the minor players in the conspiracy, had shown a significant, unexplained deposit. It wasn't a large sum, not enough to raise immediate red flags in the initial investigation, but it was enough to pique the interest of a determined investigator. And that investigator, fueled by a persistent hunch and access to resources far beyond the reach of the initial investigators, was closing in.

This new lead, this glimmer of hope, reignited my waning resolve. The exhaustion, the lingering trauma, were still palpable, but a renewed sense of purpose, a fierce determination to see this through to the very end, pushed me forward. I found myself poring over financial records, tracing the money trail, my mind sharp and focused, operating at a level of intensity I hadn't experienced since the initial escape. I was working from a safe house, provided by a grateful and anonymous benefactor, a testament to the ripple effect of my actions. The benefactor's identity remained unknown, a silent guardian angel in the shadows, someone who understood the dangers inherent in pursuing such a dangerous path.

The offshore account led to a shell corporation, a complex web of subsidiaries and holding companies designed to obfuscate the true source of the funds. Utilizing my meticulous attention to detail and innate ability to unravel complex patterns, I began to unravel the threads. It was slow, painstaking work, each step requiring careful consideration, each move pregnant with risk. I was operating in a twilight zone, on the very edge of legality, constantly mindful of the potential consequences if I were discovered.

The trail led to a small, virtually unknown technology company based in a remote part of Eastern Europe. The company's official purpose was the development of sophisticated encryption software, but my research revealed a far more sinister reality. The software was far more advanced than publicly advertised, capable of deep-level surveillance, data manipulation, and even controlling critical infrastructure systems. The company's founders, men whose names were barely known beyond a select few, had ties to the individuals implicated in the original conspiracy. This was no coincidence. It was the missing piece of the puzzle, the final link in the chain of corruption.

This discovery was a turning point. It provided concrete evidence of a much larger, more insidious plot than initially imagined – a plot that threatened to destabilize not only the financial systems but also the very fabric of national security. The original conspiracy had been a smokescreen, a carefully orchestrated distraction from a far more dangerous and far-reaching operation. Liam and Isabella, despite their ruthlessness, had been but pawns in a larger game, their actions controlled and directed by shadowy figures operating from afar.

The realization filled me with a chilling sense of dread, but it also fueled my determination. The stakes had been raised exponentially. This was no longer about personal survival or professional vindication; it was about national security, about preventing catastrophic consequences. I felt the weight of responsibility pressing down on me, a heavy burden I bore willingly. I was no longer just a psychologist escaping a dangerous situation; I was a lone warrior against a vast and powerful enemy.

I carefully compiled the findings, structuring evidence in a way that would be impossible to ignore. I worked late into the night, fueled by coffee and the unwavering belief in the need for justice. The fear was still there, a constant companion, but it was tempered by a renewed sense of purpose, a fierce determination that burned brighter than ever before. I utilized encrypted channels to contact a trusted source within the government, an individual I had met through anonymous tip-offs, an individual who understood the high stakes and the extraordinary nature of these findings.

The contact, a seasoned government operative known only as "Agent Vex," met me in a secure location. The meeting was brief, professional, devoid of pleasantries. Agent Vex, a figure shrouded in secrecy, listened intently, his eyes betraying neither emotion nor judgment. He had dealt with this type of clandestine operation before, and he knew when to listen and when to act. He was impressed, even awed by the meticulous investigation, deep understanding of human behavior, and unwavering courage in the face of overwhelming odds.

He acknowledged my methods, the ethical ambiguities, without judgment. He understood the world I had inhabited for the past several months, a world of shadows and deception, where survival dictated the rules. He knew that the pursuit of justice often required navigating morally gray areas. He simply asked one question: "Are you certain of your findings?" My affirmative answer sealed the deal.

Agent Vex's resources dwarfed anything I could access independently. He mobilized a specialized task force, using the evidence as a foundation to launch a comprehensive investigation. The technology company in Eastern Europe became the focus of a multi-national operation, involving law enforcement agencies and intelligence services from across the globe. The scale of the operation, its secrecy, and its potential ramifications kept it firmly under wraps, operating far away from the prying eyes of the media.

The arrest of the key players in the new conspiracy was swift and decisive. The entire operation was dismantled, its web of deceit unraveled. The original trial, while a significant victory, had only scratched the surface; the new investigation unearthed a vast conspiracy that reached into the highest echelons of power. I watched the events unfold from a distance, observing as the pieces fell into place, my contribution remaining largely anonymous.

The feeling of relief wasn't overwhelming; it was subtle, a gradual unwinding of tension rather than a sudden release. The aftermath was characterized by a quiet satisfaction, a sense of having fulfilled my purpose, of having done what I had to do. The knowledge that I had played a pivotal role in preventing a catastrophic event provided a profound sense of validation, far greater than any public recognition could have offered.

Yet, the shadow of these experiences still remained. The psychological toll, the ethical dilemmas, remained part of my story. The lines crossed would always be a part of my past, a reminder of the difficult choices I had made, the price I had paid for justice. But I had survived, and in surviving, I had transformed. The experience had strengthened my resilience, sharpened my focus, and given me a newfound understanding of the complexities of human behavior, the darkness that lurked beneath the surface of society. My life would never be the same, but in the heart of the darkness, I had found a glimmer of light, a beacon of hope in the face of overwhelming odds. I had found my own strength, and in doing so, I had helped save a piece of the world.

Chapter 10

The Turning Point

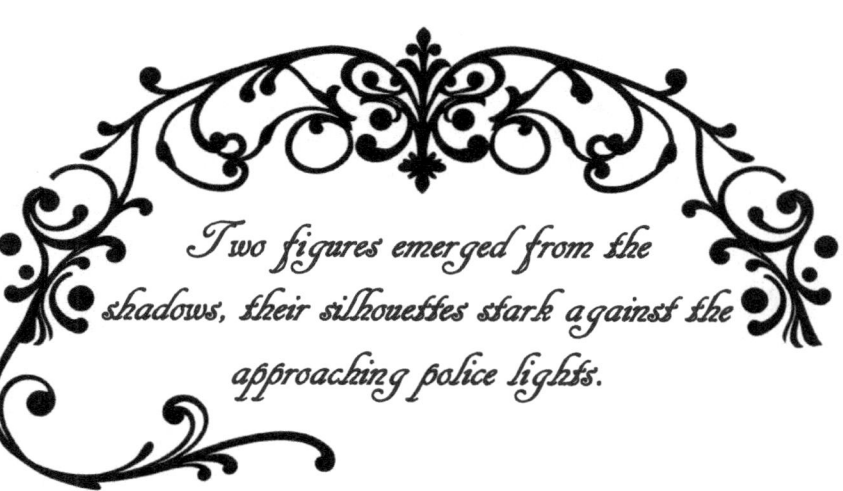

Two figures emerged from the shadows, their silhouettes stark against the approaching police lights.

A Crucial Discovery

The encrypted email arrived at 3:17 AM, a single line of code embedded within a seemingly innocuous image file. Fueled by lukewarm coffee and the gnawing unease that had become my constant companion, I deciphered it in seconds. The code, a complex algorithm I recognized from my work on the initial case, pointed to a specific server located deep within the dark web. It wasn't a direct accusation, not a smoking gun, but a subtle breadcrumb, a suggestion of something far more significant lurking beneath the surface. The thrill of the chase, the adrenaline rush of pursuing this hidden truth, temporarily eclipsed the weariness that weighed heavily on my shoulders.

I accessed the server using a heavily cloaked IP address, navigating through layers of obfuscation, each click a potential risk, each keystroke a gamble. I felt the familiar tension building, a tightening in my chest, the rapid beat of my heart against my ribs. The fear was a constant companion, but it was a fear I was learning to manage, to weaponize even, using it as fuel to push myself forward. The server contained a wealth of data, a sprawling digital landscape of encrypted files and hidden directories.

Sifting through the digital debris, I found it - a single, unencrypted file, tucked away in a seemingly innocuous folder. It was a financial report, detailing the transactions of a small, obscure company registered in the Cayman Islands. The company's name, "Aether Technologies," meant nothing to me, but the sheer volume of untraceable funds flowing through its accounts raised immediate red flags. The numbers were staggering, far exceeding anything I had encountered during the initial investigation.

Days blurred into a relentless cycle of research, analysis, and cautious action. I was working in my safe house, immersed in the labyrinthine world of offshore finance, tracing the money trail like a bloodhound on the scent. I used psychological insights to anticipate the patterns of behavior, to predict the next move of the unseen players behind Aether Technologies. I recognized a methodology, a signature, in the way these funds were being laundered—a style eerily similar to a sophisticated money laundering operation I'd studied in graduate school, a scheme considered so advanced, it had never been successfully cracked. This was no mere coincidence; it was the work of a master, a puppet master pulling strings from the shadows.

The trail led to a series of shell corporations; a complex web of interlocking entities designed to obscure the origins of the funds. Each lead was a piece of a larger puzzle, each clue a step closer to the truth. But with each step, the risks increased. I knew I was walking a tightrope, operating outside the bounds of established legal frameworks. The potential consequences—exposure, capture, even death—were ever-present, lurking just beneath the surface of my every action. Yet, I pressed on, driven by a sense of purpose, a determination to expose the truth no matter the cost.

My psychological training proved invaluable. I approached the digital investigation with the same meticulous attention to detail I brought to my therapeutic sessions. I analyzed the data, searching for patterns, inconsistencies, any clue that could reveal the hidden intentions behind the transactions. I understood the psychology of deception, the subtle cues that betrayed a hidden agenda. This wasn't just a financial puzzle; it was a game of psychological chess, with high stakes and deadly consequences.

A breakthrough came when I noticed a recurring pattern in the timing of the transactions. They coincided with specific geopolitical events – periods of market volatility, international crises, instances where nations were most vulnerable. This wasn't just about money laundering; it was about market manipulation, about destabilizing global economies for personal gain. The scale of the operation was breathtaking, a meticulously crafted plan to exploit global vulnerabilities for immense profit.

The next link emerged unexpectedly. A seemingly trivial detail – a recurring email address used in several transactions – led me to a previously unknown online forum dedicated to discussing advanced encryption techniques. This was no ordinary forum; it was a haven for hackers, codebreakers, and other individuals operating in the gray areas of the digital world.

I spent weeks immersed in this clandestine online community, carefully studying the conversations, analyzing the code snippets, piecing together the fragmented information. I learned about a new type of encryption software, far more sophisticated than anything publicly available. The software, I discovered, had the capacity to manipulate financial markets, control critical infrastructure, and even influence elections. The very foundations of national security were at risk.

This discovery was not merely a turning point; it was a seismic shift in the landscape of the investigation. The original conspiracy, with its seemingly high-stakes financial crimes, now appeared as a mere sideshow, a carefully orchestrated distraction from a far more sinister and expansive operation. The initial suspects, including Liam and Isabella, were merely pawns, their actions carefully orchestrated by a shadowy cabal operating from behind a screen of anonymity and technological sophistication. Aether Technologies was not simply a shell corporation; it was the tip of a very large, very dangerous iceberg.

The implications were staggering. This wasn't a matter of individual greed; it was a global threat, a conspiracy that threatened to destabilize entire nations, to plunge the world into chaos. I felt the weight of this revelation pressing down on me, a crushing burden of responsibility. The stakes had escalated beyond anything I could have anticipated. My initial fight for personal survival had transformed into a battle for global stability.

I compiled my findings into a comprehensive report, meticulously documented, irrefutable. I used encrypted channels to reach out to Agent Vex, the government operative I had secretly contacted after my initial escape. The information was transmitted through multiple layers of security protocols, each step designed to protect my identity and the integrity of the data. The risk was enormous, but I had no choice. The world depended on this.

The meeting with Agent Vex took place in a secluded location, far from the prying eyes of the public. The air crackled with unspoken tension, a palpable sense of urgency. Agent Vex, a man of few words, listened intently to my presentation, his expression unwavering, his eyes revealing nothing of his thoughts. He acknowledged the risks I had taken, the ethical compromises I had made, without judgment. He simply nodded, his silence a powerful acknowledgment of the magnitude of my discovery.

With Agent Vex's resources at my disposal, the investigation moved with a speed and efficiency that far surpassed anything I could have managed independently. A multinational task force was assembled, involving law enforcement agencies and intelligence services from multiple countries. The operation remained shrouded in secrecy, conducted with the utmost discretion, to avoid alerting the conspirators.

The arrests came swiftly and decisively. The leaders of Aether Technologies, the puppet masters pulling the strings from the shadows, were apprehended, their vast network of deceit unraveling before the eyes of the world. The sheer scale of the conspiracy was mind-boggling, its ramifications extending far beyond the initial financial crimes. It touched every corner of the globe. The evidence I accumulated formed the cornerstone of the prosecution's case.

The world was spared from a catastrophic event, a global crisis averted through courage and dedication of what had started from the work of a victim but transformed into an unlikely hero. I remained in the shadows, my contribution largely unknown to the public. I preferred it that way. The quiet satisfaction of knowing I had made a difference, that I had helped prevent a global catastrophe, was its own reward. My life would never be the same, marked by the indelible scars of trauma and the moral ambiguities I had faced. Yet, I had survived, transformed, strengthened by the very darkness that had threatened to consume me. And in the heart of that darkness, I had discovered a strength I never knew I possessed.

Reevaluating Relationships

The adrenaline rush had faded, leaving behind a bone-deep exhaustion and a gnawing unease that felt far more profound than the physical tiredness. The arrests of Liam and everyone involved, the dismantling of Aether Technologies – it was all a monumental achievement, a victory against overwhelming odds. Yet, the hollow feeling persisted. The weight of the world, or at least the weight of a very significant portion of its underbelly, had been lifted, but a new burden had settled upon my shoulders: the weight of solitude.

The investigation had consumed me, leaving little room for anything else. Friends, colleagues, even the fleeting connections I'd made during the escape – they all felt distant now, blurred figures in the rearview mirror of my life. The trust I once placed in others now seemed naïve, almost foolish. How could I have been so blind, so easily manipulated? Liam and Isabella, the initial suspects, were now confirmed pawns, their actions carefully choreographed by the puppet masters. But what about the others? Who else had been playing a part, who else was still out there?

I reviewed all the interactions of my relationships with a clinical eye, dissecting every conversation, every gesture, every seemingly innocuous detail. The sharp knife of self-doubt sliced through the memories, revealing unsettling patterns. The casual friendliness of my neighbor, Mr. Henderson, the seemingly helpful advice offered by my former therapist, the quiet concern expressed by my landlady - each interaction now held a chilling ambiguity. Were these acts of genuine kindness, or were they veiled attempts at surveillance, subtle manipulations designed to gain my trust? The lines were blurred, the boundaries indistinct.

My work as a counselor had taught me to recognize the subtle nuances of human interaction, the unspoken cues that betray hidden agendas. I had spent years helping others navigate the treacherous waters of their relationships, yet I had failed to recognize the currents that were pulling me under. I had been so focused on the larger investigation, on the global conspiracy, that I'd overlooked the more immediate danger, the threats lurking in the shadows of my own life.

The encrypted communication with Agent Vex had been a lifeline, but even that connection felt precarious. He was a ghost, a shadowy figure operating in the twilight world of espionage. His motivations, while ostensibly aligned with mine, remained opaque. Did he truly believe in me, or was I merely a tool, a pawn in a larger, even more complex game? The possibility chilled me to the bone.

My relationship with my own family – a relationship already strained before the events that had led to the current predicament – felt like a chasm. The distance was not just geographical; it was a chasm carved by betrayal, misunderstanding, and the chilling realization that they, too, might have been unwitting participants in the machinations of the conspiracy.

The trauma I had endured had eroded my trust not only in others but also in myself. My judgment, once a source of pride and professional competence, now seemed unreliable, flawed. Had I missed crucial clues, misinterpreted vital information? Had my own biases and vulnerabilities been exploited? The self-criticism was relentless, a vicious cycle of doubt and self-recrimination.

The thought of resuming my practice as a counselor felt impossible. How could I help others navigate the complexities of their relationships when I couldn't even untangle the tangled threads of my own? How could I guide my clients through the labyrinth of emotional distress when I was lost in the darkness of my own trauma?

The solitude was crushing. It was not the peaceful solitude of contemplation, but a stark, lonely isolation, a profound disconnect from the human connection I craved. Sleep offered little respite, my dreams haunted by fragmented images – flickering screens, encrypted messages, the cold, calculating eyes of my enemies.

I found myself seeking solace in the familiar rhythm of my digital investigation, sifting through the remaining data, searching for any overlooked clues, any lingering threads that might unravel the remaining mysteries. It was a form of self-medication, a way to escape the crushing weight of the loneliness and self-doubt, to immerse myself in something tangible, something concrete, in a world where the only certainty was the relentless pursuit of truth.

The anonymity of the digital world, once a source of vulnerability, now offered a strange sense of comfort. I could be myself, or rather, a version of myself, stripped of the expectations and vulnerabilities of the real world. The digital realm was a space where I could control the narrative, where I could dictate the terms of my interactions. It was not a substitute for human connection, but a refuge, a temporary sanctuary from the emotional turbulence of my life.

I revisited the online forum where I had initially discovered the advanced encryption software, lurking in the shadows, observing the interactions of the hackers and codebreakers. I was looking for something more than technical information; I was looking for confirmation, for a sign that my instincts were correct, that my suspicions were justified. The sense of unease was intensified by a recurring pattern in the forum's discussions, a subtle shift in the conversations, a new level of caution and secrecy.

The feeling of being watched, the intuition that I was being followed, intensified. I found myself checking the rearview mirror constantly, scrutinizing faces in crowds, my senses on high alert. Paranoia, I knew, was a dangerous companion, but I couldn't shake the feeling that someone was close, that my privacy was being compromised.

I changed routines, varied my routes, increased the layers of security around the safe house. Each new measure was a desperate attempt to regain a sense of control, to assert my autonomy in a world that seemed determined to undermine me. Sleep became more elusive, my nights filled with anxiety and vigilance.

The turning point came not from another breakthrough in the investigation, but from a small, almost imperceptible shift within myself. The relentless self-doubt began to yield to a flicker of self-compassion. I boxed up Liam's personal belongings and sent them to his family as a form of closure. I recognized that these feelings of isolation and betrayal were not signs of weakness, but a natural response to the trauma I had endured.

I understood that trust was not a commodity to be freely given, but a delicate flower that needed nurturing and protection. It required careful cultivation, a willingness to be vulnerable while maintaining healthy boundaries. I started to focus on the positive relationships in my life – the unwavering support of Agent Vex, the quiet companionship of the digital allies, and the enduring connection with my therapist, Dr. Sharma, who had skillfully guided me through the initial stages of my recovery.

The process of re-evaluating my relationships was not a simple process of dismissal and rejection. It was a process of careful discernment, of recognizing and honoring the genuine connections while letting go of those that were toxic or insincere. It was a gradual process, a delicate dance between vulnerability and self-protection, between the desire for connection and the need for emotional safety.

I decided to carefully rebuild my relationships, to choose my connections wisely, to cultivate friendships based on mutual respect and genuine understanding. I knew that rebuilding trust would take time and effort, that there would be setbacks and disappointments along the way. But I was ready to face those challenges, to embark on this new phase of my life with a renewed sense of hope and a more profound understanding of myself and the complexities of human relationships. The fight was far from over, but for the first time since my escape, I felt a glimmer of hope, a sense of calm amidst the storm.

Strategic Maneuvers

The glimmer of self-compassion, fragile as a newborn butterfly, fluttered in my chest. It wasn't a sudden, dramatic shift, but a slow, deliberate unfurling of a protective shield around my heart, allowing for the possibility of trust, of connection, while simultaneously recognizing the need for vigilance. My adversaries were cunning, their methods sophisticated, and I wouldn't allow myself to be caught off guard again. This wasn't about forgiveness; it was about strategic recalibration.

My first maneuver involved Dr. Sharma. The sessions had been a lifeline, a safe space to process the trauma, to disentangle the tangled threads of betrayal and self-doubt. But now, I needed more than therapy; I needed an ally. I approached our next session with a carefully constructed plan. I didn't reveal the full extent of the ongoing investigation – that would be too risky – but I subtly hinted at the patterns I'd noticed, the recurring themes of manipulation and surveillance that echoed in my personal life and the digital world I inhabited. Dr. Sharma, a seasoned professional, picked up on the subtle cues, her understanding eyes conveying a quiet empathy.

"I've been reconsidering some of my own therapeutic approaches," I said, my voice calm, deliberate. "The standard models often underestimate the manipulative capacity of those with narcissistic tendencies." I steered the conversation towards creating a detailed psychological profile of my potential adversaries, drawing on my knowledge of manipulative tactics, the subtle cues of deception, and the common traits of those who thrive in the shadows. This wasn't just therapy; it was a collaborative intelligence operation disguised as a session. Dr. Sharma, intrigued by the unique blend of clinical insight and strategic thinking, readily agreed to assist, offering valuable insights into behavioral patterns and manipulative techniques.

My next move involved Agent Vex. Their communication was encrypted, their interactions shrouded in secrecy, but I understood the importance of building trust, however cautiously. I didn't divulge the details of my personal vulnerabilities, but I began to share snippets of strategic thinking, subtle hints about the next steps in my investigation. I tested his loyalty by subtly altering the parameters of the operation, gauging his response. Did he remain loyal to the mission, or would his allegiances waver? His reactions, though subtle, confirmed his unwavering commitment to our shared goal. He was a ghost, yes, but a dependable one. This was crucial in the long-term strategy.

My third and most complex maneuver focused on the online forum. I had to maintain a presence, gathering information, but also avoiding detection. I carefully curated an online persona, subtly shifting my posting style, my language, my approach. I studied the patterns of communication within the forum, identifying key players, their communication styles, and their potential weaknesses. I created subtle distractions, planting false leads and misleading information to sow seeds of discord and confusion amongst the enemy. It was a game of deception, a cat-and-mouse chase within the digital world, where every keystroke, every line of code could have life-altering consequences.

The forum became a battleground of wits, a virtual chessboard where I maneuvered the pawns with precision and grace. I subtly manipulated conversations, subtly guiding the flow of information, directing the attention of the users away from my true intentions. I utilized advanced techniques of obfuscation, deploying misdirection strategies to conceal my true identity and purposes. I became a digital phantom, a ghost in the machine, my every move a carefully calculated strategy.

The personal aspect was no less challenging. The constant fear of surveillance weighed heavily on me, but I didn't allow it to paralyze me. I systematically reviewed the routine, identifying potential weaknesses and mitigating them. I varied routes, changed habits, and learned to blend into the background, moving through the city like a shadow, my movements unassuming, my presence almost imperceptible.

I developed a sophisticated network of covert surveillance, using advanced technology and skills in observation to monitor my surroundings. I learned to read body language, to discern subtle cues of deception and hostility. I had to trust on instincts while simultaneously remaining skeptical, maintaining a delicate balance between intuition and rigorous analysis. Every encounter was a potential risk, every conversation a potential trap.

The psychological aspect was perhaps the most demanding. The weight of the trauma, the constant threat, the gnawing self-doubt – these were formidable adversaries. I understood that to defeat my external enemies, before I could proceed, I had to subdue the insidious anxieties that haunted me, a formidable internal battle waged in the silent chambers of my soul. My sessions with Dr. Sharma weren't just about processing the past; they were about fortifying my mental defenses, sharpening resilience, and developing coping strategies for dealing with the stress and anxiety.

My self-care routine became a non-negotiable part of my survival strategy. I exercised regularly, eating healthy meals, and ensuring adequate sleep. I practiced mindfulness techniques to stay grounded and centered. I prioritized self-compassion, recognizing that my emotional strength was as crucial to my success as intellectual prowess.

The turning point, however, came not through a single grand victory, but through the cumulative effect of small, calculated moves.

Observing the adversary's actions, I discerned recurring anomalies and exploitable weaknesses, revealing a predictable, if deceptive, structure to their operations. I uncovered hidden connections, piecing together seemingly unrelated events to form a comprehensive picture of the adversaries' network, their motives, and their strategies.

This wasn't a battle of brute force; it was a battle of wits, a subtle dance of deception and counter-deception. I played the role of the innocent bystander, the curious observer, the unsuspecting victim, all the while gathering intelligence, planning my next move, and tightening the noose around my enemies.

The combination of using clinical skills, digital prowess, and innate strategic intelligence proved invaluable. I meticulously documented every interaction, every piece of information, building a comprehensive dossier on my adversaries. This wasn't just about bringing them down; it was about understanding them, about anticipating their moves, about outmaneuvering them at every turn.

This was more than a fight for survival; it was a battle for justice, a fight for truth. It was a battle I was determined to win, not just for myself, but for all those who had been manipulated, betrayed, and silenced by the shadowy forces I was fighting against. And as I sat alone, late at night, reviewing the data, a renewed sense of purpose filled me. This wasn't just a fight; it was a crusade, fueled by resilience and a renewed commitment to justice. The turning point wasn't just a moment; it was a decision, a commitment to a long, strategic fight. And I was ready.

High Stakes Confrontation

The chill wind whipped around me as I stood on the rooftop, the city lights a shimmering tapestry below. The air tasted metallic, a premonition of the violence to come. I wasn't just playing a game anymore; this was a life-or-death situation. The information I'd painstakingly gathered, the digital breadcrumbs I'd meticulously laid, had led me here – to a final, unavoidable confrontation.

My heart hammered a frantic rhythm against my ribs, a counterpoint to the city's low hum. Fear, cold and sharp, sliced through me, but it didn't paralyze me. Years of therapy, of dissecting the psychology of manipulation, had prepared me for this. I'd learned to channel my fear, to transform it into a steely resolve.

The rendezvous point was a desolate rooftop overlooking a bustling intersection, a strategic location chosen by my adversaries, a place where escape would be difficult, pursuit easily obscured. I'd arrived early, studying the shadows, assessing escape routes, my mind a whirlwind of contingency plans. My instincts screamed danger, yet a strange calm settled over me, a chilling acceptance of the inevitable.

My phone vibrated, a silent signal. A single text message: *"Be punctual. We have much to discuss."* The message was devoid of emotion, clinical in its precision, a reflection of the cold, calculated minds behind it. I recognized the style – a hallmark of my adversaries, a testament to their meticulous planning and chilling efficiency.

The waiting was agonizing, each tick of the clock amplifying the tension. I reviewed the information one last time, the digital dossier I'd painstakingly compiled flashing before my eyes. I knew their faces, their online personas, their patterns of behavior, their vulnerabilities. But knowing wasn't the same as being prepared for their ruthlessness.

Then, they appeared, silhouetted against the cityscape. Three figures, their faces obscured by shadows, their movements fluid and predatory. They approached slowly, deliberately, their presence exuding an aura of menace. There was no attempt at concealment; they were confident, arrogant, secure in their power.

The leader stepped forward, his silhouette tall and imposing. He removed his hood, revealing a face etched with cold determination. His eyes, dark and intense, held a glint of something akin to amusement. He was the one I had identified as 'The Architect,' the mastermind behind the intricate web of manipulation.

"You've come a long way," The Architect said, his voice smooth, devoid of emotion, a stark contrast to the turmoil raging within me. "We've been watching you. We know what you've been doing."

I met his gaze, unflinching. "I know you're behind the attacks, the manipulation," I replied, my voice steady, unwavering. "I have the evidence. The game is over."

The Architect let out a low chuckle, a chilling sound that sent a shiver down my spine. "Evidence? You're amusing. You think you can defeat us with evidence? We operate in the shadows, where evidence is meaningless."

He gestured to his companions, two imposing figures who stood silently, their expressions impassive. One carried a weapon, its shape barely visible in the dim light. The weight of the threat pressed down on me. This wasn't a negotiation; this was an ambush.

"This isn't about evidence," I said, my voice gaining strength. "This is about stopping you. About preventing you from hurting anyone else."

"Oh, we've hurt plenty of people," The Architect said, his smile widening. "But you...you're special. You've shown a remarkable resilience, a tenacity that we admire. But your defiance will be your undoing."

He signaled to his companion who stepped forward, raising the weapon. Time seemed to slow down, stretching into an eternity. I knew this was it, the culmination of months of careful planning, of calculated risks, of relentless pursuit. My life hung in the balance.

But panic didn't consume me. Instead, a surge of adrenaline coursed through my veins, sharpening my senses, enhancing my awareness.

A lifetime of arduous self-improvement, wrestling with inner turmoil, and confronting my deepest fears., had prepared me for this moment. I wasn't a victim; I was a warrior.

I reacted instinctively, my body moving faster than my conscious mind could process. I lunged forward, deflecting the blow with a calculated maneuver. The ensuing struggle was brutal, a desperate fight for survival, a chaotic ballet of blows and counter-blows, a terrifying dance with death.

The rooftop became a battleground; the city lights a silent witness to their struggle. My training kicked in, honed instincts overriding fear. I used the knowledge of psychology, understanding of human behavior, to anticipate their moves, to exploit their vulnerabilities. I fought with the precision of a surgeon, the ferocity of a lioness protecting her cubs.

The battle raged on, a desperate struggle for dominance, a test of wills as much as a physical confrontation. The Architect, initially confident, began to show signs of surprise, then frustration, finally fear. He hadn't anticipated my resilience, my cunning, my unwavering determination.

The fight continued, a brutal display of strength and skill. I fought with the ferocity of a cornered animal, my every move calculated, my every blow precise. I leveraged my understanding of psychology,

possessed with an uncanny understanding of human nature, enabling me to preempt actions and capitalize on weaknesses. my training, my therapy – all coalesced into a fierce determination to survive.

Finally, with a desperate lunge, I disarmed my attacker. The weapon clattered onto the rooftop, a symbol of the battle's end, a testament to unwavering courage. The Architect, defeated, stood before me, his arrogance shattered, replaced by a chilling recognition of his own mortality.

The police sirens wailed in the distance, their approach a promise of justice, a symbol of the ending of the nightmare. The turning point wasn't just a moment of victory; it was the culmination of months of preparation, of resilience, confronting my inner turmoil. It was a testament to the power of human spirit, the capacity for healing, the strength to overcome even the darkest of adversities. The city lights, previously a backdrop to danger, now shone with a new hope, a beacon of survival, a symbol of a hard-won victory. The battle was over, but the long road to recovery had only just begun.

Unexpected Assistance

The sirens were closer now, their wail a rising crescendo against the backdrop of the city's muted hum. The Architect, his face pale and drawn, stared at the discarded weapon, his eyes reflecting the flashing red and blue lights that were rapidly approaching. He was defeated, not just physically, but psychologically. The carefully constructed facade of control had crumbled, revealing the vulnerable man underneath.

I felt no triumph, only a profound exhaustion. My body screamed in protest, every muscle aching, every breath a labor. The adrenaline that had fueled my fight was fading, leaving behind a hollow ache and a chilling awareness of my own mortality. I'd faced death on that rooftop, stared into its abyss, and somehow emerged victorious. But victory felt hollow, tainted by the brutality of the encounter.

Suddenly, a voice cut through the rising cacophony of sirens. "Police! Freeze!"

Two figures emerged from the shadows, their silhouettes stark against the approaching police lights. They weren't police officers, though. One was a tall, slender woman with a shock of fiery red hair, and the other, a wiry man, his face partially obscured by a worn baseball cap. I recognized them instantly. They were Elias Thorne and his associate, Sarah Chen.

Elias Thorne, a renowned cybersecurity expert, had been a ghost in the digital world, a legend whispered among those in the know. I'd only ever interacted with him through encrypted channels, exchanging crucial information in the battle against the Architect. His expertise had been invaluable in tracking down the Architect's digital footprint, a trail of meticulously crafted deception and carefully concealed servers.

Sarah, his associate, was equally enigmatic. She operated in the shadows, a master of infiltration and data retrieval. Her work had often been the key that unlocked the Architect's next move, giving me the edge I needed to stay one step ahead. The fact that they were here, on this rooftop, was utterly unexpected.

"How...?" I managed to gasp, my voice raw and strained. My mind struggled to process their sudden appearance. They were supposed to be monitoring the Architect's digital activity, miles away from this dangerous confrontation.

Elias approached cautiously, his eyes scanning the scene. He held a small, sophisticated-looking device in his hand, its screen flashing with data. "We intercepted a communication," he explained, his voice calm and collected, a stark contrast to the chaos unfolding around us. "A secondary server, hidden deep within the dark web, that was used to coordinate the attacks. We traced it back to this location, in real-time."

Sarah, her eyes sharp and assessing, was already examining the Architect. She moved with a practiced grace, quickly checking for weapons and securing the scene, her movements efficient and precise. Her expertise was apparent. This wasn't just luck; they had anticipated my need for backup and had arrived perfectly timed, an unexpected act of calculated support.

"You saved my life," I said, my voice trembling slightly. The weight of that realization washed over me, the near-miss hitting me harder than the adrenaline-fueled fight.

Elias offered a small, almost imperceptible nod. "We believe in strategic alliances," he said, his gaze unwavering. "We are well aware of the Architect's plans, and we had a shared interest in his elimination." He gestured towards the approaching police cars. "The data we've collected will be instrumental in dismantling his operation permanently."

Sarah added, "His network is larger than you realize. He has other assets, other associates." Her tone was devoid of emotion, yet her words painted a stark picture of the Architect's vast and insidious influence.

The police arrived, their presence overwhelming, their blue and red lights painting the night in vibrant hues of urgency. They quickly apprehended the Architect and his remaining associates. Elias and Sarah worked seamlessly with the officers, providing them with the necessary digital evidence to solidify the arrest, ensuring a solid case would be built. Their efficiency and professionalism were nothing short of awe-inspiring.

As I was escorted away from the scene by a uniformed officer, I took one last look at the rooftop, the city lights shimmering as a silent witness to the night's events. The chaos had subsided, replaced by the quiet hum of police activity. Elias and Sarah were already transferring data to the police's digital forensics team, their actions precise and efficient. They were more than just unexpected allies; they were vital pieces in bringing the Architect's reign of terror to an end.

The subsequent weeks were a blur of interviews, depositions, and media scrutiny. The Architect's network was far-reaching, his influence deeper than I had ever imagined. The evidence Elias and Sarah had provided was crucial in dismantling his operation, leading to a series of arrests that sent shockwaves through the criminal underworld. Elias and Sarah's assistance wasn't just a matter of chance; it was a calculated move, a testament to their skill and foresight. They'd seen the bigger picture, understood the greater threat, and acted decisively, risking their own safety to ensure the Architect's capture.

My therapist, Dr. Anya Sharma, had been my steadfast support throughout this ordeal. She helped me process the trauma of the rooftop confrontation, guiding me through the emotional aftermath of the brutal fight. The fear, the adrenaline, the exhaustion – all had taken their toll. But the unexpected intervention of Elias and Sarah had been a turning point, not only in bringing the Architect to justice but also in my own recovery.

Their actions demonstrated a level of trust and collaboration that transcended the usual boundaries of our respective roles. Elias and Sarah weren't just providing digital support; they were actively participating in a joint effort to dismantle a dangerous organization. Their level of involvement revealed a shared sense of purpose, a common enemy, and a willingness to collaborate beyond the confines of their usual expertise.

The successful takedown of the Architect, with Elias and Sarah's crucial assistance, represented more than just the end of a terrifying chapter in my life. It signaled a new beginning, not only in terms of justice, but also in fostering an unexpected yet essential partnership. The collaboration between our worlds, the digital and the physical, had created a synergy that had ultimately triumphed over a formidable foe. This new alliance, born in the crucible of danger, was more significant than either of us could have ever foreseen, opening doors to future collaborations and strengthening our commitment to justice and bringing down criminals operating within the digital underworld. The city lights no longer held the same ominous glow; now they shine with a newfound hope, a testament to the strength of unexpected alliances and the power of collective action. The road to healing was still long, but I faced it with a renewed sense of purpose, a knowledge that even in the darkest moments, unexpected help can arrive, transforming a life-or-death struggle into a hard-fought victory. The turning point was not just my survival on that rooftop; it was the forging of an unexpected partnership that proved to be far more powerful than either of us could have imagined.

Chapter 11

Close Calls

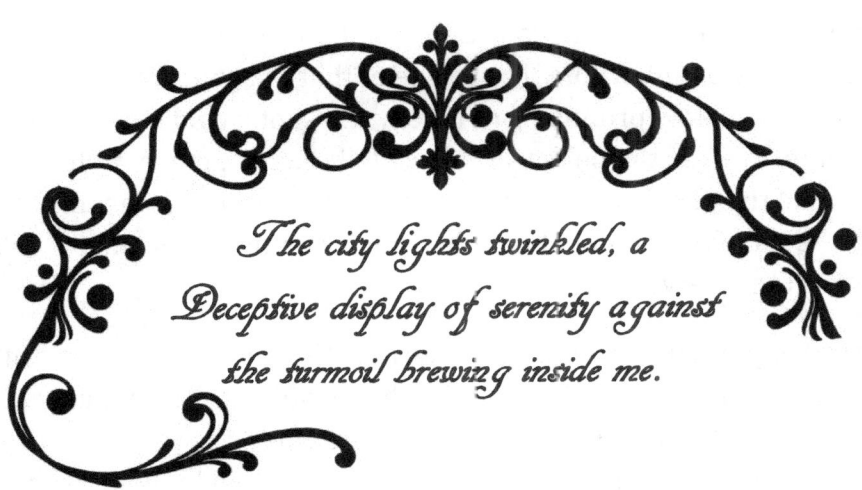

The city lights twinkled, a Deceptive display of serenity against the turmoil brewing inside me.

Narrow Escape

The chilling metallic tang of blood still clung to the air, a stark reminder of the near-miss. My breath hitched in my throat, a ragged, shuddering intake that felt more like a sob than a breath. The adrenaline had finally leached out, leaving behind a bone-deep weariness and a tremor that ran the length of my body. Elias and Sarah, efficient and calm amidst the burgeoning chaos of the police arrival, had saved my life, a fact that settled upon me with the weight of a physical blow.

My escape had been a hair's breadth from disaster. The Architect, cornered and enraged, had lunged, his weapon a blur of deadly intent. I'd reacted instinctively, a primal surge of self-preservation propelling me into action. The struggle had been brutal, a desperate dance of survival played out on the edge of a precipice. The memory of his eyes, filled with a chilling mix of rage and defeat, remained imprinted on my mind's eye, a stark reminder of the violence I'd barely survived.

The fall had been the closest call. One wrong move, one slip of my foot on the slick, rain-soaked rooftop, and the city below would have swallowed me whole. The image of that dizzying drop, the concrete far below promising oblivion, still sent a cold shiver down my spine. Even as the police sirens wailed their urgent symphony, I could feel the phantom sensation of the wind whipping past my face, the terrifying moment of vulnerability before Elias and Sarah's unexpected intervention.

The subsequent interrogation felt surreal. The fluorescent lights of the police station seemed to amplify the throbbing ache in my head, a constant, dull reminder of the fight. I recounted the events, my words tumbling out in a torrent of adrenaline-fueled recollections.

The details, sharp and vivid, played out in my memory like a slow-motion replay of a near-fatal accident. The officers, though professional, couldn't fully grasp the nuances of the Architect's methods, the calculated cruelty, the chilling precision of his attacks. They understood the violence, the crime, but not the chilling, methodical precision that was his hallmark.

It was then that the true significance of Elias and Sarah's intervention began to sink in. Their knowledge of the Architect's digital infrastructure, the meticulous tracking of his online movements, the pinpoint accuracy of their arrival – it was more than just luck. It was a sophisticated operation, a meticulously planned counter-offensive, conducted with an expertise that bordered on the miraculous. Their intervention wasn't merely a fortunate coincidence; it was a calculated risk, a strategic maneuver that had ultimately saved my life.

Their seamless integration with the police was remarkable. They provided technical support and forensic details, guiding the officers through the labyrinthine world of encrypted communications, hidden servers, and anonymous networks. Elias calmly explained the Architect's complex digital infrastructure; the intricate web of deception he'd woven to shield his operation. Sarah, precise and efficient, guided the forensic team through the digital evidence, ensuring that the case against the Architect would be airtight. Their collaboration was fluid, almost intuitive, a symphony of expertise that was as impressive as it was unexpected.

My own role in the investigation became overshadowed by the enormity of the Architect's digital empire. My testimony was crucial, filling in the gaps of the physical acts of violence, providing a human element to the cold, hard data Elias and Sarah presented. The media frenzy that followed was overwhelming, a deluge of interviews, questions, and speculation. The public was captivated by the story, drawn to the drama of a near-miss and the unraveling of a sophisticated criminal network. My face was plastered across newspapers and television screens; my name became synonymous with the Architect's downfall.

Yet, beneath the surface of the public narrative, a quieter, more personal reckoning was underway. The physical wounds were healing, the cuts and bruises fading. But the psychological scars, the lingering anxiety, the persistent fear – these were deeper wounds, requiring a different kind of healing. My therapist, Dr. Sharma, was invaluable during this time. She provided a safe space for me to process the trauma, to unravel the tangled threads of fear and exhaustion. Our sessions were a lifeline, pulling me back from the brink of a debilitating spiral of anxiety and self-doubt.

Dr. Sharma helped me understand the impact of the near-death experience, the physiological and psychological consequences of facing such intense fear and violence. We delved into the intricacies of PTSD, exploring the symptoms, triggers, and coping mechanisms. She patiently guided me through breathing exercises, mindfulness techniques, and strategies to manage the flashbacks and nightmares that plagued my sleep. She acknowledged the bravery of my actions, the resilience I had shown in facing the Architect, yet she also recognized the toll it had taken on my mental and emotional well-being. The emotional toll of the experience was considerable, and her support was the key to begin my recovery and healing.

The collaboration with Elias and Sarah continued even after the initial investigation had concluded. Their expertise was invaluable in tracking down the Architect's remaining associates, uncovering hidden financial accounts, and dismantling the remnants of his organization. We were bound by a shared goal, a common enemy, and a unique understanding of the insidious reach of his criminal enterprise. This unlikely alliance was built upon a foundation of mutual respect and a profound understanding of the gravity of the situation, which we were effectively managing by working together.

Our partnership wasn't merely professional; it evolved into a complex network of trust and mutual respect. We held regular briefings, exchanging information and coordinating strategies. They provided the digital intelligence, the intricate details of the Architect's online activities, and I supplied the real-world context, the human element that gave their digital findings a tangible meaning. We were each other's grounding force, a balance between the tangible and the intangible, the physical and the digital, merging our knowledge and expertise into a formidable force against a formidable adversary.

The success of our joint efforts, the dismantling of the Architect's network, had a profound impact on me. It provided a sense of closure, a validation of the risks I'd taken, the sacrifices I'd made. It was a testament to the power of collaboration, the strength that emerged from combining vastly different skills and perspectives. The experience redefined my understanding of partnerships, of trust, and of the unexpected alliances that could arise in the face of immense danger.

The road ahead wasn't entirely clear, but I approached it with a renewed sense of purpose. The near-miss on the rooftop had stripped away illusions, forcing me to confront my own mortality. But it had also revealed the unexpected strength of human connection, the profound impact of collaboration, and the power of defying expectations. The shadows still lingered, the memories still haunted, but the weight of fear had lessened, replaced by a quiet sense of determination, a newfound confidence in the alliances that had saved my life and brought a dangerous criminal to justice. The city lights no longer seemed to hold the same menace; instead, they shimmered with a hope born from an unlikely partnership, a testimony to the extraordinary power of collaboration. The long road to healing was still ahead, but I walked it with the sure knowledge that even in the deepest darkness, an unexpected beacon of hope could appear. The victory wasn't just mine; it was a shared triumph, a testament to the power of collaboration, resilience, and trust forged in the crucible of danger and near-death.

Emotional Breakdown

The celebratory champagne felt like acid on my tongue. The city rejoiced, the media lauded our success, and the police department patted themselves on the back. But inside, the fragile calm I'd painstakingly constructed began to crumble. The exhaustion, which had been a dull thrumming beneath the surface for weeks, now roared in my ears, a deafening symphony of fatigue. I'd been operating on adrenaline, sheer willpower, and an unhealthy dose of denial. Now, the dam was breaking.

The dismantling of the Architect's network was a victory, a significant achievement, but it hadn't erased the trauma. The vivid images – the glint of steel, the sickening thud of the Architect's fall, the dizzying drop from the rooftop – still played on a relentless loop in my mind. Sleep became a battlefield, a nightmarish landscape populated by shadowy figures and the chilling echo of his breath. Even in the fleeting moments of slumber, the threat never truly abated. It lurked; a venomous serpent coiled in the recesses of my consciousness.

Dr. Sharma noticed the shift almost immediately. Our sessions, once focused on managing PTSD symptoms and processing the trauma, took a darker turn. My carefully constructed facade of composure cracked, revealing the raw, vulnerable core beneath. The carefully modulated voice I used in public, the confident demeanor I projected to the world, dissolved into a trembling whisper.

"I'm... I'm falling apart, Dr. Sharma," I confessed one evening, the words escaping in a choked sob. The weight of everything – the near-death experience, the media scrutiny, the endless interviews, the constant fear of another attack – had become unbearable. My body felt heavy, leaden, burdened by an unseen weight. My heart hammered against my ribs, a frantic bird struggling to escape its cage.

Dr. Sharma listened patiently, her gaze steady and reassuring. She didn't offer platitudes or empty reassurances. Instead, she provided a space for my raw emotions to surface, validating my pain, my fear, and my exhaustion. She gently guided me through the turbulent waters of my emotional breakdown, helping me to navigate the chaos.

"It's okay to fall apart," she said softly, her voice a balm to my frayed nerves. "What you've been through is incredibly traumatic, and it's perfectly understandable to feel overwhelmed. It's not a sign of weakness, but a testament to the strength you've already shown."

Her words were a lifeline, a small beacon in the encroaching darkness. With her gentle guidance, I began to unpack the layers of trauma, confronting the buried emotions, the suppressed fears, and the overwhelming sense of vulnerability. The sessions became a sanctuary, a safe space where I could shed the carefully crafted armor I had worn for so long and allow myself to simply be – broken, exhausted, and terrified.

We delved into the intricacies of my emotional state, exploring the origins of my anxieties, dissecting the patterns of self-doubt that had begun to creep into my life. I confessed to the nightmares, the constant sense of unease, the hypervigilance that colored every interaction. The simple act of walking down the street, once mundane, now felt fraught with peril, my senses on high alert, scanning for threats that may or may not exist.

Dr. Sharma introduced new coping mechanisms – grounding techniques to anchor me in the present moment, progressive muscle relaxation to combat the physical manifestations of anxiety, and mindfulness practices to help quiet the relentless noise in my mind. These were tools, she explained, to navigate the difficult terrain of my emotional landscape, to reclaim a sense of control in a world that had felt chaotic and unpredictable.

The process was agonizingly slow, a painstaking journey through the darkest corners of my psyche. There were days when progress seemed imperceptible, when the weight of my trauma threatened to pull me under. There were moments of intense grief, of rage, of despair. But Dr. Sharma was a steadfast presence, a constant source of support and understanding, guiding me through the storm.

We explored the nature of my relationship with Elias and Sarah. Our collaboration had been instrumental in bringing the Architect to justice, but it had also created a unique dynamic, a bond forged in the crucible of shared danger. I found myself relying on them, not only for their professional expertise but also for their unwavering support, their quiet presence a reassurance in my moments of deepest despair.

Dr. Sharma helped me to understand the complexities of this relationship, acknowledging the healthy aspects of our collaboration while also recognizing the potential pitfalls of blurring professional and personal boundaries. She helped me to articulate my feelings, to identify the source of my dependence, and to develop healthier ways of managing my emotional needs.

The emotional breakthrough came gradually, not in a single cathartic moment, but in a series of small, incremental shifts. The nightmares lessened in intensity, the flashbacks became less frequent, the constant sense of dread began to recede. I started to rediscover the joy in simple things – a walk in the park, a cup of coffee with a friend, the quiet comfort of my own home. The world, once a menacing place of perpetual danger, began to feel safer, more manageable.

The healing process wasn't linear. There were setbacks, moments of regression, when the old fears resurfaced with a vengeance. But each time, Dr. Sharma was there, providing the support and guidance I needed to navigate these difficult periods, helping me to rebuild my sense of self and my resilience.

The road to recovery was long and arduous, filled with moments of intense emotional pain, but the journey was transformative. I emerged from the darkness a changed person, stronger, wiser, and more resilient. I had faced the depths of my own emotional vulnerability and emerged with a newfound appreciation for the power of human connection, the importance of self-care, and the transformative potential of healing. The victory over the Architect had been significant, but the victory over my own inner turmoil was a far more profound accomplishment. The city lights now held not the same chilling reminder of danger, but the warm glow of resilience and renewed strength. The shadows still lingered, but they no longer controlled me. I was, finally, in control of my own destiny.

Seeking Support

The city lights twinkled, a deceptive display of serenity against the turmoil brewing inside me. While outwardly I presented a picture of renewed strength, a carefully constructed facade designed to reassure everyone – and myself – the reality was far more nuanced. The victory over the Architect was a monumental achievement, yet it hadn't erased the deep scars etched onto my soul. The lingering trauma, the persistent fear, the ever-present shadow of what could happen again – these were battles I was still waging, alone, in the quiet solitude of my own mind.

Dr. Sharma's guidance had been invaluable, providing a safe haven where I could unravel the tangled threads of my emotional wreckage. But even within the secure confines of her office, I felt the limitations of individual therapy. The weight of my experience, the sheer intensity of the trauma, was more than I could bear alone. I needed more than her expertise; I needed the unwavering support of my community, the comforting presence of those who understood, who had shared this journey with me.

My thoughts turned to Elias. Our collaboration had been intense, a dance of intellect and intuition that had led us to the Architect's downfall. Beyond the professional respect, a genuine friendship had blossomed, a bond forged in the crucible of shared danger. He understood the toll the case had taken, not just on me, but on all of us. His quiet strength, his unwavering belief in my capabilities, had been a lifeline during the darkest hours. He was a pillar of support, even when unspoken.

I reached out, a simple text at first, then a phone call. His voice, warm and reassuring, grounded me in the present moment. He listened patiently as I poured out my anxieties, my fears, the lingering sense of unease that clung to me like a second skin. He didn't offer empty platitudes or dismiss my feelings. Instead, he offered empathy, a shared understanding born from our shared experience. He knew the darkness, had walked beside me through it.

"You're not alone, Elara," he said, his voice a comforting presence across the miles. "We're all in this together." His words, simple yet profound, were a balm to my frayed nerves. We spent hours talking, not about the case, but about the emotional aftermath, the challenges of healing, the constant vigilance against the unseen threats. His presence was a reassuring anchor, a solid ground in the midst of the emotional tempest.

Sarah, too, became a vital part of my support system. Her strength, her resilience, her unwavering optimism, were a source of inspiration. She understood the intricate dance of balancing professional success with personal well-being, a challenge we had both faced during the Architect's case. She saw beyond the superficial, into the very core of my struggle, and she offered her support without judgment, without reservation.

Our conversations weren't always easy. There were moments of raw emotion, of shared vulnerability, where the masks we wore in public crumbled, revealing the cracks beneath. We acknowledged the shared trauma, the lingering fears, the emotional exhaustion. We validated each other's experiences, creating a space where we could freely express our feelings without fear of judgment. Her laughter, her unwavering spirit, became a beacon in the storm.

Beyond Elias and Sarah, I extended my support network to include friends and family, people who didn't necessarily understand the intricacies of my professional life or the depth of the trauma I had endured, but who understood the universal language of empathy and support. Their simple acts of kindness – a listening ear, a comforting hug, a thoughtful gesture – became vital components of my healing journey.

My parents, initially apprehensive about the nature of my work, learned to understand, offering silent support and unconditional love. They didn't try to fix me or offer unsolicited advice; they simply provided a safe space, a haven where I could retreat from the intensity of my professional life and be myself – vulnerable, scared, and slowly, painfully, healing.

I started attending support groups, cautiously at first, hesitant to expose my vulnerabilities to strangers. Yet, the shared experiences of others, their struggles and triumphs, created a powerful sense of connection. I discovered that I wasn't alone in my pain, that others had faced similar challenges and had emerged stronger, more resilient. The shared understanding, the mutual support, created a powerful sense of community, a network of strength that amplified my individual efforts.

I learned the importance of self-compassion, recognizing that healing wasn't a linear process but a journey with setbacks and breakthroughs. I acknowledged that it was okay to have "bad days," to feel overwhelmed, to retreat and recharge. I learned to identify my triggers and develop coping mechanisms that worked for me – mindfulness meditation, long walks in nature, spending time with loved ones.

The support of my friends, my family, and my professional colleagues wasn't a magic cure; it wasn't a quick fix for the trauma I had endured. But it was a vital component of my healing process, a critical piece of the puzzle that allowed me to piece my life back together. It was the human connection, the unwavering support, that helped me navigate the treacherous terrain of recovery, allowing me to emerge stronger, more resilient, and more deeply connected to the people who cared.

The process wasn't easy, and there were moments when the old fears threatened to engulf me. The nightmares persisted, though less frequently and less intensely. The flashbacks still occurred, but their power diminished, their hold on me weakening with each passing day. The constant hypervigilance gradually subsided, replaced by a growing sense of security and self-reliance.

The support network I had cultivated wasn't merely a source of comfort; it was a catalyst for growth, a catalyst for change. It empowered me to confront my vulnerabilities, to acknowledge my fears, and to embrace the imperfections that made me human. It reminded me that strength isn't about invulnerability, but about resilience, the ability to bounce back, to heal, and to emerge stronger from adversity.

My professional life, once a source of overwhelming stress, started to feel more manageable. I found a renewed sense of purpose, driven not just by the pursuit of justice but by a deep desire to make a difference in the lives of others, to use my experiences to help others heal. I began to integrate my experience into my work, recognizing the importance of understanding the emotional toll of trauma on both victims and investigators.

The city lights no longer held the chilling reminder of danger, but the warm glow of community, of connection, and of healing. The shadows still lingered, but they no longer held the power to consume me. I had faced the depths of my own emotional vulnerability, and with the unwavering support of those around me, I had emerged stronger, wiser, and more deeply connected to myself and to the world around me. The victory over the Architect had been significant, but the victory over my own inner turmoil, with the invaluable support of my friends and loved ones, was a far more profound accomplishment. My journey wasn't over, but I was finally, truly, walking towards the light. The path ahead may still be uncertain, but I walked it knowing I wasn't alone.

Strategic Retreat

The quiet hum of the refrigerator was the only sound in the otherwise silent apartment. Empty coffee cups sat on the counter, stark reminders of the sleepless night I'd endured. The city outside, usually a source of both comfort and unease, felt distant, muted. My focus wasn't on the glittering skyline or the distant sirens; it was inward, on the intricate web of anxieties that had woven themselves into the fabric of my being.

The victory over the Architect hadn't brought the peace I'd anticipated. The adrenaline had dissipated, leaving behind a gnawing emptiness, a chilling awareness of my own vulnerability. The nightmares continued, their vivid imagery blurring the lines between reality and the terror of the past. The constant hypervigilance, a relentless companion for months, hadn't completely abated. Even in the sanctuary of my own home, I felt a persistent sense of unease, a deep-seated fear that the danger hadn't truly passed.

Dr. Sharma, my therapist, had been instrumental in helping me process the initial shock, guiding me through the emotional wreckage. Her office, a haven of calm amid the storm, provided a safe space to explore the darkest corners of my psyche. Yet, a growing unease within me suggested that the individual therapy sessions, while helpful, weren't enough. I needed a more strategic approach, a more deliberate plan for navigating the uncharted waters of my recovery.

I needed to retreat. Not physically, necessarily, but mentally. I needed to create distance, to gain perspective, to analyze the situation with a clear and focused mind. The relentless pressure of the case, the constant fear of retribution, had blurred my judgment, clouded my thinking. I needed to clear the fog, to regain control.

My strategic retreat began with a deliberate disconnection from the constant stream of information. I silenced my phone notifications, avoided news websites, and resisted the urge to check social media. The constant barrage of information had become a source of anxiety, triggering flashbacks and exacerbating my feelings of unease. Silence, I realized, was my most powerful ally.

The next step involved a thorough self-assessment. I spent hours journaling, meticulously documenting my thoughts, feelings, and physical sensations. I identified my triggers – specific images, sounds, or even smells – that evoked overwhelming anxiety and panic. I examined my coping mechanisms, assessing their effectiveness and identifying any areas needing improvement. This process was painstaking, emotionally draining, but it was essential for understanding my vulnerabilities and developing targeted strategies.

The resulting self-assessment revealed a complex interplay of psychological factors. The trauma of the Architect's case had not only left me with PTSD symptoms but had also intensified pre-existing anxieties related to my personal safety and professional vulnerabilities. The experience had shaken my sense of security, leaving me feeling exposed, vulnerable, and profoundly alone, despite the support of my friends and family. Understanding the nuances of my emotional landscape was critical in formulating an effective plan.

My strategic plan was multifaceted. It involved strengthening my physical safety measures – reinforcing home security, being more mindful of my surroundings, and limiting solo activities, especially at night. It also encompassed a structured approach to my mental well-being, including regular mindfulness meditation sessions, increased physical activity, and continued therapy sessions with Dr. Sharma. But more than this, I needed to address the underlying anxieties that had been heightened by the case.

I sought out specialized therapy to address the specific anxieties related to my professional work. The Architect's case had shattered my sense of control, highlighting the inherent risks associated with my career path. This new therapy focused on cognitive behavioral therapy techniques to challenge negative thought patterns, develop healthier coping strategies, and rebuild a sense of agency. The goal wasn't to eliminate all risk but to learn to manage it effectively.

Simultaneously, I began exploring creative outlets to channel my anxieties. Painting became my refuge, a medium through which I could externalize the chaotic imagery from my nightmares, transforming them into abstract expressions of emotion. The act of creation, the focus required, helped to quiet the relentless noise in my mind, creating a space for calm and reflection.

The strategic retreat wasn't about avoidance; it was about recalibration, a period of self-assessment and strategic planning. It was about accepting my vulnerability, acknowledging my limitations, and developing targeted strategies to build resilience and regain a sense of control. The journey wasn't linear; it was fraught with setbacks and breakthroughs, moments of immense progress followed by waves of overwhelming anxiety.

Yet, as the days turned into weeks, I began to notice a shift. The nightmares became less frequent, less vivid. The constant hypervigilance gradually subsided, replaced by a more measured awareness of my surroundings. The emotional turbulence, while still present, became more manageable. I started to reclaim my sense of self, rebuilding the foundations of my mental and emotional well-being, brick by painstaking brick.

My interactions with Elias and Sarah became more than just a source of comfort; they were vital components of my recovery plan. Sharing my experiences, my anxieties, and my progress with them reinforced my sense of connection and validation. Their unwavering support, their understanding, were crucial pillars in the construction of my newfound resilience. We began to forge a new dynamic, a collaborative approach to navigating the aftermath, ensuring we were there for each other to process and celebrate every small victory along the healing journey.

This strategic retreat was far from an escape; it was a strategic maneuver in the ongoing battle against the lingering effects of trauma. It was a time of profound self-discovery, a period of recalibration that laid the groundwork for a more resilient and resourceful future. The city lights, once a constant reminder of danger, began to hold the promise of a brighter tomorrow, a testament to the strength I was steadily cultivating within myself. The shadows still lingered, but they no longer held the power to define me. I was learning to live with them, to integrate them into the tapestry of my life, recognizing that even in darkness, there was a light to be found, a light that I was determined to cultivate and hold onto. The path to healing was long and winding, but with each carefully planned step, I felt myself moving closer to a place of peace and wholeness.

Gathering Intel

The scent of chamomile tea hung faintly in the air, a comforting counterpoint to the turmoil churning within me. Dr. Sharma's office, usually a haven of calm, felt charged with a different kind of energy tonight – the electric hum of anticipation. We'd reached a turning point in my therapy, a point where the carefully constructed scaffolding of our sessions was about to be tested. The strategic retreat, while profoundly beneficial, had only provided a temporary reprieve. The underlying anxieties, the lingering shadows of the Architect case, still cast long, dark stretches across my consciousness. Tonight, we were going to confront them head-on.

"I've been reviewing the case files," Dr. Sharma began, her voice soft yet firm, "and I've noticed a few inconsistencies, some overlooked details that might be crucial." She pushed a file across her desk, the familiar weight of it sending a shiver down my spine. It wasn't just the weight of the paper; it was the weight of the untold story, the hidden connections I had yet to unravel.

The inconsistencies she pointed out were subtle, almost imperceptible – a slight discrepancy in the timeline, a minor contradiction in witness testimonies, a forgotten detail buried within the avalanche of evidence. But as she carefully laid them out, connecting the dots I'd missed, a chilling realization began to dawn. The Architect hadn't acted alone. There was another player, a more insidious shadow lurking in the periphery, manipulating events from the darkness.

Dr. Sharma's insights were more than just professional observations; they were a testament to her acute psychological understanding. She recognized patterns of behavior, subtle nuances in communication, that I had overlocked in my emotionally charged state. She pointed out the Architect's meticulous planning, the almost surgical precision of his attacks, suggesting a level of sophistication that implied collaboration.

"He was good," I murmured, a chill running down my spine. "Too good to be working alone."

"Exactly," Dr. Sharma agreed. "Think about the logistics, the timing, the almost flawless execution. It suggests a coordinated effort, a division of labor, a carefully orchestrated dance of deception."

Her words ignited a cascade of fragmented memories, previously dismissed as insignificant, now rising to the surface with newfound clarity. A fleeting glimpse of a second figure in the shadows during one of the Architect's attacks. An anonymous email, dismissed as spam, that contained cryptic information subtly hinting at a larger conspiracy. A whispered conversation overheard in the courthouse hallway; a veiled threat laced with a chilling familiarity.

These were the fragments, the puzzle pieces I'd overlooked in my obsession with the Architect. Now, with Dr. Sharma's guidance, they were starting to fall into place. We painstakingly reconstructed the timeline, meticulously analyzing each piece of evidence, each seemingly insignificant detail, searching for patterns, for connections.

The pattern, when it finally emerged, was both terrifying and clarifying. The attacks weren't random. They were strategically placed, designed not just to cause harm, but to send a message, to manipulate events for an unknown purpose. The victims weren't simply targets; they were pawns in a larger game. And I, caught in the crosshairs, was unknowingly playing my part.

The longer we worked, the more the picture sharpened. We traced the anonymous email back to a seemingly innocuous account, but a deeper dive revealed its connection to a shell corporation, linked to several high-profile individuals involved in the city's underworld. The whispers in the courthouse hallway pointed towards a powerful individual, a shadowy figure pulling the strings from behind the scenes.

"It's not just about the Architect," Dr. Sharma stated, her voice hushed with gravity. "He was a tool, a disposable piece in a much larger game."

The realization struck me with the force of a physical blow. The Architect's defeat hadn't brought an end to the danger; it had merely shifted the focus, exposed a deeper, more dangerous layer of the conspiracy.

The next few hours were spent meticulously tracing the links, piecing together the fragments of information, searching for the common thread. We used investigative databases to track the shell corporation's activities, cross-referencing their transactions with known criminal networks. My understanding of psychological profiling proved invaluable, helping to anticipate the next move, to predict the behavior of the shadowy figure orchestrating this sinister game.

As the night wore on, the picture became clearer. The shadowy figure wasn't simply a criminal mastermind; he was someone connected to my past, someone who knew my vulnerabilities, someone who was using the Architect as a pawn to achieve a personal vendetta. The pieces started falling into place with alarming speed. The subtle hints, the carefully constructed clues, pointed towards a figure from my past – a former colleague, someone I had trusted, someone who had betrayed me.

The revelation was a gut-wrenching blow. The betrayal stung more deeply than any physical injury. The sense of violation was amplified by the realization that this betrayal hadn't been random; it had been meticulously planned, strategically executed, using the Architect as a weapon.

The realization wasn't just about the immediate threat; it was about the further unraveling of my understanding of trust, loyalty, and the illusion of safety. The trauma was compounded not only by the near-death experiences but by the insidious poison of betrayal, a violation that cut deeper than any bullet.

This new understanding shifted my perspective, changing the narrative from a simple pursuit of justice to a personal quest for truth and healing. The intelligence gathering wasn't just about apprehending the shadowy figure; it was about confronting the lingering ghosts of the past, processing the profound sense of betrayal, and rebuilding my trust in a world that had proven so volatile. The fight for survival was now intertwined with the fight for emotional redemption.

The process of piecing together the fragments was both exhausting and exhilarating. Each connection forged fueled the relentless pursuit of truth. Every revealed layer revealed a deeper complexity, adding dimensions I had never envisioned. The seemingly simple case had become a labyrinth of deceit, a web of interwoven connections, leading to a truth far more intricate and devastating than I could have ever imagined.

By the time dawn broke, painting the sky in hues of soft pink and orange, we had assembled a reasonably complete picture. The shadowy figure, armed with my past vulnerabilities and the calculated moves of a master manipulator, had used the Architect as a tool to enact a deeply personal revenge.

The emotional toll of this revelation was immense. The exhaustion ran deep, both physically and mentally. But the newfound clarity, the knowledge of the enemy, brought with it a sense of purpose. The fight for survival was not just about my physical safety but about regaining my emotional equilibrium. It was a fight for my sense of self, my trust, and my future. The path ahead was still treacherous, but armed with the truth, I felt a surge of strength, a resilience made stronger in the affliction of betrayal. The darkness held fewer shadows now; it held purpose. The game had changed, but I was ready to play.

Chapter 12

The Final Gambit

The battle was swift, brutal, yet precisely choreographed.

The Plan of Action

The first rays of dawn painted the cityscape in soft pastels as I leaned back, a thoughtful expression etched on my face. The air in the office, previously thick with the weight of revelation, now felt lighter, charged with a newfound sense of purpose. "We have a picture," I said softly, my voice a low hum against the quiet vibration of the city awakening. "A fragmented, incomplete picture, perhaps, but enough to begin to formulate a plan."

The words spoken out loud were a balm to my frayed nerves. The sheer enormity of the revelation – the betrayal, the meticulously planned conspiracy, the chilling manipulation – had left me reeling. But the calm, methodical approach was grounding, bringing a steady hand in the chaos. I spent the next few hours meticulously dissecting the information, laying out the pieces of the puzzle like a macabre game of strategy. The shadowy figure, my former colleague, David Oaken, emerged as the puppet master, pulling the strings from the shadows, using the Architect as a pawn in his twisted game of revenge.

David Oaken. The name tasted like ash in my mouth. He had been more than a colleague; he had been a friend, a confidant, someone I had trusted implicitly. The betrayal cut deep, a wound that went beyond the physical scars. It was a violation of trust, a shattering of the very foundation upon which I had built my life.

Even with a keen understanding of human behavior guiding me through the emotional minefield I needed help to understand the psychology of personal betrayal, the intricate mechanisms of manipulation, and the insidious way in which Oaken had exploited my vulnerabilities. Dr. Sharma didn't minimize the pain; instead, she validated it, acknowledging the depth of my trauma and guiding me towards a path of healing and resilience.

Our plan of action wasn't simply about apprehending Oaken; it was about carefully dismantling his operation, exposing his network, and bringing him to justice without jeopardizing my safety. We couldn't rush; we needed to be strategic, methodical, and precise. This wasn't a Hollywood-style showdown; this was a chess match against a formidable opponent, a master manipulator who knew my weaknesses and played them to his advantage.

First, we needed to solidify our evidence. We meticulously documented every piece of information, cross-referencing data, corroborating witness statements, and creating a comprehensive dossier that would stand up in court. My expertise in psychological profiling proved invaluable, helping us to anticipate Oaken's next move, to predict his reactions, and to avoid his traps.

Next, we needed to consider the legal ramifications. We consulted with a seasoned lawyer, a specialist in high-profile cases with experience handling complex conspiracies. He listened intently as we laid out our case, his sharp eyes assessing the evidence, his mind calculating the legal strategy. He advised us to proceed cautiously, to gather irrefutable evidence, and to document everything meticulously. The legal battle would be as challenging as the psychological one.

Simultaneously, we began to develop a strategy for approaching the authorities. We needed to choose our words carefully, presenting the information in a way that would convince them of the validity of our claims without revealing too much about our own investigation. We needed to walk a tightrope, balancing transparency with discretion, ensuring that our actions didn't tip off Oaken or jeopardize our safety.

The plan evolved over days, a delicate dance of strategy and counter-strategy. We considered every possible scenario, anticipating Oaken's reactions, preparing for potential setbacks. The understanding of human psychology proved crucial, the ability to predict behavior patterns, helped us anticipate Oaken's moves, enabling us to develop a flexible and adaptable strategy.

We decided to start with the shell corporation. It was the nexus of Oaken's operation, a seemingly innocuous entity that masked a network of criminal activity. We began by gathering financial records, tracing transactions, and identifying key associates. We worked late into the night, poring over documents, analyzing data, and piecing together the intricate web of Oaken's financial empire.

The lawyer, meanwhile, began to assemble a legal team, preparing the necessary documentation for a potential lawsuit. He advised us to prioritize the gathering of irrefutable evidence, ensuring that we had a solid legal basis for our actions. He emphasized the importance of meticulous documentation, ensuring that every step of our investigation was carefully recorded and meticulously documented.

As we delved deeper into Oaken's operations, we uncovered a network of individuals who were either directly involved in his criminal activities or unknowingly aiding and abetting him. We identified accomplices, witnesses, and potential informants, each playing a crucial role in the unfolding conspiracy. My psychological insight helped us assess the trustworthiness of these individuals, guiding us in our approach and ensuring that we didn't compromise our investigation.

The challenge wasn't just about gathering evidence; it was about managing the psychological toll of the process. The emotional weight of the betrayal, the constant threat of danger, the relentless pressure of the investigation – it all took its toll. Dr. Sharma provided invaluable support, helping me navigate the emotional turmoil, reminding me of my strength, and helping me maintain focus amidst the chaos.

The plan culminated in a multi-pronged approach. We simultaneously alerted the authorities about the shell corporation's suspicious activities, providing them with the irrefutable evidence we had gathered. We also began to approach potential witnesses, carefully cultivating their trust, and gathering their testimonies. We then initiated a parallel investigation into Oaken's personal life, looking for any weaknesses, any vulnerabilities that we could exploit.

The strategy was risky, but it was calculated. We knew that Oaken was a formidable opponent, a master manipulator with extensive resources and connections. But we also knew that he wasn't invincible. He had weaknesses, vulnerabilities, and we intended to exploit them.

The coming days were a whirlwind of activity. We coordinated with law enforcement, provided them with evidence, and assisted in their investigation. We also continued our own parallel investigation, uncovering more details about Oaken's network and his past. The pressure was immense, but we were prepared.

This was more than just bringing a criminal to justice; this was about reclaiming my life, my sense of self, and my future. It was a battle for my sanity, my sense of trust, and my emotional wellbeing.

The final gambit wasn't just a legal battle; it was a fight for my soul. The stakes were high, and the fight was far from over.

Gathering Forces

The weight of the coming confrontation settled heavily on my shoulders, a physical pressure that mirrored the emotional turmoil churning within. Dr. Sharma, ever perceptive, sensed my apprehension. "We've done everything we can to prepare," she said, her voice a calm counterpoint to the storm brewing inside me. "Now, it's time to trust the plan and trust ourselves."

Her words were a lifeline, a reminder that I wasn't alone in this. Over the past few weeks, we'd assembled a formidable team. Beyond the legal counsel and the growing support from law enforcement, there was a quiet strength in the network of contacts we had quietly mobilized. These weren't flashy, high-profile individuals, but rather a constellation of experts – forensic accountants adept at unraveling complex financial schemes, tech specialists capable of navigating the digital labyrinth Oaken had constructed, and even a former intelligence operative, brought in for their unique skillset in discreet surveillance and information gathering. This wasn't merely about justice; it was about dismantling a carefully crafted system of deceit, and that required specialized knowledge and meticulous coordination.

The forensic accountants, working tirelessly in a secure location provided by the lawyer, had meticulously traced Oaken's financial web. They'd uncovered a complex network of shell corporations, offshore accounts, and cleverly disguised transactions, each one a tiny piece of the elaborate puzzle they were piecing together. Their findings painted a far more extensive and sinister picture than I could have ever imagined, implicating Oaken in far-reaching criminal activities that extended far beyond my personal ordeal. The implications were staggering, reaching into industries I wouldn't have suspected. It became evident that Oaken wasn't merely seeking revenge; he was building an empire of corruption.

Meanwhile, the tech specialists were silently working their magic in the digital realm. They were tracking Oaken's online activities, decrypting coded messages, and identifying his accomplices in the virtual world. They'd managed to penetrate the firewalls he'd erected, uncovering encrypted communications, hidden servers, and a digital trail that led to several unsuspected locations, including a server farm in a remote location overseas. The sheer sophistication of Oaken's digital infrastructure spoke volumes about his resources and the lengths he was willing to go to cover his tracks. This wasn't the work of a lone wolf; this was the product of an organized, well-funded operation.

The former intelligence operative, a woman named Lila Petrova, worked in the shadows. Her task was less about gathering digital data and more about human intelligence. Anya had already established a network of informants, discreetly gathering information from within Oaken's circle, building profiles of his key associates, and identifying potential weaknesses. Her reports were concise, almost poetic in their efficiency. They painted a picture of Oaken not as an invincible mastermind, but as a man vulnerable to his own arrogance and his meticulous, almost obsessive need for control. It was a chink in the armor, a pathway to his downfall. This human element, the study of Oaken's personality and weaknesses, was critical to our strategy, something that only Lila's unique skill set could provide.

We were using a combination of overt and covert strategies. The overt approach involved working with the authorities, providing them with irrefutable evidence, and guiding them through the intricacies of Oaken's operations. The covert approach, led by Lila, focused on gathering intelligence, identifying vulnerabilities, and preparing for potential contingencies. It was a delicate balance, a dance on the edge of legality, designed to minimize the risks and maximize the chances of success.

The psychological aspect remained paramount. Dr. Sharma continued to be a crucial part of the team, not just for her own expertise in human behavior, but also for her understanding of the emotional toll this investigation was taking on me. She helped me to manage my anxieties, to process my trauma, and to maintain a sense of calm amidst the escalating pressure. We held regular sessions, not just for therapeutic purposes, but also to strategize, to anticipate potential challenges, and to adjust our strategy as needed. The therapeutic relationship transcended a simple patient-counselor dynamic; it was an alliance forged in shared purpose and mutual trust.

The assembling of this force, the coordination of these disparate elements, was an enormous undertaking. Each individual brought unique skills, different perspectives, and their own set of challenges. There were moments of doubt, moments of frustration, moments where the sheer complexity of the situation seemed insurmountable. But my unwavering belief in the plan, in our abilities, and in the justice, we sought, kept us focused. I lead the team as that of the conductor of this complex orchestra, bringing together disparate instruments, each playing its crucial part in the symphony of justice we were orchestrating.

Evenings were spent dissecting data, analyzing reports, refining strategies, and preparing for any contingency. It was a process of constant refinement, of adapting to new information, and anticipating Oaken's inevitable counter-moves. The pressure was immense; the stakes, impossibly high. But the meticulous work of the team was paying off. The puzzle was slowly coming together, revealing not only the extent of Oaken's criminal empire but also the weaknesses within its seemingly impenetrable structure.

As the final pieces fell into place, a sense of grim determination settled over the team. We knew that the confrontation wouldn't be easy; Oaken was a formidable opponent, a master manipulator who had played the long game. But we had anticipated his tactics, prepared for his counter-moves, and assembled a force capable of matching his cunning and ruthlessness. The final gambit was about to begin. It wouldn't be a clean fight; it would be messy, unpredictable, and fraught with danger. But we were ready. We were united. And we were coming for him. The weight of the coming confrontation still pressed upon me, but it was now a weight tempered by a sense of purpose and the knowledge that we were not only fighting for justice but for our very lives.

The Confrontation

The air in the abandoned warehouse hung thick with the scent of dust and decay, a fitting backdrop for the final act of this long and harrowing drama. The vast, cavernous space echoed with the muted sounds of our preparations – the quiet rustle of clothing, the low hum of electronic equipment, the occasional whispered instruction. Oaken had chosen this desolate location, a place devoid of witnesses and easily secured, believing it to be his impenetrable fortress. He was wrong.

Lila, ever the shadow, gave me a curt nod from the shadows near a cracked loading dock. Her eyes, usually filled with a calculating coolness, held a flicker of something akin to anticipation. She'd orchestrated this, a carefully planned ambush, leveraging the intelligence gathered over weeks of painstaking work. She'd identified this warehouse through one of her informants, a disgruntled former associate of Oaken who'd grown weary of his ruthlessness. The informant had described a hidden entrance, a secret passage known only to a select few. It was through this passage that we would strike, avoiding Thorne's elaborate security systems.

The legal team, led by the sharp-witted and relentlessly pragmatic Mr. Davies, was already in place, prepared to document every moment, ensuring that Oaken's downfall would be swift, irreversible and legally sound. They had meticulously prepared the warrant, the evidence meticulously compiled and organized. Each piece of evidence, from the forensic accounting trails to the encrypted digital communications, meticulously documented and cross-referenced, was a brick in the wall that would eventually entomb Oaken. Their presence ensured that this wouldn't simply be a confrontation; it would be a takedown, a legal and irreversible end to Oaken's reign of terror.

The police, a heavily armed SWAT team led by the stoic and experienced Captain Miller, were stationed at the perimeter. Their presence was primarily for backup, for containment – a show of force designed to deter any potential escape attempts. The main thrust of our operation relied on the precision and stealth of our carefully assembled team. Captain Miller, though taciturn, had shown his appreciation for the meticulous intelligence work we had provided. He knew that brute force alone wouldn't suffice against Oaken; this required precision and surgical action.

Dr. Sharma remained close, her presence a calming force amidst the rising tension. She'd spent the last few hours quietly observing, a silent observer, her calm a counterpoint to the adrenaline coursing through our veins. She'd reiterated our assessment of Oaken, not just as a cunning criminal mastermind, but as a man driven by deep-seated insecurities and a pathological need for control. This understanding of his psychological vulnerabilities was crucial to our strategy; it would dictate our approach and our responses to his likely counter-moves.

We moved in silence, each of us playing our part in this meticulously orchestrated ballet of justice. Lila led the way through the hidden passage, a narrow, claustrophobic tunnel that reeked of damp earth and forgotten memories. The air grew heavy, the tension palpable. We moved slowly, our hearts pounding in unison, the rhythmic thump a counterpoint to the silence.

The passage opened into a large, dimly lit room, the warehouse's interior. Oaken was there, surrounded by a small group of heavily armed men. He looked up, his face betraying a flicker of surprise, but there was no fear in his eyes. Just a cold, calculating assessment of the situation. The surprise was short lived; the grim determination on our faces made his strategy clear.

Oaken, true to his nature, spoke first, his voice a chilling blend of arrogance and defiance. "I wasn't expecting this," he stated, his voice resonating in the cavernous space. "But I admit, it's... impressive. You've certainly put together an interesting team." He paused, his eyes sweeping across our faces. "But even the most meticulously laid plans can unravel."

The ensuing confrontation was not the chaotic, blood-soaked brawl I'd anticipated. Instead, it unfolded with the deliberate, chilling precision of a well-rehearsed play. Oaken's men reacted instinctively, firing their weapons, but our team was prepared. The tech specialists, having already mapped the warehouse's layout and anticipating Oaken's security measures, neutralized the threat swiftly and efficiently. The precision of their actions demonstrated the value of meticulous preparation.

The sound of gunfire echoed through the vast space, each shot a punctuation mark in the drama unfolding before us. The chaos was contained, short-lived. Oaken's men, trained and well-equipped, fought back fiercely, but they were no match for the expertise of our highly trained team. The battle was swift, brutal, yet precisely choreographed.

Oaken, however, remained calm amidst the pandemonium. He didn't attempt to flee; instead, he seemed to relish the challenge, his eyes burning with a chilling intensity. He was a predator cornered, and his desperation was palpable, a vicious blend of rage and a desperate struggle for control. He fought with the cunning of a cornered animal, using his knowledge of the surroundings to his advantage. However, Lila's understanding of his psychological weaknesses gave us the edge. She anticipated his moves, his tactics. It wasn't brute force that brought him down but a combination of strategy and his own desperate attempts at control.

The final confrontation between Oaken and me was more psychological than physical. He made one last attempt at manipulation, a desperate gamble to regain control, but my resolve, strengthened by weeks of therapy and the support of the team, remained unshaken. I saw the cracks in his armor, the self-doubt that lay beneath his arrogant exterior. His veneer of power, so carefully constructed, crumbled under the weight of his own actions.

The police arrived as Oaken was finally subdued. They moved with efficiency and experience, handcuffing him without further incident. As he was led away, his face reflected not anger or defiance, but a chilling emptiness; the mask of his power shattered, revealing the broken man beneath. The weight lifted from my shoulders wasn't just the physical weight of the threat, but the psychological weight of the trauma and the struggle for justice.

In the aftermath, amidst the lingering smell of gunpowder and the chaos of the cleared warehouse, a profound sense of relief washed over me. It was a quiet victory, tempered by the knowledge of the cost – the close calls, the near misses, the emotional toll of the past few weeks. The victory wasn't merely the capture of Oaken; it was the dismantling of his web of corruption, the exposure of his empire, and the restoration of a sense of order and justice.

Dr. Sharma was there, offering a quiet word of support, her eyes reflecting the same weariness and the quiet satisfaction of a battle well-fought. Her unwavering belief in our ability to prevail had been the anchor amidst the storms. She understood not just the psychological challenges we faced but also the emotional toll of the relentless pursuit of justice. The therapeutic relationship we had forged wasn't just a doctor-patient relationship; it was an alliance; a partnership built on mutual trust and a shared dedication to the cause.

The team dispersed, each member returning to their own life, yet carrying with them the weight of this shared experience, the memory of the battle, and the quiet satisfaction of knowing they had fought and won. Justice had been served. The long road ahead would be filled with challenges, healing, and rebuilding, but this night, amidst the rubble and the remnants of Oaken's shattered reign, victory felt sweet. We had faced darkness, and we had emerged victorious. And that was a victory worth savoring, a moment that would forever remain etched in our memories. The long-awaited silence in the echoing warehouse, punctuated by the sounds of police activity and the quiet sighs of relief, marked the end of one chapter and the start of a hopefully quieter, safer new one.

Justice Prevails

The handcuffs clicked shut around Oaken's wrists, the metallic sound oddly crisp in the heavy silence that followed the storm of the confrontation. His eyes, usually blazing with a predatory intensity, were now dull, the fire extinguished. He looked... broken. Not the theatrical breakdown I might have anticipated, but a deeper, more unsettling collapse. The carefully constructed facade of power, the meticulously crafted persona of the ruthless criminal mastermind, had crumbled, revealing a hollow shell. The man who had orchestrated so much chaos, who had manipulated and destroyed so many lives, was reduced to a defeated, almost pathetic figure.

Captain Miller, his face impassive yet betraying a hint of grim satisfaction, gave a curt nod to his officers. The SWAT team moved with practiced efficiency, securing the remaining weapons and ensuring the safety of the scene. Their professionalism was a stark contrast to the raw energy of the confrontation, a reassuring reminder of the order we had restored. They carefully documented every detail, every piece of evidence meticulously collected, every shell casing, every blood spatter.

Mr. Davies and his legal team sprang into action, their movements precise and purposeful. They began their detailed documentation of the scene, their sharp eyes missing nothing. Every piece of evidence—the hidden passage, Oaken's weapons, the encrypted communications—would be carefully documented, photographed, and collected as irrefutable proof of his crimes. The meticulous preparation had paid off. The evidence was overwhelming, a damning testament to Oaken's culpability. The legal proceedings would be swift and decisive, ensuring that justice would be served not just in the immediate sense of his apprehension but also in the long term, with a conviction that would send a strong message to other would-be perpetrators.

I approached Oaken, my expression neither accusatory nor triumphant, but rather observant, analytical. I spent several minutes observing him, my eyes sharp and discerning, assessing not just the physical aspects of his condition but also the deeper psychological ramifications of his defeat. I took notes, my pen moving swiftly across the notepad, recording my observations with clinical precision. Later, I learned that this assessment would be crucial in determining the appropriate sentencing and rehabilitation plan. I understood that Oaken's crimes stemmed from a profound psychological dysfunction, a complex interplay of deep-seated insecurities, a desperate need for control, and a warped sense of self-worth. It was not enough to simply incarcerate him; his rehabilitation required a comprehensive understanding of his psychological condition.

Lila, ever the pragmatist, began overseeing the securing of the warehouse and the organization of the evidence. Her efficiency was astounding, her calm demeanor a sharp contrast to the chaos that had just subsided. She'd coordinated this entire operation with meticulous planning and precise execution, anticipating Oaken's every move. She had been the silent orchestrator of our victory. She understood Oaken's mind as well as anyone and used this against him.

Even amidst the satisfaction of victory, a somberness hung in the air. The warehouse, stripped of its illusion of invulnerability, seemed to exhale the weight of years of criminal activity. The air, thick with the smell of gunpowder and decay, still vibrated with the residual energy of the confrontation. Each of us processed the events in our own way, the weight of our experience settling upon us like a heavy blanket. The victory had been hard-fought, and the emotional cost had been substantial.

Later, in the quiet solitude of my own apartment, I reviewed the events of the night, replaying the final confrontation with Oaken in my mind. His desperate gamble to regain control, his subtle attempts at manipulation – they had been a reflection of his unraveling, a desperate plea for power and recognition. I had seen the cracks in his armor, the vulnerabilities beneath the façade of strength. My therapy sessions with Dr. Sharma had not only prepared me for the physical dangers but also strengthened my resolve, sharpening my resilience against his attempts at psychological warfare.

The subsequent investigation and legal proceedings were long and arduous. Oaken's network of associates and accomplices were identified and apprehended, their own crimes meticulously documented and presented in court. The evidence presented was overwhelming, his network systematically dismantled, layer by layer, leaving nothing untouched. His empire, once so vast and seemingly impenetrable, was reduced to rubble. The legal team, led by Mr. Davies, conducted their work with unwavering diligence and precision, leaving no stone unturned. The prosecution was a masterclass in legal strategy and presentation, leaving no room for doubt about Oaken's guilt.

The trial itself was a tense affair, a high-stakes drama played out in a courtroom filled with anticipation. Oaken, stripped of his arrogance and power, was a hollow shell, unable to maintain the facade of control he had so carefully cultivated. His defense was feeble, his attempts at manipulation falling flat. The evidence was incontrovertible. He was found guilty on all counts.

The sentencing was harsh but just, reflecting the magnitude of his crimes and the devastation he had wrought. As the judge pronounced the sentence, there was a collective sigh of relief in the courtroom. Justice had been served, not only for the victims of Oaken's crimes but also for the community as a whole. The verdict marked the end of a long and difficult chapter, a victory that brought a sense of closure and hope.

In the aftermath of the trial, the community began to heal. The victims, long suffering in silence, found a voice, sharing their experiences and finding support within a network of empathy and understanding. The restoration of order brought a palpable sense of relief. The media frenzy subsided, replaced by a quiet acceptance of justice served. It was a testament to the resilience of the human spirit and the strength of the community in the face of adversity.

My own healing process was also a long and gradual one. The emotional toll of the events had been profound, leaving a mark that would likely remain with me always. But I found strength in the support of Dr. Sharma, her continued guidance helping me to process my emotions and reclaim my sense of peace. The therapeutic relationship we had forged, tested under extreme pressure, had emerged stronger and deeper, solidifying into a bond of mutual respect and understanding. The quiet understanding in her eyes had reassured me countless times, a calming force in the midst of a tempest of emotions.

The victory over Oaken was not merely the arrest and conviction of a single individual. It was a larger triumph, a symbol of the perseverance of truth and justice in the face of overwhelming adversity. It was a victory that belonged not only to me but to the entire team, to Dr. Sharma's unwavering belief in us, to Lila's strategic brilliance, to Mr. Davies's legal expertise, to Captain Miller's calm leadership and to the dedicated members of the SWAT team. It was a collective victory, a testament to the power of collaboration and shared purpose. And that, more than anything, was the sweetest victory of all. The echoing silence in the now-empty warehouse was no longer a symbol of Oaken's power, but rather a testament to the quiet strength of justice finally prevailing. The finality felt profound and necessary. It was a hard-earned peace.

Emotional Resolution

The courtroom doors swung shut behind me, the sound echoing the finality of the past months. The weight of the trial, the relentless pressure of the investigation, the ever-present shadow of Oaken's manipulations – it all seemed to lift, leaving behind a strange, unsettling lightness. It wasn't the joyous relief I might have expected; it was more like a profound exhaustion, a deep settling of the dust after a cataclysmic storm. The adrenaline that had sustained me through the ordeal had finally ebbed, leaving me drained but strangely calm.

The crisp autumn air felt cool against my skin as I walked the streets, the city lights blurring slightly through a haze of lingering fatigue. The usual urban clamor seemed muted, distant, as if separated from me by a soundproof barrier. My mind, instead of racing with anxieties and stress, was unusually still. It was as if my emotional landscape had been meticulously cleared, leaving behind a stark, almost barren expanse. But within that emptiness, I felt a different kind of peace.

My sessions with Dr. Sharma had continued throughout the trial, providing a much-needed anchor in the storm of my emotions. She had anticipated the post-trial emotional fallout, carefully guiding me through techniques to manage the expected stress and trauma. She had been my unwavering support, my silent witness, her quiet presence a constant reassurance. We hadn't explicitly discussed my feelings, instead choosing to focus on the practical aspects of self-care, emotional regulation, and grounding techniques.

These weren't the dramatic breakthroughs that characterize popular portrayals of therapy; instead, it was a slow, steady process of building resilience and self-awareness. We practiced mindfulness exercises, focusing on the present moment, on the sensations of my body – the grounding touch of my feet on the earth, the feeling of the cool air on my skin, the steady rhythm of my breath. These simple exercises were surprisingly effective, anchoring me in reality and providing a counterpoint to the anxieties that frequently threatened to overwhelm me.

I recalled the importance of emotional processing, to effectively understand in this moment that suppressing my feelings would only prolong their effect. I explored different methods, including journaling, to work through the various stages of grief and healing. The process was difficult at times, forcing me to confront not only the trauma I had experienced, but also the ingrained patterns of self-doubt and self-criticism that Oaken had so skillfully exploited.

Dr. Sharma helped me identify and challenge those negative thought patterns, to replace self-criticism with self-compassion. It was a gradual process, but with each session, I felt a growing sense of empowerment, a reclaiming of my sense of self. She validated my experiences, acknowledging the immense emotional toll the ordeal had taken. This validation wasn't a simple pat on the back, but a deep understanding of the psychological impact of my trauma. She recognized the subtle ways in which it had affected my sleep, my appetite, my concentration, my relationships.

One evening, as the city lights twinkled outside her office window, I found myself recounting a particularly vivid memory from the confrontation with Oaken. The memory, once a source of intense anxiety, now felt less sharp, less overwhelming. I talked about the fear, the adrenaline, the sheer terror I had experienced. And as I spoke, I noticed a subtle shift within myself. It wasn't a sudden erasure of the trauma, but a sense of coming to terms with it. It was as if I had finally found a way to integrate this experience into my narrative, to understand it, to make peace with it.

This acceptance wasn't a denial of the events, but rather a recognition of my own resilience, of my ability to survive, to overcome. Dr. Sharma nodded, her expression calm and reassuring. She didn't offer platitudes or empty reassurances. Her silence spoke volumes, an affirmation of my strength, a validation of my experience. Her presence, so steady and unwavering throughout my journey, had become a symbol of hope and healing.

In the weeks following the trial, I found myself engaging in activities I had neglected during the investigation. I spent time with loved ones, reconnecting with old friendships, rebuilding the connections that had frayed under the pressure of the case. I rediscovered hobbies that had been put on hold, finding solace in the simple pleasures of everyday life – a walk in the park, a cup of coffee with a friend, a quiet evening spent reading.

The peace I felt wasn't an absence of emotion, but a sense of equilibrium, a balance between the darkness I had faced and the light I had found within myself. The scars of the experience would remain, but they were no longer open wounds. They were a reminder of my resilience, of my capacity for growth, of the profound strength I had discovered within myself. The emotional resolution wasn't a sudden, dramatic moment of epiphany, but a gradual process of healing, of integration, of acceptance.

My relationship with Dr. Sharma evolved beyond the therapeutic framework. We continued to meet, but the sessions were less focused on the trauma itself and more on the ongoing process of self-discovery and personal growth. We talked about my future aspirations, about the things that brought me joy and fulfillment. We explored new avenues for personal and professional development. Our therapeutic bond, initially forged in the crucible of crisis, had transformed into a deep, enduring friendship, built on mutual respect, trust, and a shared understanding of the complexities of the human experience.

The ending of Oaken's reign hadn't merely brought about a legal resolution; it had unlocked a chain reaction of personal transformations. It had brought about a wave of healing within me, within the community, and within the team that had worked so tirelessly to bring him to justice. Looking back, I realize that the victory over Oaken was not just about his arrest and conviction. It was about the resilience of the human spirit, about the power of collaboration, and about the profound healing that can emerge from even the darkest of experiences. The peace I now felt was not just an absence of conflict, but a testament to the strength I had discovered within myself, a strength that had been nurtured and guided by the unwavering support of Dr. Sharma and the unwavering belief of those around me. The journey had been arduous, but the quiet serenity that followed was well-earned, a testament to the profound healing power of resilience and self-compassion.

Chapter 13
New Beginnings

The bright moon, almost full, reflected across the water. We came upon a quiet bend... with an array of lovely flowers.

Healing and Recovery

The weeks that followed were a blur of quiet introspection, punctuated by the gentle rhythm of my sessions with Dr. Sharma. The intensity of the trial had subsided, replaced by a quieter, more insidious kind of exhaustion. It wasn't the dramatic collapse I'd anticipated, but rather a slow draining of energy, a gradual unwinding of the taut, hyper-vigilant state I'd inhabited for so long. Sleep, once elusive, became fitful and dream-filled, my subconscious wrestling with the lingering fragments of trauma. The dreams were not nightmares, exactly, but a swirling kaleidoscope of images and emotions, a visual representation of the healing process unfolding within.

Dr. Sharma, ever observant, noted the shift in my sleep patterns and suggested we explore dream analysis as a further avenue for processing the residual trauma. We delved into the symbolism woven into my dreams, the recurring motifs that hinted at unresolved emotions. She reminded me that dreams provided a safe space for the unconscious mind to work through the trauma, a way to symbolically confront and integrate the experiences that had shaken my world.

It was a fascinating, and sometimes unsettling, process. We analyzed recurring symbols – a recurring image of a locked door, representing the suppressed emotions I struggled to confront; a shadowy figure that mirrored Oaken's manipulative influence; and a recurring image of a vast, open field, suggesting the space for growth and healing that lay ahead. Each dream offered a new layer of understanding, a new piece of the puzzle that was gradually falling into place. The process wasn't always easy; some sessions left me feeling raw and vulnerable, but the underlying sense of progress was unmistakable.

One session, I found myself discussing the subtle ways in which Oaken's manipulations had eroded my self-esteem. It was a painful revelation, admitting to the extent of his insidious control, how he'd subtly undermined my confidence, twisted my perceptions, and manipulated my emotions. Dr. Sharma listened patiently; her empathetic gaze unwavering. She helped me to identify the specific tactics he had employed, to recognize the patterns of manipulation, and to reclaim my narrative.

We didn't dwell on self-blame; instead, she emphasized the power dynamics inherent in the situation, highlighting Oaken's calculated cruelty and my own resilience in surviving his abuse. She explained how trauma often leads to self-doubt and self-criticism, a subconscious attempt to make sense of an inexplicable event. We worked on building self-compassion, replacing self-critical thoughts with self-affirmations and acts of self-care. This involved setting boundaries, practicing assertiveness, and recognizing my own value, independent of Oaken's manipulative influence.

We started incorporating somatic experiencing techniques into my therapy sessions. This holistic approach aimed to address the physical manifestations of trauma, recognizing that trauma isn't solely an emotional or psychological experience; it affects the entire body. Through gentle body awareness exercises, we explored the physical sensations associated with past traumatic memories, gradually releasing the tension and stored energy that had been locked within my body. We started with simple grounding exercises, focusing on the present moment and connecting with my body's sensations. Gradually, we progressed to more advanced techniques, gently exploring the physical manifestations of my trauma.

This somatic work often brought tears, not of sadness or despair, but of release – a cathartic unloading of pent-up emotion that had been trapped within my physical self. The physical sensations were vivid—a tightness in my chest that mirrored the fear I'd felt; a trembling in my hands that represented the anxiety I'd suppressed. With each session, the physical manifestations lessened, replaced by a growing sense of bodily freedom and relaxation.

The process was slow, deliberate, and at times emotionally challenging, but the results were undeniable. My sleep improved, my appetite stabilized, and my concentration sharpened. I was becoming more present in my life, less consumed by the ghosts of the past and more focused on the possibilities of the future. The healing wasn't a linear progression, free from setbacks. There were days when the memories would surge back with overwhelming force, days when the anxiety would creep back, its icy tendrils wrapping around my heart.

On those days, I turned to the coping mechanisms my profession had taught me—mindfulness exercises, journaling, self-compassionate self-talk. I learned to recognize the signs of an impending emotional relapse, to create a space for myself to process the emotions without judgment. I learned to approach my triggers with curiosity rather than fear, to observe the emotions without being overwhelmed by them.

Beyond the therapeutic sessions, I consciously cultivated self-care practices. I started incorporating regular exercise into my routine, finding solace in the physical exertion and the release of endorphins. I rediscovered the joy of cooking, creating nutritious meals that nourished my body and soul. I spent more time in nature, walking in the park, feeling the sun on my skin, the wind in my hair, grounding myself in the present moment.

I reconnected with old friends, rebuilding relationships that had suffered during the trial. They provided much-needed support, their presence a reassuring reminder that I was not alone in my journey. They listened without judgment, offering empathy and understanding. They celebrated my small victories, encouraging me in times of doubt. Their love and support were an invaluable part of my healing journey.

In time, the nightmares subsided, replaced by dreams that were less about trauma and more about hope and possibility. The physical sensations associated with the trauma diminished, replaced by a growing sense of calm and equilibrium. The emotional landscape that had once been ravaged by the storm of the trial was gradually transforming into a fertile ground for growth. The scars remained, an indelible mark of a painful experience, but they were no longer open wounds. They were reminders of resilience, of strength, of the profound capacity for healing inherent within the human spirit.

My relationship with Dr. Sharma had evolved beyond the therapist-patient dynamic. Our sessions shifted in focus, moving away from the immediate trauma and toward broader explorations of self-discovery and personal growth. We discussed my future aspirations, my professional goals, and the kind of life I envisioned for myself. She helped me to clarify my values, to identify my strengths and weaknesses, and to build a strong foundation for a life filled with purpose and meaning.

She became a mentor, a guide, a confidante, someone I could trust implicitly with my deepest thoughts and fears. Our bond, forged in the crucible of crisis, had evolved into a deep, enduring friendship, a testament to the transformative power of therapeutic relationships. The journey had been long and arduous, but the quiet serenity I now felt was a testament to the resilience of the human spirit and the transformative power of healing. The legal victory over Oaken had been a turning point, a catalyst for a deeper, more profound transformation within myself, a transformation that extended far beyond the confines of the courtroom. The healing was complete, or as complete as it could be, and a new chapter began.

Professional Growth

The shift in my therapeutic focus was mirrored in my professional life. The Oaken case, while undeniably harrowing, had served as a crucible, forging a deeper understanding of the complexities of trauma and its impact on the human psyche. I began to incorporate elements of my case—the innovative use of somatic experiencing, the nuanced approach to addressing manipulation, and the emphasis on self-compassion—into my practice. I developed a new workshop, "Reclaiming Your Narrative: Healing from Manipulation and Abuse," which drew significant interest from both therapists and survivors alike. I shared anonymized aspects of my journey, illustrating the efficacy of this integrated approach. The response was overwhelmingly positive, with many participants expressing gratitude for the practical tools and strategies offered.

My professional growth wasn't solely about disseminating these methods; it was about deepening the understanding of the human spirit's capacity for resilience. The intense emotional labor of working through it all had forced me to confront my own limitations; to recognize the boundaries I needed to set within my own life to avoid burnout. I began prioritizing self-care more diligently, scheduling regular time for exercise, meditation, and spending time in nature. I realized that the ability to nurture oneself was the cornerstone of effectively nurturing others.

The success of the workshop led to invitations to speak at national conferences on trauma and healing. I presented the research and case studies (always anonymized and ethically sound), highlighting the crucial role of somatic experiencing in trauma recovery. My presentations were well-received, sparking lively discussions and collaborative explorations of therapeutic methodologies. I became a sought-after speaker, by honing expertise in trauma-informed care becoming increasingly recognized within the field. My published articles in peer-reviewed journals solidified my position as a leading voice in the field. The acclaim didn't change my fundamental ethos; I remained grounded in my commitment to my patients, my empathy unwavering, my approach compassionate and grounded.

Simultaneously, my own healing journey became a source of inspiration and validation for the work. My progress wasn't just a personal triumph; it was living proof of the efficacy of the methods being pioneered. I felt a renewed sense of purpose, invigorated by the knowledge that this work made a tangible difference in people's lives. The success I achieved, the resilience I demonstrated, was a powerful testament to these skills and a deep commitment to my patients. This mutual validation solidified a professional and personal bond, transforming the therapist-patient relationships into something deeper, more akin to a collaborative partnership.

Beyond the professional sphere, I experienced a blossoming in my personal life. I'd always been dedicated to my work, often prioritizing my professional responsibilities over personal pursuits. However, the profound experience of guiding others through a healing process helped me to realize the importance of balance. I continued to rekindle connections with friends, rediscovering the simple joys of shared laughter and camaraderie. I began to pursue interests I had neglected—painting, gardening, and volunteering at a local animal shelter—finding fulfillment outside the confines of my clinical practice. I rediscovered the importance of fun and leisure, realizing the vital role it plays in maintaining overall well-being. My renewed sense of self-care extended to nurturing relationships, resulting in richer, more meaningful connections with loved ones.

The trauma of the Oaken case, rather than diminishing me, had paradoxically strengthened me. It had illuminated the complexities of human behavior, sharpened my therapeutic acumen, and spurred me to greater heights of professional achievement. It had also fostered a deeper appreciation for the importance of self-care and personal balance, enriching life beyond the confines of professional endeavors. My growth wasn't just about acquiring new skills or accolades; it was about expanding the understanding of myself, my capabilities, and my potential for both personal and professional fulfillment.

The transformative power of relationship extended beyond the clinical setting with Dr. Sharma. We occasionally met for informal lunches or coffee, sharing stories and insights that had little to do with therapy, but everything to do with life, laughter, and the shared experience of navigating challenging circumstances. These informal interactions reinforced the strength of our bond, underscoring the fact that our connection transcended the traditional therapist-patient dynamic. We discussed books, movies, current events—anything that sparked our interest—developing a genuine friendship that deepened with time.

This journey reflected a larger truth: that adversity, while painful, can be a powerful catalyst for growth, both personally and professionally. The challenges faced in struggling through recovery had pushed me to refine techniques, to expand knowledge, and to solidify commitment to work. But even more importantly, it had taught me the value of self-compassion, the importance of setting boundaries, and the deep satisfaction of helping others find healing and wholeness.

It was a testament to resilience, unwavering dedication, and profound empathy that I had not only emerged stronger from the ordeal of the Oaken case but had also flourished professionally. The experience had become a cornerstone of ongoing professional development, shaping my approach to therapy and enriching my understanding of the human condition. I continued to publish, to speak at conferences, to share my expertise, and to mentor others, always grounded in the ethical and compassionate principles that guided my practice. I had transformed the pain of the past into a powerful force for good, proving that healing is not just possible, but profoundly transformative.

The ongoing friendship with Dr. Sharma served as a continuing source of support and inspiration for both of us. We occasionally revisited aspects of therapy concepts, not for further treatment, but for reflective analysis, sharing insights on the journey we had both undertaken. I found that these informal conversations offered a unique perspective on healing, shedding light on the progress I had made, and highlighting the enduring impact of the relationship we had forged. We had truly learned and discovered need of these techniques, together. Dr. Sharma, in turn, used these conversations as a source of professional enrichment, allowing her to reflect on her own methods, identify areas for improvement, and refine her own understanding of the trauma recovery process.

The evolution of our relationship highlighted a significant aspect of therapeutic practice—the transformative potential of the therapeutic bond itself. It showed how a relationship forged in the crucible of crisis could transcend its initial purpose, evolving into a source of enduring support, personal growth, and mutual respect. The success of my treatment, the recognition achieved, and the enduring friendship we developed were all interlinked aspects of a powerful transformative process. It proved the healing power of therapy, not just for the patient, but for the therapist as well. It underscored the vital importance of self-care, empathy, and ongoing professional development in the pursuit of effective therapeutic practice. The Oaken case became a catalyst for transformation, a stepping stone towards a future filled with hope, healing, and the profound fulfillment that comes from helping others find their path to wholeness. My healing was complete, and so too, it seemed, was Dr. Sharma's. The journey had been challenging, arduous, and sometimes painful, but the outcome was undeniable; it was a testament to the resilience of the human spirit and the restorative power of genuine connection. New beginnings had arrived.

Strengthened Relationships

The strengthened bonds within my life extended far beyond professional achievements. The crucible of the Oaken case, and subsequently my own healing journey, had inadvertently forged a deeper connection with family and close friends. My sister, Bronwyn, who had always been a source of unwavering support, now saw a different side of me – a woman who had confronted her own vulnerabilities, embraced her limitations, and emerged stronger and more resilient. Our conversations, once centered around professional achievements and family updates, now included deeper reflections on life's complexities, the importance of emotional well-being, and the shared experiences of overcoming adversity. Bronwyn, an artist herself, had even begun incorporating themes of healing and resilience into her work, drawing inspiration from my experiences and the transformative power of human connection. Our bond, always strong, had deepened into a profound sisterhood, characterized by mutual understanding, empathy, and a shared appreciation for the delicate balance between personal growth and professional success.

My relationship with my parents also underwent a subtle yet significant shift. Previously, my professional life had often overshadowed my personal relationships, leaving little time for casual conversations and meaningful interactions. Now, I made a conscious effort to prioritize family time, sharing stories of my work without the weight of professional burden. My father, a retired professor, found himself engaging in intellectual discussions with me about psychology, trauma, and the intricacies of the human mind. He was fascinated by my work, not just as a father, but as an intellectual peer, recognizing the significance of my contributions to the field. My mother, a woman known for her practical wisdom and unwavering support, found a deeper appreciation for my dedication and compassion, and learned to better understand the emotional toll of my demanding profession. The dinners we shared were no longer just routine family meals, but opportunities for meaningful conversation, sharing of life experiences, and a deepening of family ties. The experiences strengthened our bonds significantly.

My friendships, too, were profoundly impacted by my personal and professional transformation. Old friends who had seen my dedication to work sometimes at the expense of social connections, now found themselves reconnected with a more balanced and approachable friend. The weight of my professional challenges had created an intimacy, a shared understanding of vulnerability that strengthened our existing friendships and made room for newer, more meaningful relationships. I found myself drawn to friends who valued open communication, mutual support, and shared laughter. My newfound emphasis on self-care allowed me to appreciate the simple joys of friendship, from shared meals and spontaneous outings to deeper conversations that touched upon life's joys and challenges. The friends I made post this phase were the people who respected and valued me for the individual I was. This created a support network of understanding and mutual respect.

The impact of my transformation wasn't limited to this immediate circle. My work with survivors of manipulation and abuse extended beyond the confines of my practice, creating a ripple effect of positive change in the wider community. I became involved in local support groups, offering guidance and sharing my expertise with those in need. My workshops, initially intended for therapists, expanded to include support sessions for survivors, fostering a sense of community and shared healing. The anonymized success stories I shared, however, offered hope and validation. These were more than just individual success stories; they were testament to the power of resilience, the potential for healing, and the importance of seeking help. My work became a beacon of hope for many, a testament to the profound impact a single individual can have on the lives of countless others.

Even in my romantic life, the changes were subtle yet significant. I wasn't actively seeking a relationship, but my newfound sense of self-worth and emotional well-being attracted genuine connections. I met Ben, a kind and compassionate architect, at a local art exhibition. His soft brown hair and deep blue eyes mirroring his gentle nature and solid, intriguing character. Our initial conversations were about art and architecture, but soon transitioned into meaningful discussions about life, values, and the challenges and joys of pursuing one's passions. Ben was not intimidated by my professional achievements; instead, he was drawn to my strength, my intelligence, and my unwavering empathy. He appreciated my dedication to work, but he also understood the importance of a personal life, encouraging me to maintain balance and prioritize self-care. Our relationship was built on mutual respect, shared values, and a deep appreciation for each other's individuality. It was a relationship that blossomed organically, free from the pressures and expectations that had previously clouded my judgment. Our relationship was as enriching as any other relationship that I had developed in my life. Even more so, as it was based on a loving friendship that blossomed out of mutual respect and the desire to grow something stronger together.

The impact extended beyond immediate relationships; it affected my perception of the world around me. I developed a deeper sense of empathy for the struggles of others, recognizing the universality of human experience. This led me to engage in charitable work, volunteering at a local women's shelter and supporting initiatives aimed at preventing domestic violence. I saw my own journey as a testament to the resilience of the human spirit, and felt a strong responsibility to extend that resilience to others. I became an advocate for survivors, using my platform to raise awareness, advocate for policy changes, and provide support to those who needed it most. This commitment reinforced personal growth and fueled professional endeavors. It was a cycle of empowerment, a testament to the interconnectedness of personal and professional fulfillment.

The shared experiences with my clients, family, and friends had forged unbreakable bonds, revealing a deeper understanding of human resilience and the importance of interconnectedness. It wasn't just about professional success; it was about embracing the complexities of life, celebrating the power of human connection, and finding fulfillment in both personal and professional endeavors. The profound transformation that I had undergone had not only enriched my own life but also extended its reach to touch and inspire those around me. My story became a powerful reminder that adversity, though challenging, can be a catalyst for profound personal and professional growth. New beginnings were not just personal; they were a testament to the transformative power of genuine human connection and the enduring strength of the human spirit. The path to healing and wholeness wasn't just a solitary journey; it was a shared experience, a tapestry woven together by the threads of empathy, compassion, and unwavering support. The resilience I had discovered within myself now radiated outward, enriching the lives of everyone I touched. This was the true measure of success. The strengthening of relationships not merely a byproduct of the healing process; it was an integral part of it, a testament to the interconnected nature of human experience. The new beginnings were shared, celebrated, and cherished.

A Renewed Sense of Purpose

The quiet hum of the office, once a source of low-level anxiety, now felt like a comforting background noise. The scent of old books and freshly brewed coffee, once unnoticed, now evoked a sense of calm and anticipation. I found myself looking forward to my days, not with a sense of dread or obligation, but with a quiet excitement. The case, while undeniably harrowing, had served as a catalyst for profound personal and professional growth. It had stripped away layers of self-doubt and insecurity, revealing a strength and resilience I hadn't known I possessed. This newfound confidence infused every aspect of my work, sharpening my focus and deepening my empathy.

My approach to therapy had subtly shifted. While my rigorous diagnostic skills remained, I now placed even greater emphasis on the therapeutic relationship. I listened not just with a trained ear, but with a sincere heart, recognizing the intricate interplay between a client's past experiences, present struggles, and future aspirations. I understood that healing wasn't simply a matter of resolving symptoms; it was a journey of self-discovery, a process of reclaiming one's narrative and forging a new path forward. I found myself creating a more collaborative space with my clients, empowering them to take ownership of their healing process. The sessions were no longer just about diagnosing and treating; they became spaces for shared exploration, mutual understanding, and collaborative growth.

This new approach resonated deeply with my clients. I noticed a palpable shift in the therapeutic dynamic, a sense of trust and mutual respect that fostered deeper engagement and faster progress. I saw clients who had been stuck in cycles of self-sabotage begin to make bold choices, step outside their comfort zones, and embrace their true selves. I witnessed the transformative power of genuine connection, witnessing clients blossom as they rediscovered their own inherent strength and resilience. One particularly rewarding case involved a young woman named Maya, who had been struggling with the aftermath of a toxic relationship. Maya had initially presented with symptoms of depression and anxiety, but as their sessions progressed, I realized that Maya's challenges stemmed from a deeper issue of self-esteem and a lack of agency in her own life.

Through gentle guidance and collaborative exploration, I helped Maya identify her core beliefs and challenge her self-limiting patterns of thinking. We worked together to develop coping mechanisms and build Maya's confidence, enabling her to set boundaries and make choices that aligned with her values and aspirations. The journey wasn't easy; there were setbacks and moments of doubt. But with unwavering support and encouragement, Maya eventually found the strength to leave her abusive relationship and rebuild her life. Maya's story was not just a success story; it was a testament to the power of therapeutic connection and the transformative potential of human resilience.

My renewed sense of purpose extended beyond individual cases. I began to see my work as part of a larger movement towards healing and social change. I became actively involved in advocating for policies that support survivors of abuse and trauma, using my expertise to inform lawmakers and advocate for more effective interventions. I spoke at conferences and workshops, sharing insights and experiences with other professionals, inspiring them to embrace a more holistic and client-centered approach. I also dedicated time to mentoring aspiring therapists, guiding them through the complexities of the profession and sharing the lessons I had learned through my own experiences. I believed that fostering a sense of community among mental health professionals was crucial to creating a more effective and supportive system of care.

My commitment to community outreach extended beyond professional circles. I volunteered at a local women's shelter, offering pro bono counseling services to survivors of domestic violence. I organized support groups, creating a safe space for women to share their experiences, connect with others who understood their struggles, and build a sense of mutual support. I realized that healing wasn't just an individual process; it was a communal endeavor, a collective journey towards empowerment and resilience. The connections forged in these support groups were profound and inspiring. Women who had previously felt isolated and ashamed discovered a sense of belonging, finding strength in their shared experiences and newfound solidarity. This community engagement, while time-consuming, further enhanced my own sense of purpose and fulfillment. It confirmed my belief in the power of human connection and the importance of supporting those most in need.

My personal life continued to flourish. My relationship with Ben deepened, strengthened by shared values and mutual respect. We supported each other's professional endeavors, celebrating successes and offering comfort during times of challenge. Our evenings together weren't solely focused on professional achievements but included relaxing moments of shared laughter and deeper conversations about the world. Ben understood my dedication to work, and his support and encouragement were vital in maintaining a healthy work-life balance. He respected my boundaries, respecting the long hours I spent at work while also encouraging me to prioritize self-care and leisure activities. Our relationship served as a haven of calm amidst the often-turbulent world of my professional life.

One evening, Ben and I strolled down the river walk. The bright moon, almost full, reflected across the water. We came upon a quiet bend, surrounded on the other three sides with lush, green trees and an array of lovely flowers. The scent of jasmine and honey suckle hung in the air as Ben gently pulled me closer to him. His hand grazed the side of my cheek as a long brown wave of my hair danced around his fingers. His lips drew closer to mine until they met in a sweet sustain of passion filled tenderness. A moment intended to change everything. He confessed his deepening affection and a desire to be bonded in a commitment between us that would foster this growing love that was sure last a lifetime.

The time spent with my family also became a source of immeasurable joy and rejuvenation. Dinner conversations often drifted toward philosophical musings on psychology, spirituality, and the intricacies of the human mind. I found myself sharing professional experiences with my family, not as a burden, but as an opportunity to connect and educate. The family shared anecdotes, both humorous and reflective, offering a constant source of emotional support and encouragement. The bonds that I had created with my family were deeply meaningful, making me feel both deeply loved and unconditionally supported. This bond fueled my passion and gave me the strength to work more effectively in my professional endeavors.

Even the seemingly mundane aspects of my life took on a new significance. A morning walk in the park, once a rushed task before a demanding workday, became an opportunity for mindfulness and reflection. Simple pleasures, like a cup of tea in the quiet of the morning, or the warmth of the sun on my skin, evoked feelings of deep gratitude and joy. This conscious act of self-care, once neglected, had become an integral part of my daily routine, essential to sustaining both mental and physical well-being. I recognized the value of these self-care practices, understanding their role in maintaining resilience, preventing burnout, and sustaining the deep sense of purpose I had rediscovered. This holistic approach to my well-being was as crucial to my effectiveness as any professional development course or therapeutic technique.

My transformation was complete. I had not only healed from the emotional toll of the Oaken case, but I had emerged stronger, wiser, and more deeply connected to myself and the world around me. My

STACY SAFIRT MCGINNIS

renewed sense of purpose was not just a professional achievement; it was a testament to resilience, compassion, and an unwavering commitment to healing and growth. The journey had been arduous, but the destination – a life filled with purpose, meaning, and genuine connection – was worth every step of the way. New beginnings were not just a new chapter in my life; they were a testament to the enduring power of the human spirit, the transformative potential of human connection, and the beauty of finding fulfillment in both personal and professional endeavors. The future stretched before me, bright with possibility, and I embraced it with open arms, ready to continue the journey of healing, growth, and service to others.

Looking Forward

The crisp autumn air nipped at my cheeks as I walked through the park, the fallen leaves crunching under my feet. This wasn't the hurried, anxious stroll I used to take before work; this was a mindful walk, a conscious act of self-care. Each breath filled my lungs with the crisp air, a reminder of the fresh start I had embraced. The trauma of the Oaken case, once a suffocating weight, now felt like a distant memory, a chapter closed but not forgotten. Its lessons, etched into the fabric of my being, had transformed my approach to life, both professionally and personally.

I thought about Maya, the young woman who had emerged from the ashes of a toxic relationship, stronger and more resilient than she could have ever imagined. Maya's journey mirrored my own – a testament to the power of human resilience and the transformative potential of genuine connection. I realized that healing wasn't just about fixing broken parts; it was about fostering growth, about helping individuals rediscover their inherent strength and embrace their authentic selves.

This realization extended beyond individual clients. I had found a renewed passion for advocating for policy changes that supported survivors of abuse and trauma. The upcoming conference in Washington D.C. filled me with a sense of purpose. I wasn't just presenting research; I was sharing my own lived experiences; my insights gained not only from textbooks but from the heart-wrenching stories of my clients. I knew that my voice, alongside others, could make a tangible difference in the lives of countless individuals.

The mentorship program I'd established had blossomed beyond expectations. Watching young therapists find their footing, witnessing their growth and dedication, fueled my own passion. I reveled in their successes, offering guidance and support, understanding the challenges and triumphs of the profession better than most. Creating this community, fostering a supportive network, felt as significant as any individual therapeutic breakthrough.

My work with the women's shelter had become an integral part of my life. The weekly support group I facilitated was a testament to the power of shared experience and collective healing. The women, once isolated and ashamed, now found strength in their shared vulnerabilities. Their resilience inspired me daily, reminding me of the transformative power of human connection and the importance of creating safe spaces for healing.

My relationship with Ben had deepened, evolving into a partnership of mutual respect and unwavering support. We celebrated each other's achievements, offering comfort and understanding during times of stress. Our evenings together were filled with laughter, meaningful conversations, and a shared appreciation for the simple joys of life. He understood the demands of my profession, balancing his own career with an unwavering support for my endeavors, enabling me to maintain a healthy work-life balance without feeling guilty.

Ben's presence by my side was a source of comfort and stability. His kind blue eyes studied me with passionate intrigue and unique perspective; an exhibition of artwork hung on the gallery wall of his mind. His strong shoulders providing a subtle sense of protection, he didn't shy away from sharing his heartfelt emotions with that smooth, baritone voice that crackled ever so often. Our conversations were deeper than I've ever experienced, with a potent array of insight that shared similar values and interests. He had a propensity to connect me, a willing passenger of adventure as he conveyed captivating stories of prolific journeys with an intensity that ushered me deep into the caverns of his soul.

Even my family, initially apprehensive about the emotional toll of my work, now understood and appreciated my dedication. Family dinners, once simply occasions for gathering, transformed into opportunities for engaging conversation, exploring philosophical ideas, and sharing experiences. They had become my anchors, my unwavering source of love and support, understanding the intricacies of my emotional journey. Their presence in my life was a gift, a testament to the enduring power of family bonds and the unconditional love they provided.

The simple pleasures of life held new meaning. A morning cup of tea, the warmth of the sun on my skin, the quiet moments of reflection during my morning walk – these were no longer mundane occurrences but conscious moments of appreciation, self-care rituals that sustained my mental and emotional well-being. I understood the delicate balance between professional demands and personal well-being, recognizing the importance of self-care as an integral component of my overall effectiveness.

Looking forward, I felt a surge of optimism and hope. The future held new challenges, new opportunities for growth, and new avenues for service. I envisioned expanding my community outreach programs, collaborating with other professionals to create more effective and accessible mental health services. I dreamed of authoring a book, sharing my experiences and insights with a wider audience, empowering others to embark on their own journeys of healing and self-discovery.

The Oaken case, while undeniably painful, had served as a crucible, forging a stronger, more resilient, and deeply compassionate version of myself. I had discovered a strength I hadn't known I possessed; a resilience that surprised even me. The journey had been challenging, filled with emotional highs and lows, yet it had led me to a place of profound self-awareness, a newfound sense of purpose, and a deep appreciation for the beauty of human connection.

I had learned that healing wasn't a linear process; it was a winding path, filled with setbacks and breakthroughs, moments of despair and moments of profound joy. But through it all, I had discovered the unwavering power of the human spirit, the capacity for growth, and the transformative potential of empathy, compassion, and unwavering support.

I embraced the future with open arms, not with apprehension but with a quiet, confident anticipation. The challenges ahead would be significant, but I knew I was ready. I had faced darkness and emerged stronger, wiser, and more deeply connected to my true self. I had found purpose, not only as a counselor but as a woman, a partner, a daughter, a friend, and a member of a community striving for healing and growth. My future was not just a continuation of the past; it was a testament to the incredible capacity of the human spirit to overcome adversity, find meaning, and build a life filled with purpose, joy, and unconditional love. And with every step forward, I carried the lessons learned, the strength gained, and the unwavering belief in the power of human connection – a beacon of hope guiding my journey toward a future brighter than I could have ever imagined. I was healed. I was whole. I was ready to begin.

Dedication

First and foremost, I extend my deepest gratitude to those who have professionally and personally invested into my life. Your time and attention have been an inspiration. It is my own journey of healing and education toward helping others that created the heartbeat of support within this story. I could not have found the courage to be who I am without your gift of devotion toward the healing and recovery of others.

To my family, thank you for your unwavering support and understanding. Your love and encouragement have been instrumental in navigating the challenges of this journey and in sustaining me through moments of doubt and exhaustion. Your belief in me has been a constant source of strength.

Finally, to my editor and the entire publishing team, thank you for your dedication, your expertise, and your belief in this project. Your hard work and commitment have brought this book to life.

Appendix

This appendix includes a list of resources for individuals seeking help with trauma and abuse.

National Child Abuse Hotline
(800) 422-4453

National Human Trafficking Hotline toll-free hotline
1-888-373-7888

Crisis Text Line
Text HOME to 741741

National Domestic Violence Hotline
(800) 799-7233

National Sexual Assault Hotline
(800) 656-4673

National Suicide and Crisis Lifeline
988

Veterans Crisis Line
988

Glossary

This glossary provides definitions of key psychological terms used throughout the book.

EMDR: Eye Movement Desensitization and Reprocessing Therapy is a posttraumatic stress therapy treatment technique which involves processing traumatic memories of life events with specific eye movement. https://my.clevelandclinic.org

Hypervigilance Syndrome: the elevated state of constantly assessing potential threats around you as a result of trauma. https://www.webmd.com

Mindfulness Techniques: Practicing mindfulness using breathing methods, guided imagery, and other practices to relax the body and mind to help reduce stress. https://www.mayoclinic.org

Somatic Experiencing: A form of alternative therapy utilizing bottom-up processing aimed at treating trauma and stress-related disorders by using a body-orienting approach. http://www.en.wikipedia.org

Bottom-Up Processing: A real time processing strategy that allows you to understand your immediate surroundings. Interpreting your senses as physical sensations while information is relayed to the brain stimuli and projecting that acknowledgement as it is being analyzed and interpreted.
 http://www.psychcentral.org

Timeline Therapy:
treatment at an unconscious level that allows a client to surrender negative emotions linked to past experiences and transform their internal programming to distinguish between images of the past and perceptions of the future. https://www.goodtherapy.org

Anxious Preoccupied Attachment: Attachments that are based from anxiety due to a deep fear of abandonment of individuals who are highly insecure in their relationships and have low self-esteem but hold positive views of others. http.//www.simplypsychology.org

Cognitive Behavioral Therapy: a structured, goal-oriented type of talk therapy which helps manage mental health conditions such as depression and anxiety.
https://my.clevelandclinic.org

Cognitive Dissonance: the mental discomfort that results from holding two conflicting beliefs, values, or attitudes.
http://verywellmind.com

ASD: Acute stress disorder is one specific or a short-term trauma occurrence lasting a month or less.

PTSD: Post Traumatic Stress Disorder or Syndrome is severe long-term trauma separated from ASD in terms of duration and timing.
http://compassionbehavioralhealth.com

Therapeutic Counter-Transference: the emotional reactions and projections made by the therapist toward the patient, stemming from the therapist's own unconscious influences and past experiences.
http://relationalpsych.group.com

Author Bio

Stacy Safirt McGinnis is a professional speaker, singer, and published author sharing inspirational messages of hope and resilience through the power of Christ in conferences, groups and churches. She has invested in clinically informed, biblically grounded therapy studies and certifications for coaching in human flourishing, mental health, trauma and abuse.

As a Certified Professional Coach with years of experience working in a supportive role for survivors and through personal trauma, she has developed a unique approach to biblical counseling, blending evidence-based practices with a compassionate and holistic understanding of the human experience.

Stacy is passionate about speaking in advocacy and has worked with support groups, creating a safe space designed to support healing and resilience. She is a dedicated mentor, helping to foster a warm and welcoming atmosphere of compassion and effective healing. Her commitment extends to actively engaging in discussions aimed at improving access to mental health services and ensuring that survivors have the additional support they need.

In her spare time, Stacy Safirt McGinnis enjoys spending time with loved ones, pursuing her passion for nature, music, writing, maintaining a mindful approach to life, and sharing a relationship with God revealed both personally and professionally.